There was a rush for the upper-deck and the emigrants crowded to the ship's rails to wave farewell to the land. Some were cheering, some shouting, nearly all were joyously excited, and only here and there could be seen any tears or sadness. For most of those on board, this ship was taking them from nothing but poverty and suffering.

Grainne stared up at the great brown sheets of the weather-stained canvas sails swelling out as they filled with wind and felt the deck beneath her moving like a living thing. Her heart pounded with excitement, and she clung to Con's arms and laughed exultantly, 'We're going, Con. We're going to America. At last, we're going to America.'

SARA FRASER

The Harsh Noontide

Futura

A Futura Book

First published in Great Britain in 1990 by
Macdonald & Co (Publishers) Ltd
London & Sydney

This edition published in 1990 by Futura Publications
Reprinted 1990

ISBN 0 7088 4766 8

Reproduced, printed and bound in Great Britain by
BPCC Hazell Books
Aylesbury, Bucks, England
Member of BPCC Ltd.

Futura Publications
A Division of
Macdonald & Co (Publishers) Ltd
Orbit House
1 New Fetter Lane
London EC4A 1AR
A member of Maxwell Macmillan Pergamon Publishing Corporation

Introduction

In the middle decades of the nineteenth century the great port of Liverpool was the gateway to the New World, the fabled lands of America.

The dispossessed, the destitute, the starving, the desperate flocked to Liverpool in their thousands, seeking a way to escape their sufferings. Their way of escape lay across the wide wastes of the ocean.

Grainne Shonley came to Liverpool to make her escape. This is the story of what she found in that mighty city.

Chapter One

Liverpool, 7 August, 1848

The paddle steamer *Athlone* had taken thirty-six hours to make the crossing from Cork to Liverpool, wallowing through high seas and driving rain, and all through those hours more than a thousand men, women and children had remained crammed together on its upper deck without shelter, many without food, and some without even a drink of water except for the rain that ran down their faces and into their mouths.

Beneath them in the holds, the ship's cargo of pigs squealed and grunted in concert with the pounding of the engines and the frothy slashing of the great paddle wheels. Even the gusting winds could not dispel the stench that rose from the lower decks but added to the shared miseries of saturated clothing, bodies shivering with cold, stomachs heaving with sea-sickness, and heads aching, giddy from lack of sleep.

When the vessel entered the calmer waters of Liverpool Bay crossing Great Burbo Bank and into the Crosby Channel, its plunging progress eased, but this brought little relief to the masses on its upper deck who were too immersed in their sufferings to want anything other than a release from their pitching, heaving prison.

The tall funnel belched out its plumes of thick smoke, answered from each side of the broad estuary by the chimneys of Liverpool and Birkenhead. Mingling with the falling rain, the smoke and soot cast a murky pall across the early evening sky.

Grainne Shonley stood staring over the bows of the ship, her shawl covering her black hair, her thin face intent, her green eyes marvelling at the scene before her. The estuary was a mile wide at this point and across the black-grey waters small ferry steamers and tug-boats constantly criss-crossed, weaving their way between the big, anchored sailing packets and the tiny red and tan sailed fishing boats. On the Liverpool side the shoreline was a continuous forest of masts and rigging, granite docks and massive warehouses, and as she stared the young woman fancied that the pulsating energy of that waterfront was already reaching out to envelop her, and the excitement of adventure welled up in her.

'Con! Maggie! Denis! Just look! Stand up and look,' she beseeched, as the steamer's bows slowly swung towards the Liverpool shore.

Huddled at her feet on the wet deck her companions reacted in different ways to her summons. Con, her husband, smiled at her excitement and rose to join her. He was tall, with a lean muscular body, swarthily handsome and at twenty-two a year older than his pretty wife. He wore a dark blue hip-length jacket, narrow velveteen trousers with a peaked forage cap rakishly cocked on his black curly hair, and thick-soled boots on his feet. Shaggy-haired Maggie Nolan lying on her side in a foetal position, groaned piteously and drew her shawl over her face, while beside her Denis Callaghan's bright blue eyes twinkled in his plump red face, and he took a long swig from the bottle of gin in his hand before telling Grainne in his hoarse, throaty, chuckling voice, 'By Jasus, honey, there's time and enough to view bloody Liverpool when I'm offa this hell-ship. I'll be seeing all I want to of it through the windows of the nearest shebeen just as soon as this bloody pig-palace kapes still long enough for me to jump off it.'

A crew member came pushing through the crowd of

8

passengers and Grainne asked him, 'Where is it we're docking, mister?'

The man's hard, weather-beaten features softened a trifle as he saw her youthful beauty. 'We'll be berthing in the North Docks. Regent Road lies behind them. You take care when you gets ashore, Missy, as there'll be thieves aplenty waiting for you'se lot to land.'

His head turned as he looked at the crowded deck of shabby people, many in rags, and nearly all of them showing the ravages of hunger and hardship. He spoke again to Grainne. 'You'd think by the looks of this lot that there 'udden't be any pickings to be got from 'um, but them bastards ashore 'ull strip whatever bit is left to these poor souls afore they can blink.' He shook his head. 'I never gets used to seeing the poor women and kids, knowing like I does that their troubles is only just beginning.' He nodded at the young couple and went about his duties.

Con Shonley put his arm around his wife and hugged her. 'Don't you worry, sweetheart. I'll take care of you. Our troubles are mostly behind us.'

'Oh God, I hope that's so, Con,' Grainne murmured fervently, 'I hope that's so.'

'They are, you'll see. We'll be in America soon, and there we'll make our fortune.'

Grainne leaned against Con's body, drawing comfort from his strong arm encircling her, and her green eyes moved thoughtfully across the surrounding mass of people, now beginning to stir from their inactivity, as the steam tugs brought the ship through the dock entrance and nudged it towards the quayside beneath the towering warehouse walls.

'They call us emigrants but really we're all fugitives. Every soul on board this ship is trying to escape,' she thought, 'to escape from starvation, disease and death.'

She stared at the faces around her, faces gaunt with hunger, she listened to the racking coughs and retching, and reluctantly glanced at the shrouded corpse around which a mother and her children were

9

sitting in silent despair. 'We're trying to escape, but we're bringing all those things with us, and most of these poor souls are already too weak to outrun them. How many will finally manage to get to America, I wonder?'

The news that the *Athlone* was docking had spread like wildfire along the waterfront and from Regent Road and Waterloo Road, Cotton Street and Carlton Street, Goree Piazza, New Quay and the Strand, Boundary Street, Great Howard Street and Tithebarn, from all the narrow, fetid alleys of the dockside came the packs of human wolves.

The moment the ship had been tied up the crew began to drive the emigrants onto the quay, and men, women and children went over the sides humping their boxes and bundles, milling around like bewildered cattle. Swarms of tough-looking men came among them, badgering the new arrivals to accompany them to hotels and lodging houses, grabbing their arms and pulling the hapless people along the quayside, carrying off chests and bundles of baggage so that the owners were forced to run after them. The quay was in uproar and confusion.

Grainne Shonley and her party had two chests of clothing and other belongings, which Con handed down to Denis Callaghan from the low deck. As Denis placed the first chest on the granite slabs and turned to take the second from Con Shonley a big rough-looking man laid hands on the first chest and heaved it onto his shoulder.

Grainne, who was supporting the moaning Maggie Nolan, shouted at the man, 'put that down.'

The man leered at her. 'I'm only trying to help you, missus.' He spoke with the thick brogue of Galway. 'I'm taking you'se to a dacent hotel, where you'll not be robbed blind by these bloody English.'

Grainne stared at him doubtfully, noting the brawl-scarred features, the filthy clothing and the unshaven jowls, but before she could speak two more tough, unsavoury characters joined the first, who continued to say, 'Come on now, missus, and the rest o yez, let's be getting on.'

One of the newcomers snatched the second chest from short, plump Denis Callaghan. The third man was a giant with a close-buttoned black frockcoat straining across his bulging chest and a tall battered tophat on his long sandy hair. When Con Shonley jumped down onto the quay and moved to take back the chest he interposed his bulk, grinned ferociously down into the young man's face and baring brown fang-like teeth, he said, 'Come now, sor, ye'll be needing lodgings won't ye, and you'se have dropped lucky, so ye have. We'll be taking ye to the best lodgings in Liverpool, so we will.'

His accent was a mixture of Dublin and Liverpool, and Grainne wondered where he had been born.

While he was speaking his two companions were moving off with the chests and although Con tried hard to push the big man aside, he was powerless to move his huge bulk, and when Grainne would have gone to his aid, Maggie Nolan, sick from the voyage, wept piteously and clung to her, crying, 'Don't leave me, Grainne! Don't leave me.'

From the deck above, the crewman who had spoken to them earlier shouted, 'Just go wi' 'um, missus, because if you don't go wi' this lot, then you'll not get a minute o' peace from the others. Just look about you.'

Grainne's eyes flickered frantically about the lamenting, shouting, disputing, weeping, struggling mass of people and for a moment imagined she was trapped in a madhouse. The rain became a downpour, and she saw a passenger suddenly get punched to the ground by two men who kicked him unmercifully. While he shouted and his womenfolk screamed and children shrieked in terror, Grainne's senses started to swim sickeningly.

'Come on, Con. Let's go with these men,' she begged. Her husband saw her distress and after a moments hesitation nodded glumly.

The huge man was instantly effusively affable. 'Jase!

11

You're a wise woman, missus. We'll look after you'se, never fear. Come now, time's wasting, and ye'll be needing to get outta this bloody rain and into a nice cosy room. Tommy Tracy is me name, and youse 'ull not find a fairer landlord than me in the whole o' Liverpool. 'Tis off to Amerikay ye're going, is it? Well, 'tis God himself who'se sent yez to me, because I know the very gentleman who can get you passage on a fine ship, and I know another gentleman who'll be able to provide yez with everything youse 'ull be needing for the voyage.'

The party joined the stream of bedraggled humanity passing through the mighty dock gates and out into the murk of Regent Road. Despite the comparative early hour the gas lamps were already alight, the rain hissing and steaming on their heated glass and iron frames, and that same rain had driven the usual swarm of street dwellers into shelter so that apart from a few carts and wagons trundling over the stone setts of the roadway, the street seemed almost deserted. Grainne looked about her curiously, marvelling at the profusion of posters that covered every available surface, and at the numbers of spirit vaults, pubs, eating houses and agents' and brokers' offices that faced the tall dock walls.

The men carrying the chests suddenly disappeared into a narrow alleyway and as Grainne, still supporting the stumbling Maggie Nolan, followed them her nostrils were filled with a vile stench, and her feet sank deep into an oozing mud compounded of rotting matter, sodden filth and human and animal excreta.

'Dear God, what is this place?' she protested. At her side Tommy Tracey laughed and told her gaily, 'It's called Paradise Alley, missus.'

The alley widened and the blank wet walls gave way to rows of mean tenements, with rag-stuffed windows and gaping doorways through which could be glimpsed the matted heads of dirty, ragged, human beings who more resembled sub-human savages than

12

the citizens of one of England's richest ports and its second largest city. They traversed a jumble of other mean narrow streets, where open cellar flaps emitted light and noise from packed lodgings and battered placards advertised beds and board, old clothes, ironware, pots and pans, provisions, and a myriad of life's other necessities. Soon the rain slackened, then ceased and like a disturbed ant-hill the inhabitants boiled out into the thoroughfares, filling the close confines with noise and bustle. Grainne could not help but marvel at the strident vitality of her surroundings, a vitality that even these depressing manmade warrens could not smother.

The beggars came scurrying at the sight of the group. Some were armless, other eyeless or legless, some were scrofulous or had ulcers. There were those who were naked and then there were those who were so emaciated that they appeared like human skeletons. Of all ages, men and women, their stinking bodies emitting an almost tangible miasma as they clustered together clamouring for alms. To clear a way through Tommy Tracey produced a cudgel from beneath his wide-skirted frock coat and waved it threateningly so that the nightmarish crew fell back snarling and cursing, while behind the group a pair of youthful sneak thieves changed their minds about attempting a quick robbery and instead skulked away down a side alley.

The chest carriers turned into a doorway and Tommy Tracey pointed his cudgel at the crudely lettered sign above it. 'This is my place,' he declared with an air of pride.

Grainne looked up at the sign, so weathered as to be almost illegible. 'Tracey's Hotel,' she spelt out, 'beds sixpence a night.'

At first look she could see no difference between the 'Hotel' and any of the adjoining terraced hovels, but the big man was quick to assure her. 'It's a lot bigger inside than it looks, Missus. It's three o' these houses knocked into one. You come on in now.'

13

He followed his men through the doorway, and Con took Grainne's arm. 'I don't like the look of this place, sweetheart.' His face was troubled. 'I reckon we should look further for somewhere better.'

Grainne stared at him uncertainly, then clinging to her other arm Maggie Nolan whispered brokenly, 'For the love o' God, Grainne, take me in to lie down somewheres. I feel like death, so I do.'

The woman's broad features were grey and sweaty, and Grainne could feel the violent shivering of her body. 'Maggie's ill, Con,' she whispered to her husband. 'We can't drag the pooor soul through the streets any longer. Let's go in and find her a bed, if only for the one night. We can always leave here tomorrow and find somewhere else.'

As if to reinforce her plea the rain suddenly lashed down once more, so the young man shrugged helplessly and said, 'Alright then, honey, but come the morn I'm going to find us a better lodgings. What say you, Denis?'

The other man grinned displaying his toothless gums, and lifted the half-full bottle of gin. 'So long as I've a drop o' the cratur, then I'm not caring where we slape, my jewel.'

The street door opened directly onto a small room furnished only with some wooden benches and a table, behind which Tommy Tracey had seated himself, with the chests of the new arrivals on the floor beside him. Several men were lounging around the walls, smoking short clay pipes and periodically hawking and spitting onto the muddy bare boards of the floor. Grainne looked nervously at them for they were uniform in their villainous appearances. But none of them spoke or even appeared to pay too much attention to the proceedings.

'Well now, let's get to business.' Tommy Tracey smiled genially. 'Ye'll need to pay in advance for your beds and for your grub.'

'But we might not choose to eat here,' Con Shonley objected.

The huge man's smile did not falter. 'No dear, man,

14

ye'll not be eating here on the premises. I'll be giving you tickets to get your meals at an eating house just along the street there. It's great prog, isn't that so, boys?' He directed his question to the lounging men, who grunted affirmation.

'All my boys looks well fed enough, don't they, sor?' He sought Con Shonley's agreement, but the young man only frowned uneasily, and made no answer.

Now Tracey's brown-fanged grin hardened, but his manner was still affable.'I reckon I'd best explain to youse how this game is played. Ye'll need to buy a passage, and for that you must go to a Broker. Then ye'll need clothing and provisions for the voyage, and perhaps other things for when you land in Amerikay. Then ye have to pass the examination of the doctors afore ye can get aboard ship.' His shrewd eyes briefly examined the grey-faced, shivering Maggie Nolan. 'That poor cratur looks to be taken badly, and she'd not get aboard any ship.' He paused, watching to see what reaction that information would bring from the small group, and satisfied by their look of concern, chuckled with satisfaction, and reassured them expansively, 'But wi' Tommy Tracey behind yez, then you won't have a care in the world,' he said winking slyly, 'because Tommy Tracey knows the needful and he can get anybody on any ship whensoever he chooses. And there's another thing: if you was to take sick on the trip, then ye'd need a bond afore you could land in New York or Boston. Well, I'll take care o' that for yez too. And then there's also the question of ready tin for when ye get to Amerikay. English money is no good to ye there, so ye'll be needing American Dollars I can change your money for ye afore ye take ship and give ye a better exchange than anybody else can give ye.'

Maggie Nolan suddenly groaned and vomited sour smelling bile down the front of her dress, and before Grainne could tighten her grip, sagged to the floor.

Tommy Tracey was the first to react. 'Pat, Murphy,

15

put her in number six, as there's a couple of empty bunks there.'

The two men lifted the moaning woman by her shoulders and legs and carried her out of the room, with the bemused Grainne and Denis Callaghan following, leaving Con Shonley alone with Tracey and the rest of his henchmen.

'Right, young feller. Ye can pay me now for your bed and prog, and for the porterage and something on account for your passage money. Ten Sovereigns 'ull do to be going along with. I'll take the rest when I've fixed your berths.'

'Ten sovereigns?' the young man questioned suspiciously. 'That seems a hell of a lot for a night's lodgings, and I'd have carried my own chest if your men hadn't prevented me from doing so.'

The men around him suddenly tensed, and Con sensed danger, but Tommy Tracey remained affable. 'Now, young feller, don't be offending me,' he said easily. 'That's if you don't want to end up lying in the street with a broken head, or worse. I'm an honest man, and half of what I'm asking is deposit money for your passage to Amerikay. Now you've a sick woman on your hands, and there's not another hotel or lodging house in this city 'ull take her in, if Tommy Tracey tells 'um not to.' He nodded towards the open door through which the sound of pouring rain came drumming. 'The poor soul 'ull be in sore straits if she's to spend the night out there. Still, if you want to leave, then I'll not lift a hand to stop ye. Ye can just pay me the five sovereigns, and you can go and take the others wi' you.'

Con Shonley was a brave man, and an intelligent one, and he realised that at this moment in time he was virtually powerless against these men, but still he felt constrained to argue further. 'Listen Mr Tracey, if you took five sovereigns from me now, then that would amount to virtual robbery. I'm sure the police would be very interested to hear about it.'

16

The huge man threw back his top-hatted head and roared with genuine amusement, and all the others in the room joined in his laughter.

Con Shonley flushed hotly and cursed himself for being a fool. It was obvious that these men had no fear of the police, and indeed were probably paying them to turn a blind eye to whatever they did.

Tracey sobered abruptly, and told the young man, 'Get wise to yourself, my bucko. I'm running a business here. If we'd chosen to we could ha' stripped you and your friends stark naked and left yez in a pile of shit, and nobody would ha' lifted a finger to help yez, not the peelers, not anybody. There's thousands o' you bowsies coming through this city, and there's hundreds goes missing, and hundreds more that gets robbed of everything they have. With me you'll get fair dealing and you'll get a passage, and when they know that you're one o' mine, then nobody else 'ull be bothering you. Now I'm not wasting any more o' my time wi' ye, so either give me the ten sovereigns and stay, or pay me the five and take your chests and your friends out from here.'

Con Shonley glanced at the savage, bestial faces of the men surrounding him, thought of Grainne and sick Maggie Nolan, and what might happen to them should he choose to go, and reluctantly accepted what seemed to him to be the inevitable. 'We'll be staying, Mr Tracey,' he said.

Chapter Two

The room was on the top floor of the three-storeyed house and its walls were lined by narrow two-tiered wooden bunks which had nothing on their bare boards. A wooden table and some benches were the sole furnishings and all available floor space was covered with the piled bundles and boxes of the twenty-odd people already packed into its close, musty-smelling confines, lit only by a single dirty skylight and a hissing yellow-flamed gas jet hanging from the rafter.

When Con joined them, Grainne and Denis Callaghan were crouching by the lower bunk on which Maggie Nolan lay, grey-faced and moaning. The people in the room looked shabby and weary, most appearing to be family groups with old and very young among them. They sat on the rough benches or lay in the narrow bunks, staring at the newcomers, but offering no greeting. Only the whimpering of a baby being nursed by its wan-faced mother broke the silence.

Con nodded to them in general, saying, 'Good day to ye all.'

There was a mumble of replies and then the occupants lapsed once more into their mute apathy.

'How did you get on?' Grainne whispered, as her husband knelt by her side.

'I had to pay them the ten sovereigns,' he told her disgruntledly. 'It was either that, or pay the buggers five sovereigns and have us all out on the street again.'

18

He saw the look of concern in her green eyes and hastened to reassure her. 'But half of the money is towards our tickets, honey.' His handsome face frowned disconsolately. 'Jesus Christ, Grainne, I feel so damned helpless here, like a pigeon ripe for plucking!'

A hoarse laugh greeted his last words, and Con stared at a young man seated on the nearest bench. 'Do I amuse you?' he challenged hotly.

The man was dressed in a threadbare black frockcoat with a high-winged collar and black cravat around his scrawny unshaven throat. He wore pantaloons and a tall black tophat and his long lank greasy hair hung down to his narrow shoulders. His thin sallow face was mottled with a skin eruption and the backs of his long bony hands were likewise disfigured. However, despite the general seediness of his appearance there was something prepossessing about this man as he smiled, disclosing good even teeth, and his hazel eyes clear and steady. As they met Con Shonley's angry glare the man replied, 'Pray don't take offence, Sir, for I assure you none was intended. I laughed solely because I found myself in complete agreement with your statement. I was seated here thinking the very same thing about myself.' He rose from the bench and, removing his hat, bowed slightly. 'Allow me to present myself, Septimus Prendergast, your servant, Sir, and yours also, Ma'am.' He bowed towards Grainne. His accent and manner were those of a gentleman, and Con Shonley's hot temper cooled as quickly as it had risen.

'I am Conrad Shonley and this is my wife.' He also rose upright and bowed in return. 'This is my good friend, Denis Callaghan, and the lady on the bunk is Miss Margaret Nolan.'

Prendergast smiled and bowed again, then indicated the empty spaces on the bench beside him. 'Won't you join me, Mr Shonley? I am thirsty for intelligent conversation.'

Denis Callaghan nudged Con and Grainne. 'You set

yourselves down, I'll stay with Maggie. Look, she's nearly aslape.'

The sick woman's eyes were closing and she seemed to be easier now that she was lying down, so Grainne joined her husband and their new acquaintance on the bench.

'Do you go to America or to one of the colonies?' Prendergast asked.

'To America,' Con told him. 'We've just landed from the Cork steamer.'

'From Cork?' The young man's charming smile caused Grainne to forget the unsightly facial eruptions, and she thought him quite personable. 'I'm English myself, of course, but I've been to Ireland several times. My father had connections in Meath.' He sighed regretfully. 'A most unhappy country these past years, I fear.'

'I think unhappy is an understatement, Mr Prendergast,' Con said bitterly. 'Ireland is in purgatory.' He paused, then unable to contain himself went on, 'The Irish people are dying from starvation, and yet we have just come over here on a boat carrying a cargo of pigs. How many poor wretches could have been saved from death if that cargo had been distributed among them, I wonder, instead of being brought here to be sold to the damned English for profit?'

The other man smiled sardonically. 'You have seen a good many of those damned English in the streets you have just walked through, who will not be buying any part of that cargo, Mr Shonley. Starvation is not the sole prerogative of the Irish. There is enough hunger and hardship abroad in England to satisfy the most exacting connoisseur of misery.'

'That may well be, sir, but I doubt that food is being robbed from this country to feed other nations, as is happening in Ireland.'

'Perhaps not,' the Englishman accepted. 'But let me ask you who it is that is exporting cattle, pigs and other

20

foodstuffs from Ireland at this time?' He did not wait for a reply but answered his own question. 'It is your own Irish landlords who are carrying out the evictions of their own peasantry, and it is native-born Irishmen who are depriving those tragic people of the roofs over their heads.'

'Protected by English soldiers and police,' Con interrupted heatedly.

'Protected by this present Government's soldiers and police, Mr Shonley,' Prendergast corrected with equal warmth. 'And those police are mainly Irishmen and the soldiers can as equally come from Ireland, as from England, Scotland or Wales.'

In his heart of hearts Con Shonley knew that the man was speaking the truth, but still he argued stubbornly, 'Ireland is ruled by a foreign tyranny and will never know any happiness until those foreign tyrants' soldiers and policemen are driven into the sea. Then the Irish people will be free.' In his excitement Con's voice had risen and Grainne, fearful of what might happen, told him sharply, 'Stop this now, Con. Haven't we troubles enough, what with poor Maggie being ill?'

It was the Englishman who answered her. 'Don't worry, Mrs Shonley.' He smiled and shook his head. 'I doubt that there are any "agents provocateurs" in this house. What is said between us, stays between us. However, I do apologise most sincerely if my conversation causes you any unease. I do have this confound predilection for political disputation, I'm afraid. Please excuse me.'

He uncoiled his long skinny body from the bench and went to a bunk at the end of the room, into which he hoisted himself, and removing his tall hat appeared to fall instantly asleep.

Grainne and her husband sat in silence, and the girl was grateful for that silence because her mind was full. Only a matter of days before, Con, her husband, had stood in the ranks of rebellion during the ill-fated and almost farcical uprising of the Young Ireland movement. After the rout of the pathetic rebel force, and the flight of its leaders, Con had come to join her, and their friends Maggie and Denis at Cork, and all four of them were now intending to go to America in search of a new life. Grainne herself was apolitical, as were Denis and Maggie, and although to help her husband she had at times aided the rebels she held no more sympathy for them and their cause, than she held for Queen Victoria and the British Government. All Grainne wanted was to live her life in peace together with her beloved Con. She smiled wryly to herself now, as she considered the irony of the fact that Con, who was half English should be a rebel, whereas herself and the other two who were all full-blood Irish, did not give a damn for the cause of Young Ireland, and had little or no respect for the rebel leaders, such as William Smith O'Brian, Gavan Duffy, Thomas Meagher and John Mitchell.

'Are you angry with me, sweetheart?'

Con's whispered question brought her from her reverie, and she took his hand in hers and squeezed gently. 'No, I'm not angry with you. But I wish you could put the past behind you now. You made your stand, and you've played your part for the cause. Can't you now forget about what can't be changed, and concentrate instead on our new life.'

He chuckled ruefully. 'I'm trying to do so, Grainne. But I'm finding it sore hard.'

Grainne smiled tenderly at him, feeling at this moment immeasurably older and wiser. 'Listen Con, I know well how deeply you love Ireland, and that you truly believe that once the English have been driven out then all will be well with her. But you can't spend your life hating another nation. Don't be forgetting that before we were wed I used to work over here in this country. The English are the same as all the other people in the world, some are good and some are bad. Your own mother is English, and you have English

22

blood in your veins as well as Irish, and let's face one fact shall we ... We've both of us been done more hurt to by our own Irish people than we've ever been hurt by any Englishman. I don't care what flag waves above my head, Con, just so long as you and I can live a happy life together.' She leaned forwards and kissed him lightly on the lips, then asked, 'And now, what do you intend doing about getting to see your mother before we sail?'

Con's father had died some time previously, and despite Con's initially strong objections his mother had re-married, and had taken her other children, Con's younger brothers and sisters, to England to live with her new husband. The man, James Mahoney, a graphic artist, had wanted Con to go with the rest of his family but the bitterly resentful young man had rejected all his offers and so Mahoney had left money in Ireland for Con's use. Although at first Con had refused to touch the money, events had eventually brought him to use it to carry himself, Grainne and their two friends to America.

Con was very serious as he told Grainne, 'I feel that whatever else might happen, I must go and see my mother and family before we leave this country. I need to make my peace with her, Grainne, and with her new husband. Now, when I think of how I behaved towards them, I am deeply ashamed.'

'When will you go?' Grainne wanted to know, and her husband corrected her.

'When will we go, sweetheart, for you must come with me to see them.'

'Very well, if that's what you want, Con. So, when will we go?'

'Let's get our passages arranged first, and then Denis and Maggie can wait for us here. I don't think we'll have sufficient money to take all four of us to London and back, that's if we're to have anything left in our pockets when we land in America.'

The heated stale air of the overcrowded room was

now beginning to affect Grainne, who felt increasingly drowsy. Con smiled fondly at her as she yawned.

'You lie down now, and get some sleep, Honey.'

She was uncomfortably aware of the dampness of her clothing, and she told the young man, 'I could do with changing into something dry.'

He glanced about him and joked, 'There doesn't seem to be any dressing room here, sweetheart.'

She pouted momentarily, then shrugged and said, 'Ah well, it won't be the first time I've slept in a wet shift. My mother's cabin didn't have a very sound roof. But how about you, aren't you tired?'

It was his turn to shrug. 'Not really.' He noted that the only unoccupied bunk was that above Maggie Nolan's. 'Anyways, it looks as if we'll have to take turns at the bed, so you go first.'

Waves of sleepiness overwhelmed Grainne and gratefully she clambered up onto the bare boards of the vacant bunk. Removing only her ankle boots she pillowed her head on her arms and within moments was sleeping soundly.

Denis Callaghan joined Con on the bench and proffered the bottle of gin. 'Take a dram outta this, Con dear. It'll cheer ye up,'

The young man patted his friend's shoulder. 'I'll not be feeling cheery until we're on the boat out from here. From what I've seen of John Bull's island up to now, the people are as hard done by as the poor souls at home.'

'Isn't that what I've been telling youse ever since I first met you, Con. It's not only us Paddies that are having hard times. It don't matter where you live. If you're poor, then ye might as well take comfort from the bottle, for it's the only comfort ye'll ever find. Now take a wee sip, and stop feeling so bloody sorry for yourself.'

Con Shonley grinned somewhat shamefacedly, and accepted the invitation. The raw spirit burned its way down his gullet and he was forced to suppress a cough.

'Are you hungry?' he asked.

'Jasus no! That bloody pig-boat has soured me

24

stomach agin' all food. I'll need to get me landlegs afore I'll be able to ate anything.'

'Me too,' the young man agreed fervently. 'God help us when we sail. It takes a month or more to cross to America, so I'm told.'

His friend's plump red face was solemn as he looked at Maggie Nolan sleeping restlessly. 'Then God help my poor wee girl there, for this trip's near killed her.'

Nearly all the room's occupants were sleeping by now, crammed in the narrow bunks, lying on makeshift bedding on the floor or balancing precariously on the benches. After a few more sips of gin Con Shonley and Denis Callaghan laid their own heads down upon the table and slept too, mingling their own snores with the discordant grunting, muttering, farting, snoring chorus of their fellow lodgers.

Down below in the small room that opened onto the street, Tommy Tracey sat alone with only the hissing of the gas-jet for company as he pored over a big, battered leather-bound ledger. His spatulate, black-nailed fingers ran down the crude notations that covered its open pages, and the sums of money entered against the lists of names. A bottle of brandy stood on the table top at his elbow, and periodically he would raise it to his lips and take a noisy gulp, then belch with resounding satisfaction. When his finger stopped at the name 'Shonley' he smiled wolfishly and murmured to himself, ' 'Tis always a pleasure to do business wi' a man who has ready money like yourself, Con Shonley. But I'd sooner do business wi' that swate missus o' yours, and that's a fact!'

His bloodshot eyes fell upon another name, and he scowled doubtfully. 'Septimus Prendergast? Now there's summat about you that don't ring true, my bucko! You've been here for nigh on a week, and ye've never pestered me about your passage yet. Now why should that be, I wonder?'

The street door opened and a young girl dressed in bedraggled clothes and a tawdry feathered bonnet came in.

'Are you'se ready for me now, Mr Tracey.'

The huge man stared at her until she began to fidget uneasily, and her hand nervously touched her swollen, badly bruised right eye. Then nodding he said, 'Bolt them doors, and get your clothes off.'

Silently she obeyed.

Chapter Three

Grainne awoke and for a few moments lay staring up at the dirty cracked skylight through which the grey light of early dawn struggled to enter. She moved her body and grimaced at the stiffness of her chilled muscles, then turned her head to look down at her husband and Denis Callaghan sprawled upon the table top. The air in the room smelled badly and Grainne herself felt stale and unclean. As she climbed down from the bunk a sudden itching erupted around her armpits and disgusted she realised that the room was badly infested.

Maggie Nolan's broad features seemed to have shrunk and aged during the night hours and as Grainne bent to speak to her the sick woman begged in a cracked voice, 'For the love o' God, give me a drink o' water, Grainne. I'm terrible parched.'

'I'll get you one, honey,' Grainne promised, and looked about her for a receptacle in which she might carry the liquid.

Everyone appeared to be sleeping, except Septimus Prendergast, who called softly, 'Mrs Shonley, give your friend some of this.' He climbed from his bunk and came to Grainne to proffer an opened bottle of pale ale. 'It's wisest not to drink the water in this district Mrs Shonley.'

'Many thanks, Mr Prendergast.' Grainne took the bottle gratefully and supported Maggie Nolan while she drank greedily. Then the sick woman slumped back upon the bare boards of her bunk, gasping for breath.

27

Grainne looked at her friend with troubled eyes. 'How are you feeling, Maggie? Is there anything I can do to ease you?'

'No, I just want to lay here. I'm feeling terrible weak, and me head is aching fit to bust.'

'Do you know of a doctor hereabouts, Mr Prendergast?' Grainne wanted to know.

The man shrugged his narrow shoulders. 'There are some who term themselves doctors, Mrs Shonley, but for the most part they are quacks who do more harm than good.'

Grainne glanced about her at the noisome room and its gloomy denizens.'Sure, this place is not good for Maggie to be in. We'll needs find other lodgings which are cleaner, more healthy and not so crowded.'

The Englishman smiled mirthlessly. 'Believe it or not, Mrs Shonley, this place is one of the better sort of lodgings, unless you have sufficient means to stay at one of the grand hotels. There are nigh on forty thousand poor souls dwelling in cellars in this city, and over eighty thousands in slum courts. I could take you to emigrant lodgings where there are forty people crammed into a cellar, or where a hundred people sleep in places licensed to take twenty.'

He paused and Grainne asked him, 'Then what should I do with Maggie, for we've only money enough to get us to America? But if necessary I'll use that money to get her better.'

The man's hazel eyes were warm as he said, 'She is indeed fortunate in her friend. I would advise that for today at least you let her lie here and rest, if her condition should worsen then there are several charitable institutions which take in fever cases and the infirmary also. But frankly, more go into those places than come out cured.'

While the conversation was taking place Con Shonley and Denis Callagham had roused themselves, and listened quietly to the exchange. It was Con who now joined in the conversation. 'Would it not be best

28

for us to take passage as soon as we can, Mr Prendergast? Surely the sea air would be good for Maggie?'

The Englishman's narrow features mirrored his uncertainty. 'I doubt that the air of the steerage is any more salubrious than it is here, Mr Shonley. Some of the emigrant ships are kept clean and well conducted, but the vast majority can truly be termed plague ships. Last year there were many thousands who died from the fever during the voyage. The overcrowding on board can be truly termed criminal, the food is very bad, and sometimes the water also, Miss Nolan would get no rest whatsoever. A passage in the steerage class of an emigrant ship should really only be undertaken by people in full health and strength.'

'By Christ, but ye're not offering us much comfort.' Denis Callaghan's normally cheerful face looked angry and resentful. 'How come ye know so much about all this?'

'I know because I have made it my business to know, Mr Callaghan,' Prendergast told him quietly. 'And what I have said is only the truth. Whether you believe me or not is your own choice. And now, if you'll excuse me, I shall go to my breakfast.' He bowed courteously, placed his top hat on his greasy hair and went from the room.

By now the rest of the occupants were stirring themselves, and babies were crying, men and women disputing irritably, children complaining of hunger and thirst. People were leaving the room and one man, dressed in the short blue cloak and caubeen of an Irish countryman stopped to speak to Con Shonley. 'Have ye the tickets for your food, Man?'

Con nodded, and the man informed him, 'Well, ye'll needs look sharp and get your breakfast at the eating shop, else ye'll get nothing until this night.'

Con thanked him, and told Denis and Grainne. 'Look, I'll stay here with Maggie while you two eat and go when you come back. We'll decide what's to be done next when we've got something in our bellies.'

Denis Callaghan shook his head. 'No, I want to stay

here with Maggie. Ye can bring us something back.'

By daylight Grainne was able to see that Tracey's Hotel was a honeycomb of rooms similar to the one she had slept in and she marvelled at the amount of people crowded in them. 'If this is one of the better lodgings, then God help the poor souls in the other places,' she thought.

Outside the narrow street was swarming with dirty, ragged, barefoot children and equally shabby adults. Grainne clung onto Con's arm and carefully picked her way amongst the filth underfoot. With equal care she avoided the open flaps of the cellars from which foul stenches and raucous noises denoted the presence of a pullulating subterranean population. The foul air was a hubbub of different accents. Grainne was struck by the all pervading ugly brutality of the faces surrounding her and by the amount of women with bruises and cuts. She shivered involuntarily and pressed ever closer to her husband's strong body. She had been in the slums of Cork, Skibereen and Schull where she had seen and experienced the terrible sufferings of famine-stricken Ireland, but she had never before sensed the threatening menace which pervaded these mean streets. In the west of Ireland, even during the worst periods of the famine, women could walk safely through the streets, but here, in this city, Grainne felt afraid.

The eating house was packed with emigrants seated on narrow benches eating thick chunks of brown bread and salt butter, and slurping gritty unsweetened coffee from tin mugs. The coffee was dispensed by a huge negress from steaming brass urns behind the stained dirty counter in exchange for the cardboard tickets issued by Tommy Tracey. Clustered around the eating house's doorway was a collection of human wrecks begging for any leftover crusts, but if any of them attempted to enter in pursuit of food, the negress shrieked and came from behind her counter to belabour them with a cudgel driving them back into the street, while cursing them in the ripest of Scouse accents.

Con and Grainne handed over their tickets, and Grainne wrapped the bread and butter for Denis and Maggie in a clean piece of cloth. They sat side by side and ate their own portions. Despite the staleness of the bread and the tainted taste of the butter Grainne realised she was ravenously hungry, and relished the poor food. Con looked at her with concern and said in a low voice, 'I'm sorry for bringing you to this, honey. If I'd known what it was like here, then I'd have waited and taken ship from Cork. We could have sailed direct from there.'

She squeezed his arm affectionately. 'No, Con, we were right to come here. Every hour we were in Cork I feared that you'd be taken up by the peelers or the soldiers for having been fighting in the rebellion. We're safe from that here.'

He grinned wryly. 'But we're not safe from a hundred other things, are we? I wish I'd got me pike with me, or at least a bloody big shillelagh. I'd be feeling a whole lot safer then.'

'Aren't you the big bold rebel,' she teased, and they both laughed.

Then Grainne sobered, and told him, 'Listen Con, you must go to see your mother by yourself. I can't leave Maggie while she's so ill. Denis, bless him, is not really capable of caring for her, especially if he takes a drink or two.'

Disappointment instantly showed on Con Shonley's face and he began to protest, but Grainne placed her finger against his lips, and told him firmly, 'No, Con! You'll go by yourself, and we'll wait here for you. You needn't be gone more than two or three days. You know that what I'm saying is right. I can't leave Maggie here with only Denis to care for her. If the situation was reversed you'd not want Maggie to leave me, would you?'

With bad grace he was forced to acknowledge the truth of what she said, and Grainne went on to urge him, 'Go today, Con. There'll be trains to London from here. If you leave today then the sooner you'll be back with me.'

After more badgering from Grainne and with evident reluctance, he finally agreed. 'Very well, honey. But you take great care while I'm gone. Don't go out by yourself at night, will you.'

It was her turn to smile wryly. 'Jesus! I'd sooner walk through a lion's den than through these streets at night. This city gives me the shivers, so it does.'

32

Chapter Four

Guided by Septimus Prendergast, Grainne accompanied her husband to the terminus of the London and North-Western Railway Company at Lime Street. The Englishman took them from the wretched stinking streets west of the Scotland Road and by a roundabout route so that he could show them another side of the city. Opulent Castle Street, Bold Street, Dale Street, St George's Crescent and Abercrombie Square, the Town Hall and Mansion House, the Exchange Building and Custom House, the gigantic Albert Docks and its warehouses, and the Goree Piazza where behind the mighty warehouses of George's Dock merchants had dealt in human cargoes of African slaves that had laid the foundations of the present city's commercial preponderance.

The streets and thoroughfares pulsated with bustle, noise and a constant stream of traffic. Long lines of wagons and carts were piled high with bales of raw cotton, baulks of timber, loads of palm oil, jute, rice and rum, tobacco, sugar, molasses and a thousand other commodities carried from all over the world on the twenty-five thousand ships that traded in and out of this port every year. Going towards those vast acres of docks and shipping were the cotton goods and woollen goods, the coal and the pottery and all the varied products of iron and steel manufactured in the industrial towns of Great Britain.

This was Con Shonley's first time in England and despite himself, he was impressed with what he saw and awed by what it represented. Grainne had been brought to England some five years previously as a lady's maid in the service of Lady Dunsmore and although she had not been in Liverpool she had seen other cities in England and knew something of its mercantile and military strength.

Now she smiled up at her husband's solemn face and teased him gently, 'You and your friends were trying to chew a big mouthful when you took on this crowd weren't you, honey.'

Momentarily he frowned, then chuckled and pretended to aim a blow at her, saying, 'Don't you be making mock of me wife, or it'll go hard with you.'

Septimus Prendergast had proved an easy and entertaining companion on their walk, and the young couple both experienced a growing liking for the young man, seedy though he appeared. He had caught the interchange between them and asked pleasantly, 'You were involved in the late unpleasantness in Ireland then, Mr Shonley?'

He saw the sudden doubt in both of their expressions, and laughed easily. 'Don't take my question amiss, I beg of you. I myself was and indeed still am, a physical force Chartist. I can understand anybody who driven by desperation finally takes up arms.' A sudden flash of bitterness twisted his features, and when he next spoke it was as if he was talking to himself. 'We are a peculiar race, we English. You may take the lowliest and most wretched of us and we still hold ourselves to be superior to any foreigner, regardless of his degree. We go abroad in our hundreds of thousands in red coats and blue jackets to fight, even die for Queen and Country, and by fire and sword we spread our dominion worldwide. At this present day we are recognised as the richest, most powerful nation in the world.' He shook his head as if bewildered and continued, 'But here at home there are millions of people suffering inconceivable hardship every day of their lives; born to wretched poverty, existing in wretched poverty and dying in wretched poverty. And when men like myself try to rouse the poor to fight against those who oppress them, we are reviled as Red Republicans, evil men, even regicides by those same poor.' He came to a standstill and asked Con Shonley, 'Are we insane Mr Shonley, or can it be that the whole world excepting us is so afflicted with insanity that they cannot see the truth in what we tell them?'

As Prendergast had been speaking Con Shonley had found himself increasingly drawn to the man, despite him being a comparative stranger. He patted his companion's narrow shoulder, noting the frailty of bone and muscle beneath the threadbare cloth of the black coat. 'If we are insane Mr Prendergast, then we are insane with the best of motives. Yes, I took up arms as at the time I believed in the justice of the cause for which I was going to fight. But to speak frankly, the uprising was a farce and those leaders that I trusted and followed failed me and others like me. Now I only wish to create a new life for Grainne and myself across the seas. I'll follow no more flags, and fight for no more causes.'

Grainne's tense body relaxed and she emitted a heartfelt sigh of relief.

Prendergast smiled at Grainne's reaction, and remarked quietly. 'Had I been so blessed with such a wife I declare I would echo your sentiments, Mr Shonley.'

At St George's Hall which was massive though still under construction, facing the ornate façade of the Lime Street Railway Station, Prendergast told them, 'I'll wait here for Mrs Shonley and see that she gets back to our lodgings safely. I wish you God speed, Mr Shonley and a happy return.'

Inside the station Grainne took charge of the arrangements for the journey as Con had never before been in a railway station. She bought a third class ticket to London for sixteen shillings and nine pence and ascertained that the journey should take approximately nine to ten hours. Swarms of green-coated, peak-capped porters hauled luggage of all descriptions through the crowds of passengers. Railway policemen dressed in top hats and green frock coats, patrolled the station, alert for pickpockets and sneakthieves. Train guards, with silver-buckled black patent leather crossbelts, white buttons and frogging overlooked the stowage of their vans. Resplendent superintendents and inspectors moved like monarchs along the platform and concourse, while grease-stained underlings scurried to attach a continuous chain to the long line of the train. It would be needed to haul the train through the steep tunnel leading to Edge Hill by means of a massive stationary steam engine at that latter station.

Con kissed his wife tenderly. 'I'll be back as soon as I can, honey. Now you've money enough for all your needs. If Tracey pesters you for anything tell him he'll get paid when I come back.'

All around the young couple was bedlam and with a final hug Con left her and took his seat in the carriage.

Grainne didn't wait for the train to depart, but walked out from the station, deriding herself for the tears which were stinging her eyes. 'Sure he'll only be gone a few days. I'm behaving as stupidly as a booby,' she murmured.

Septimus Prendergast escorted her back to the rancid slums west of the Scotland Road, and left her at the door of Tracey's Hotel.

'I'll needs be about some personal business, Mrs Shonley,' he said. 'But I'll return shortly, so if you need any service I'll be available to you then.'

Grainne thanked him, and to her own surprise was loth to see him go. In the entrance hall she met Tommy Tracey, and stopped to ask him, 'Have you any idea how long it will take to book a passage, Mr Tracey?'

He grinned and told her, 'Just as soon as I can, my

36

pretty, I'll have ye on a fine big ship. But what a fine looking crayture like you needs to go off to Amerikay for, I can't for the life o' me figure out. You could earn your fortune in this city.'

Grainne regarded him steadily and for a moment was tempted to make a sharp reply. But deciding against it she only nodded coolly and walked on past him, through the labyrinth of dark passageways, odourous doorways and cubby holes and mounted the steps to the room in which she lodged.

> 'On the banks of the ro'ossesss me love and I
> sat down,
> And I took out me fiddle
> For to play me love a tune . . .'

It was Denis Callaghan's voice she could hear singing drunkenly, and her heart sank. 'Dear God, Denis, do you have to get drunk so early in the day?' she muttered despairingly, beneath her breath.

'Well now, if it ain't me own swate colleen bawn come back to see us. Set yourself down here, my lovely, and have a spot o' this.'

He was seated at the table with two other men, bareheaded, his face flushed and sweaty, his coat and shirt open to display his pallid flabby chest. He lifted the black bottle of gin and proffered it to her. 'Come now, little Grainne. Take a wee drop for your own dear Mammy's sake. By the Christ, the woman did the world a great favour when she birthed you, Grainne, because ye're the prettiest crayture that ever walked this earth, and that's including me own darling Maggie, so it is.'

Grainne glanced at the table, noting the other empty bottles that littered its surface and annoyance flared within her as she turned to Maggie Nolan. The woman was lying on her back, apparently unconscious, mouth gaping, her breathing harsh and laboured, her grey face sheened with sweat. What caused Grainne's annoyance was the bottle that the sick woman clutched in her hands. She took it from the flaccid fingers and checked its almost consumed contents, then angrily turned on Denis Callaghan, crying, 'Why have you been giving her gin? She's ill, and this poison can only make her worse!'

The man grinned blearily. 'Arragh sure now, my jewel, a drop o' the blue ruin ne'er killed anybody yet. And it's a sovereign cure for any sort o' fever. I should know, because 'twas all that kept me and your own man alive when we was working as burial men. And sure, you know that yourself. If it hadn't been for the gin and the poteen then me and Con would have been stretched in our graves long since.'

'Where are you getting all this drink, Denis?' Grainne demanded, knowing that neither he nor Maggie had any money whatsoever, because she and Con were paying for everything for the pair.

He winked slyly. 'Sure now, there's no call for you to worry your pretty little head about that, my jewel. These gentlemen here are working for Mr Thomas Tracey, and they get it for me cheap.' He sought confirmation from his companions. 'Isn't that so, boys?'

Grainne glanced briefly at each man in turn. Unshaven hulking brutes, dressed in dirty clothing, both with battered hats pulled down low on their greasy, matted hair, they grinned back at her in drunken fuddlement, and one of them beckoned to her with his filthy swollen hand, saying, 'Come here to me and see what I've got for yez.' His hand went to his groin and he kneaded it in lewd suggestion. 'I reckon I could do you a bit o' good, my little judy. Arter you'd had a taste o' what I've got here rammin between your legs, you'd be beggin' for more.'

Grainne's anger flared. 'If my husband was here it's you who'd be begging. Begging for mercy, you disgusting animal!' she shouted.

The man's heavy features twisted in vicious threat and he struggled to rise to his feet. 'You stroppy cunt! '

he mouthed, saliva spraying from his loose blubbery lips. 'I'll kick your fokkin' head in for yez.'

But his friend grabbed him by the tail of his coat and pulled him down again onto the bench. 'Lave her be, you thick-skulled bastard. Tracey's took a fancy for her.'

The first man backed down reluctantly, but remained glaring at Grainne, mouthing a stream of filth at her.

Denis Callaghan stared blearily, shaking his head, mystified by the proceedings, and Grainne, who was more shaken by the sudden eruption of the incident than she cared to show, bent over Maggie Nolan, busying herself by wiping the sweat from the woman's face and throat while waiting for the pounding of her own heart to ease.

As she calmed down, Grainne realised with a sinking heart that without Con here to protect her, she was in ever present danger of both verbal and physical assault. A sense of anger and disgust towards Denis Callaghan filled her. When sober, he was not a bad man, and had proven a good friend to both her and Con in the past, but now, with the drink taking an ever increasing toll on him he was fast becoming a liability, and whatever respect or liking Grainne had had for him was rapidly disappearing. Now, with resentment, she heard him wheedling. 'Grainne my jewel, d'ye think ye could let me have a few shillings to buy me round with? Only me and these gentlemen want to take the air elsewhere, and it's my turn to divvy-up.'

Her first impulse was to refuse him, but mindful of the fact that she could not begin to care for Maggie Nolan while having to be watchful of another outburst from the man who had insulted her, she stealthily fumbled for a few coins in the small pouch concealed in her bodice, and handed them to Callaghan muttering, 'Here, take this, but you'll get nothing more from me to waste on the drink, Denis. And if you pester me for more, then I'll be telling Con when he gets back.'

He grinned and jerked his head at his companions. 'That's it, boys. Lets go and take a look at what the town's got to offer.'

To Grainne's intense relief both men stumbled out of the room with him, and she was left alone with the sick womn. The absence of the other people who shared the room momentarily puzzled Grainne, but when she realised that the boxes and bundles which had cluttered the floor space were also gone she assumed that they had been shipped out that morning on a vessel.

The door opened and a ragged bent-bodied old woman came in. Upon seeing Grainne and Maggie Nolan she confirmed Grainne's assumption. 'Another lot went this morn, but ye'll have plenty o' company directly, missis. This place niver stays empty what wi' all the poor souls coming over from Ireland, and all the other parts. Now which is your stuff, missis?'

Grainne pointed out her own party's luggage, and the crone's withered, dirt-grimed feaures evinced a glum disgust.

'Fuck 'em!' she grumbled fiercely. 'Them bastarts hasna left sweet fuck-all for poor Old Bridie.' She picked up the empty bottles from the table and stowed them away beneath her multi-layered smelly rags. Then, going down on her hands and knees she scurried along the filthy floor peering and feeling beneath the bunks with her stick-thin arms. Muttering all the time, the old crone worked her way around the narrow room. Then groaning painfully she straightened up and came to look down at Maggie Nolan. 'That one won't be staying on this earth for too much longer by the looks on it. Poor cow's got the hand o' Death on her already ... Old Bridie knows when they'm done for. Old Bridie's seen fuckin' more on 'um go than she'd care to remember.'

She peered at Grainne with red-rimmed rheumy eyes. 'I used to look like you when I fust come 'ere to this cursed city.' She preened grotesquely and twitched her broken-brimmed bonnet. 'I was a pretty maid, I was. A sweet pretty virgin maid. 'Til these fuckin' devils in this city got ahold o' me.' She shook her crooked misshapen fingers in Grainne's face. 'Don't you bide here, my maid. You get out whiles you can. They anna men in this place, but fuckin' devils.'

'Gerrof away from here, you dirty old bat!' One of Tracey's men came through the door, and following him up the staircase could be heard a party of new arrivals. He savagely kicked the old crone on her backside, sending her stumbling into Grainne, who instinctively interposed between the pair to shield the old woman from further brutality.

'Devils they am. Fuckin' devils!' the old crone shrieked in her cracked voice and with a speed surprising in one of her age, darted through the door, dodging the further blow the man aimed at her.

The new arrivals filed into the room, speaking in the soft rustic burr of Gloucestershire. A man, dressed like a farmer in a good broadcloth coat, low-crowned tophat, corduroy breeches and leather gaiters entered with his plump, pink-faced wife, and a brood of children of varying ages, each one carrying either bundle or box, and father himself toting a large wooden chest on his broad back.

Grainne felt relieved when she saw her new roommates. 'They look decent souls, thank God.' But having thought that, she became uncomfortably aware that she had not washed herself or changed her underclothing since leaving Cork city. 'Here's me worrying about having decent folk in the room, and I must be looking like a tinker-woman myself.' She was also uncomfortably aware that her sick friend was beginning to smell unpleasant. 'I'll needs get us both cleaned up, and the sooner the better,' she thought.

She waited until the newly arrived family had settled themselves and then said to the woman, 'Forgive me for troubling you, ma'm, but my friend is ill, and I need to fetch water to wash her. Could you please keep an eye on her and on our baggage while I go to try to find water?'

41

The woman's plump motherly features beamed assent. 'O' course I can, my dear. You go along now. I'll see that the poor wench comes to no harm, nor your baggage neither.'

Downstairs in the entrance hall Tommy Tracey was taking money from more new arrivals, and these, unlike the family in Grainne's room, showed all the ravages of poverty. With stunted bodies, pallid faces, they were refugees from the slums of Lancashire given funds from some parish poor chest to take them to the New World.

As Grainne stood quietly waiting for the business to be finished, she admitted to the truth of Septimus Prendergast's assertion, that the Irish did not hold the monopoly of starvation when she saw the emaciated bodies, the rags, and hollow eyes of England's own children.

'What can I be doing for you, sweet thing?' Tommy Tracey grinned at her, when the newest arrivals had gone into the warren under the charge of another of his henchmen.

Although made uncomfortable by the lust so openly displayed in his expression, Grainne asked him politely, 'Please where can I get water, and a bucket to carry it in?'

He made a show of pushing his tall black hat back upon his head and scratching his matted sandy hair. 'Water, is it? Now then, that might be a problem, sweet thing. We've a standcock in the court at the side of us, but mostly it's not working. There's a cart comes once a day up the corner there, and you can buy a pail full for a ha-penny, but it might have been and gone already. Why do you want water anyway? Isn't the porter good enough to drink?'

She could not help but rise to his baiting. 'I want to wash myself and my clothes. Don't people do such as that round here?'

Her sarcasm appeared to delight him, and he laughed heartily before telling her, 'Now you've mentioned it, honey-lamb, the answer is no. They don't do much in the way o' washing their clothes. They might throw a drop o' water on their head sometimes, but mostly they just waits 'til it rains, and stands out in it for a bit.' He paused and regarded her closely for a couple of seconds, his eyes gleaming with amusement. Then he went on, 'Mind you, spaking for meself, I'm summat of a jack-dandy. I have the shave at least once a week, and I've been known to wash me face and neck every so often. But I'm a man o' business, and I have to look smart and clean. It's not the same for these other bowsies. They're just scum really, and most of them lives like pigs.' Again he laughed heartily, then added, 'O' course, it's a sight warmer that way, isn't it now? Particularly in the bloody winter. A bit o' dirt helps kape the cold out.'

Grainne kept a rein on her fiery temper, knowing that until Con returned she was very much at this man's mercy. 'Look Mr Tracey, my friend is very ill, and I need to wash her. I'll pay you for the use of a bucket, and also for the water.'

He regarded her for a long moment, his expression ambiguous, then said with apparent sincerity, 'Listen girl, if I could give you water at this time, then I would. But I'm only spaking the truth when I tell ye that I've none to give yez. There's only three taps in this street, and sometimes there's no water runs from 'um for weeks at a time. When it's regular, then we only get the water maybe twice or thrice a week, and then its only running for maybe half an hour. Believe me, I don't like it either, because I still have to pay bloody rates for it, being the householder here.'

Grainne stared at him disbelievingly, and in the face of her disbelief he became irritated, and snarled, 'I'm not lying to yez, so don't you be looking at me like that. If you need water so bad, then ye'll have to go to the bloody Water Company and fetch it back wi' you!'

'Mr Tracey is telling you the truth, Mrs Shonley.' Septimus Prendergast had come to the street door while the exchange was taking place and had heard what passed between them.

'But how can people live without water to wash with?' asked a mystified Grainne, and Prendergast's even teeth gleamed in a mirthless smile. 'The short answer to that, Mrs Shonley, is that a deal of them don't. They die with great frequency in these streets. I do believe that this city has the highest mortality rate in the kingdom. When people get really desperate for water, they steal it, from wherever they can. Is that not so, Mr Tracey?' He sought confirmation from the big man, who nodded sullenly.

'God, I wish we'd never come to this city!' Grainne exclaimed in anger and disgust, and turning on her heel went back to her room.

Septimus Prendergast joined her there after a few minutes and seated himself on the bench beside her. He nodded towards the comatose Maggie Nolan and whispered, 'I see that your friend's condition has not improved, Mrs Shonley.'

Grainne bit her lips worriedly. 'I don't know what to do for the best, Mr Prendergast. Con may not be back here for several days, and Denis is off somewhere drinking. She needs a doctor to look at her, of that I'm certain, but how can I know which is a good doctor to attend her, even if I should find one willing to come to this place? I would think that any gentleman would be feared to penetrate these streets.' Aware of her own stale body she added ruefully, 'And what gentleman would accompany me here, with me being unwashed for days, and looking like a tinker-woman myself.'

It was the Englishman's turn to grimace ruefully. 'Your appearance is at least more respectable than my own, Mrs Shonley.'

Grainne experienced instant embarrassment. 'I meant no offence, Mr Prendergast. I believe you to be a gentleman yourself, indeed I do.' She flustered lamely and, unable to say anything else which might not equally embarrass him, fell silent.

'I was not always in such straits,' he said softly. 'Indeed, there was a time not so long past, when I was considered a gentleman.' He paused, and an expression of regret clouded his eyes. 'But I have no one else to blame but myself for being brought so low.' He shook himself as if to dispel his mood, and told her briskly, 'Now let us consider what's to be done. You need to bathe and to change your clothing, do you not? Well, that at least is easily remedied. There is a public bath that I know of not above a mile from here by George Dock. Of course it is salt water, but it will suffice you. And in Frederick Street there is a large public wash house, where for a few pence you may obtain the services of a laundress. I shall escort you to both those places. Then, when you are cleansed and refreshed, we may consider what's best to be done for your friend here. Fortunately the day has turned warm, so you'll not be shivering too much in the bath. What say you to that?'

Grainne was tempted by his suggestions, but reluctant to leave Maggie for so long. Nevertheless, she asked the motherly farmer's wife if she would continue to look over the sick woman for an hour or two. 'I'll not be any longer away than I can help,' she finished. The plump woman smiled, saying, 'You goo on off, my duck, and take no concern for this poor wench. I'll take care on her. You get off wi' your young man now.'

Grainne blushed and would have explained that Septimus Prendergast was only befriending her, but before she could answer the tall Englishman bowed and said jokingly, 'Alas, Ma'am, to my deepest regret this lady and I are but acquaintances. Her husband is unavoidably absent at this time, but will be returning in a few days.'

Grainne sorted out fresh clothing from her chest and made a bundle of it. Then together with Septimus Prendergast she set off for the public bath and wash house.

Again as they traversed the city Grainne was struck

by the extremes of wealth and poverty it demonstrated: the smart carriages, glossy horses, and elegant people promenading, the glittering shops and fine buildings, and the festering courts and alleys seething with disease, hunger and want that lay behind those majestic façades.

After the wash house and the baths, refreshed and feeling clean once more, Grainne accompanied the Englishman along the great swathe of the Waterloo Road bordering the docks. It was by now early evening and the crews from the hundreds of ships lining the quays were coming ashore in search of their evening entertainments. Americans, British, Spanish, Italians, Greeks, Russians, Scandanavians, Germans, Lascars, Hindoos, Moslems, Chinese, Africans; it seemed to Grainne's enthralled eyes that every nationality in the world was represented among their colourful, swaggering array. And to meet the seamen came the touts, the bully-boys, the prostitutes, beggars, musicians, acrobats, tumblers, tricksters and vendors of every conceivable object or service that human ingenuity could devise. Waterloo Road and the streets that led off it were a swirling, brawling, shouting, singing maelstrom of humankind in all its shapes and all its forms, and despite her fear of this city, Grainne felt excitement building in her as all this rampaging vitality reached out to enfold her senses.

Looking down at her flushed, excited face, Septimus Prendergast smiled and told her, 'With all its dreadfulness this city is still a living pageant, is it not, Mrs Shonley? I do declare that much as I hate it, yet it holds for me a fascination that binds me here amongst its cruelty and filth, as surely as the chains held the slaves in their bacaroons. I hate it, yet I love it. I want to escape from it, yet cannot bear the thought of leaving it. Is that not a bizarre state of mind to be in?'

Involuntarily, and to her own amazement, Grainne shook her head. 'Oh no, Mr Prendergast, no,' she murmured, almost as if to herself. 'I don't find it bizarre, for at this moment I feel that I could live here always and never ever tire of it.'

That feeling remained with her as they made their way back to Tracey's Hotel, where she found beside Maggie Nolan's bunk a bucket filled with discoloured, musty-smelling water.

The farmer's wife smiled at her surprised expression. 'A man brought it up not half an hour since, my dear. He told me to tell you that Mr Tracey sent it with his compliments.'

Grainne shook her head with bemusement and Septimus Prendergast smiled saying softly, 'He's a strange man, Tommy Tracey.'

'Indeed he is, Mr Prendergast,' Grainne echoed. Then putting the matter of Thomas Tracey from her mind she used the water to clean her friend as best she could.

Later that night, lying on her hard narrow bunk, listening to the snores and the night-noises surrounding her, Grainne's thoughts once more turned to Tommy Tracey, and again she found herself puzzled by the man. 'I must ask Septimus what he knows of Tracy,' she decided, 'for he really does intrigue me.' Then as sleep overcame her, she realised with a shock of disgust that she had not thought of Con, her husband, for many hours. 'Forgive me, Con, my darling,' she prayed in her mind, 'And God keep you safe, wherever you might be this night.' And then she slept ...

Chapter Five

London

'Hey! Wake up, matey! It's Euston. We all gets out 'ere, my cocker.'

Con Shonley awoke with a start, and for a second or two stared blankly at the bewhiskered face hovering above him.

'It's Euston Station,' the bewhiskered face repeated, and as Con came to full awareness, he realised that his legs were blocking the opened carriage door.

'Sorry,' he mumbled, and rose to step down onto the platform. Carrying his small bundle he walked several paces, then halted amidst his fellow passengers scurrying around him to gaze at the scene in wonderment.

The wide platform was a gentle curve fully nine hundred feet in length covered by a massive vaulted metal and glass roof supported by great iron pillars, and brightly illuminated by large flaring gas lamps suspended from the roof and pillars. All along its offside was a seemingly interminable line of cabs, private carriages, gigs, dog carts and omnibuses. Opposite the omnibuses there were small black notice boards on which their destinations were chalked: Oxford Street, Regent Street, Charing Cross, Cheapside, Holborn, Fleet Street and the Strand and every other part of Central London and its environs.

Porters off-loaded the passengers' baggage from the roofs of their carriages, liveried servants came searching for their masters and mistresses, men scurried to engage cabs, friends and lovers greeted each other with hugs and kisses and parents wept for joy as sons and daughters came hurrying to meet them.

Con Shonley let himself be swept on amid the streams of foot passengers out of the departure gates through which the cabs came trotting, the drivers calling out the number of their vehicle and their destination to the checkmen waiting to note down the information in their books. Con passed under the great portico of the station and along the front of the Euston Hotel, still hardly able to grasp the fact that less than ten hours previously he had been in Liverpool, over two hundred miles away. Never in his life had he imagined that he would have been able to travel at such speed.

Immediately outside the station concourse and away from its watchful policemen, were numbers of raddled prostitutes, shabby touts, beggars, street vendors, ragged loungers and street urchins who pestered the new arrivals for money, or proffered doubtful services and dubious delights. The tiny shoeless, bare-legged urchins turned cart-wheels, walked on their hands and performed somersaults in the hopes of reward, recklessly putting their lives in jeopardy from the passing traffic.

Although the dusk was only now beginning to fall, a heavy blanket of cloud made the evening gloomy, and the smoke filled air held a sulphurous taste which bit at Con's throat causing him to cough until he accustomed himself to its acridity. He beckoned to a small ragged boy who was standing in the gutter holding out a box of lucifer matches and chanting in a hoarse high-pitched monotone, 'Penny a box for a poor orphin! Penny a box for a poor orphin! Penny a box for a poor orphin!'

'Which way to Somers Town?' Con asked.

'Take yer there for a tanner, mister!' the urchin offered, and Con grinned acceptance.

The house he sought stood in a quiet cul-de-sac of detached villas. As the urchin ran off hooting happily, the coin clutched in his grimy paw, Con Shonley stood in the gathering dusk outside the neat front door, throat thick with nervous anticipation. Then, drawing a deep breath to dispel the flutterings of his stomach he mounted the steps, gripped the brass bell pull and tugged hard.

The elderly man clad in funereal black stared suspiciously down his long red nose, then gestured with thin fingers, saying, 'Tradesman's entrance is at the side, my man.'

'I'm no tradesman,' Con told him indignantly.

The man scowling asked, 'What's your business here then?'

'I'm here to see Mrs Mahoney.' Con tried to control his fast mounting irritation at the other man's aggressive manner.

'What could the likes o' you be wanting wi' Mrs Mahoney?' the man snapped, and for a brief moment Con was strongly tempted to take him by the throat and shake the superciliousness from his scrawny body. Instead, he managed to say quietly, 'My name is Conrad Shonley. I'm Mrs Mahoney's eldest son.'

The manservants's close-set eyes bulged visibly, and bowing, said to Con, 'Please to step inside, Mr Shonley, and I'll inform my mistress of your arrival.'

Con entered the large hallway with its ornate furnishings, and looked ruefully down at his heavy boots, clogged on their soles with the filth of the streets. Flustered, he stepped back onto the steps, searching for the footscraper, and finding it at the bottom immediately began cleaning the bottoms of his boots.

'Con?' The soft voice caused his heart to pound furiously, and sweeping his peaked cap from his head in two strides he was at the door and hugging the small, fair-haired woman to him. For a moment or two neither of them could speak. Then laughing and crying at the same time, Charlotte Mahoney pushed herself away from her son's embrace and cradled his face in her hands, her eyes searching his features with an avid intensity, while he for his part stared lovingly at her thin, still girlish face and figure.

'You've become a man, Con,' she told him in a tremulous voice. 'And I am so very, very happy to see you.'

Con swallowed hard, his eyes bright with tears, and once more hugged her to him. 'And I am so very, very happy to see you Mother,' he whispered, 'So very happy.'

For a while they stayed locked in each others arms, and then the man standing further back in the hallway coughed discreetly, and Charlotte Mahoney broke the embrace and turned to her husband.

James Mahoney was a handsome man of middle age, his curled hair still black and his long side whiskers only flecked with grey. His dark brown eyes were warm as he saw mother and son side by side, their hands still entwined, and now he came forward with his own hand outstretched. 'Welcome, Con, I am truly pleased and happy to see you here in this house.'

Con Shonley gladly took the proffered hand and shook it heartily. 'Can you forgive my past behaviour towards you, Sir? I am truly sorry for it.'

Mahoney clapped the young man's shoulder with his free hand. 'There is nothing to forgive,' he said forcefully. 'Let us regard this moment as our beginning. But come! Come and sit by the fire and take some refreshment.' He pulled the pair of them with him into the warm cosiness of the drawing room, calling out as he did so, 'Jenks, tell Cook to prepare something hot and savoury, and tell Madge to make up the bed in the guest room.'

When Con and Charlotte Shonley were seated comfortably and Con had a glass of wine in his hand, James Mahoney smiled fondly at his wife. 'Charlotte, my dear, I am going to leave you and Con by yourselves for a while because you will have much to impart to each other. When I return I want to see this young man stuffed to bursting with food, and rosy with wine.' To Con he said simply, 'This is your home, Con. Use it as such, or I will be mortally offended.' With that, he left mother and son to their reunion.

Now that the first shock of that reunion was passing, Con was able to regard his mother a little more objectively. The lines of suffering and privations that he remembered had softened and smoothed now and, dressed in her long-waisted, wide-skirted gown of rich dark velvet, her fair hair parted in the centre and falling gently back from her broad brow, her blue eyes lucent in the glow of the lamplight, it was hard to believe that she had borne five children, four of whom still lived, and that her eldest, Con, was a full grown man.

'Where are Sean and Mairead and Martin. I'm longing to see them?' Con asked, eager to know news of his younger brothers and sister.

'They are visiting Portsmouth as Sean has a passion to enter the Navy. James arranged for him to go there to go on board some of the warships in the dockyard. Mairead and Martin couldn't bear to miss the chance of such an adventure, and pestered to accompany him so much, that in the end James allowed all three to go.' She saw Con's disappointment, and smiling, was quick to tell him, 'Don't worry that you'll not be seeing them, Con dear, for if I'm not mistaken, James has gone now to the Electric Telegraph Office at Euston Station to send them the news that you are here. They are staying at his brother's house in Southsea, so they will have the news of your arrival before this night ends, of that you may be sure.'

'James Mahoney is good to the children then?' Con sought to know, and his mother smiled radiantly.

'He is good to all of us, Con. I have had cause many times to bless the day that I wed him. Although James can never ever take the place of Daniel in the children's hearts, yet all three of them love him dearly, as I do myself. It is not that I do not still carry the love of Daniel in my heart, for that I shall ever do. Your father was my first love. But thanks be to God, I have found love with James Mahoney also. He is truly a good and gentle man, and is kindness itself.'

A shading of jealousy touched Con Shonley, but even as it did so he inwardly castigated himself for feeling such an emotion. 'You should be thanking God that mother has got a good man, and that the children have found someone who is a kind protector to them,' he thought.

Charlotte Shonley's eyes studied her son's face, and some of what she saw there disturbed her. 'I fear you have suffered much, Con,' she said softly. 'Tell me now, all that has passed with you since we last met. I will tell you that all the time I have been here I have corresponded with Doctor Donovan at Skibereen concerning you and what you are doing. I know much of what befell you, and I know also that you are now married, and that your wife lost the babe she carried. But good though he was to write me, Doctor Donovan obviously could not tell me all I wished to know. Tell me now, Con.'

Con's love for this woman overwhelmed him, and once more tears blurred his eyes. He drew a long, long breath to steady his voice and then opened his heart and poured out his memories to her, while she sat silent and intent; and as he talked their world shrank to the soft pool of lamplight and each other ...

Before they went to their beds Charlotte Shonley told her son about her own imminent departure from London. 'James is taking up a position with the East India Company in their Bengal Presidency, and the children and I are to go with him. If Sean cannot enter the Royal Navy, then he can always try to obtain a cadetship in the company. That is why your coming

53

here tonight is an answer to my prayers Con, my dearest boy. We did not know ourselves until two days since that we were going out to India. I wrote post haste to Doctor Donovan, but of course he has probably not yet received my letter.'

Con heard this news with mixed feelings, but only said, 'India is a long way away, Mother.'

'And so is America,' she retorted. 'And if you wish to seek adventure there, would you not be happy for me to do the same in India?'

'Do you really want to go there?' he asked her, and she answered with shining eyes.

'I do, Con. With all my being, I do. I've always wanted in my secret heart to make voyages and visit strange lands. This is a dream come true for me.'

'Then I am happy for you,' he told her, and with a last tender embrace they parted for the night.

Chapter Six

Liverpool

Maggie Nolan's flesh seemed to have wasted from her body during the dark hours of the night, and Grainne stared down with horror-filled eyes at the gaunt face of her friend, whose own frightened eyes glittered feverishly in their sunken bony sockets.

'Holy Mother o' God, what's wrong wi' me, Grainne?' Maggie's voice was a weak breathless croak, and she had to force the words from her parched throat. 'Am I dying, Grainne? Am I?'

'No, of course you're not dying!' Grainne assumed a confidence she was far from feeling. 'It's just a fever you have, that's all. So stop this silliness. You're no nearer dying than I am.'

'But I'm burning up, Grainne. Me head feels like it's on fire, so it does, and I'm so weak I can't stir me body.'

Grainne laid her hand on her friend's forehead, and was forced to hide her dismay as she felt the terrible throbbing heat radiating from the tight-stretched flesh.

'Yes, you're a bit hot, that I won't deny, honey, but sure that's only the fever coming out from your body. That means that you're already beginning to get better.' She tried to soothe the sick woman. 'I'll bathe your head and cool you.'

Utilising the dirty water in the bucket, she tore a piece of rag in two parts and started to dip them in the musty-smelling liquid, laying the wet cloths in turn on

55

her friend's temples. 'There now honey, this will ease it for you,' she comforted. 'Try to sleep again. Just close your eyes, and try to sleep.'

Sprawled across the table next to her, Denis Callaghan grunted and snored in his sleep. Grainne looked at him resentfully. She had been woken by his drunken entrance in the early hours of the morning, when he had fallen headlong through the door cursing and bawling. He had then draped himself across the table and had fallen instantly into a deep slumber, punctuated by his hiccuping, belching and farting. He had made so much noise that Grainne herself had not been able to get back to sleep for hours.

The room was crammed again with transients, and its air was foul with the stench of dirty bodies, clothing, and the exhalations of its sleeping occupants. As Grainne tended her friend she knew that somehow or other she must get Maggie Nolan away from here, and into better quarters.

There came a tap on her shoulder, and she looked up and smiled to see Septimus Prendergast. He jerked his chin in mute enquiry towards Maggie Nolan, whose eyes were now closed again, and Grainne shook her own head sadly. The Englishman pointed at the door and indicated that Grainne was to follow him, then went quietly out into the dark passageway. When Grainne joined him there, he whispered, 'Your friend is worsening, is she not?'

Grainne nodded glumly. 'I fear so.'

'Then do you not think it better that she should be removed to the infirmary, Mrs Shonley?'

She sighed, and shook her head uncertainly. 'I don't know what to do for the best. Certainly she needs medical treatment. Can you find a doctor and bring him here to examine her? I'm feared to leave her alone any more. You may tell whoever you find that there's money enough to pay his fee, even though we're in such a place as this.'

Prendergast nodded. 'I'll just get my hat, Mrs

56

Shonley, and I'll find a doctor and bring him back with me, even if I have to drag him here by main force.'

On impulse Grainne reached out and took the man's thin hand in her own to squeeze it gently. 'You are proving a good friend to me, Mr Prendergast, and I am very grateful to you.'

His fine teeth showed briefly as he smiled. 'Then, if we are good friends, would it not be permissible for you to call me by my christian name, and for me to call you by your own?'

She returned his smile. 'Of course it would, Septimus, and when my husband returns I hope that you will still be here, for I wish him to know how well you have befriended me.'

The man's smile momentarily faltered, and he murmured, 'I must confess there are brief moments when I forget that you are a happily married woman. Thank God you remind me when needful, or I might well make embarrassing declarations.' Before Grainne could make any reply, he went on, 'You return to your friend, Grainne, and I'll go directly to search for a doctor.'

Grainne had bought several bottles of porter which she kept hidden in her chest, and now she went to extract one of these so that Maggie could have something to drink when she awoke again. She was reclosing the chest when Denis Callaghan snorted loudly and suddenly pushed himself upright in to a sitting position. His bleared eyes blinked slowly several times, finally focusing on the bottle in Grainne's hand.

'For the love o' God, gissa sup o' that, honey,' he begged in a hoarse cracked voice. 'I'm dyin' wi' the thirst, so I am.'

Grainne experienced a rush of disgust and anger. 'You'll get nothing from me, Denis, until you sober up,' she snapped curtly. 'Can't you see that Maggie is ill? I've sent out for a doctor to come and look at her.'

He lifted his hands and rubbed his eyes, then peered blearily at the bunk on which Maggie lay. 'Sure now, what's up with her?' he questioned anxiously.

'She is burning with fever.' Grainne felt a pang of pity for him, and softened, 'Here, you'd best have this. Perhaps it will clear your head.'

'Jase, but you're a good girl, so you are Grainne. A good swate girl.' With that, he snatched the bottle from her outstretched hand and, fingers trembling, uncorked it, greedily sucking at its contents, his glottle bouncing up and down in his flabby throat as he gulped it empty. Then belching loudly he wiped his lips with the back of his hand.

'By the Christ, but that was a bloody life-saver, so it was, and ye're a bloody angel o' mercy, my jewel.' His hands were visibly shaking as he rose and came to bend over Maggie Nolan's bunk. 'Dear God!' he exclaimed in fearful surprise as he saw the sick woman's face. 'Dear God! My wee girl is real bad, isn't she now!'

Grainne successfully withstood the temptation to upbraid him for the tardiness of this realisation, and instead asked him, 'How do you feel about Maggie going into the infirmary, Denis? Because in all truth I think that it would be the best thing for her. This place is not good for a sick person to be in.'

His broad red face was troubled. 'I don't know about that, Grainne. Them places kills more than they cures, don't they?'

By now the rest of the room's occupants were rousing themselves, and the confined space became a hubbub of noise and bodies bumping and impeding each other as people moved about their affairs.

Grainne grimaced and spread her hands in appeal. 'But she will have no chance of getting better if she stays here, Denis, and we haven't money enough to get her a private room somewhere.'

The man suddenly groaned loudly and sank down upon the bench next to Grainne, burying his face in his hands. 'Jasus, me head is killing me. It feels like it's fit to burst.' He stared at Grainne with wild eyes. 'I must have a drop o' summat or other, girl, afore I'll be fit for anything. Me head is killing me, so it is. I swear to God

58

and all His Saints, it's like to drive me bloody mad it's pounding so hard.'

Grainne stared at the man worriedly. His normally red face had darkened alarmingly, becoming a livid purplish hue, and sweat was streaming down it. His chest beneath his open shirt and coat rose and fell with a frightening rapidity as he gasped for air.

'Lie down on my bunk, Denis,' she begged him, but he shook his head and choked out, 'That just makes it worse. I've had this before. I must take a drop o' spirits, Grainne. It's the only cure for this. I'll be better once I've had a drop o' the cratur.'

Even while her logic told her not to do so, Grainne was already reaching for coins from the pouch nestling between her high firm breasts. Before she had time to reconsider, Denis grabbed the money from her. 'I'll be back directly,' he gasped and wheezing loudly made an unsteady exit from the room.

'You bloody fool,' Grainne told herself bitterly. 'You've given him more money for drink, after you'd sworn that you would not. But then, supposing you hadn't given him anything, and he'd took a fit or something, how would you feel then?' Forcing the matter from her mind, she settled herself to wait for the advent of the doctor with what patience she could muster.

The doctor was a fatter, more florid version of Denis Callaghan in physique. His clothing was grubby and liberally bespattered with the remnants of past meals, while his tall black top hat bore proof of past crushings. Even at this early hour of the morning his breath reeked of brandy and his diction was slurred.

He made a cursory examination of Maggie's mouth and tongue, and asked a few questions as to the onset of the disease and its length. Then, opening his cracked and battered leather bag, he extracted four large sticky blue lozenges from its unsavoury contents. 'She has the Wasting Fever,' he told Grainne, and

59

showed her the lozenges on his grimy open palm. 'You'll needs give her one of these every four hours, and as much liquid as she can take down. Port wine would be most suitable.' He suddenly appeared to take notice of his surroundings, and his blackened teeth showed fleetingly as if he smiled in apology for some social gaffe. 'Porter or ale will do equally well. I should not advise water. On this side of Scotland Road it ain't got the sweetest of tastes. In fact, it normally tastes pretty horrid.'

As Grainne reached for the lozenges, his fat fingers closed on them, and he told her, 'I'll take my fee now, missy. Five shillings, in cash. There's no tick in these matters.'

Grainne paid him and he relinquished the lozenges to her. 'How can she have been struck by this disease, and the rest of us have not been?' she queried, and the man shrugged his meaty shoulders.

'Well, most times it comes from a miasma, missy. Foul vapours rising from the filth and corruption that abound in the slums. Some are more susceptible to that miasma than others. Anyway, give her one of those every four hours.'

'And if she is no better after taking them, what can I do then?'

Again the meaty shoulders shrugged. 'I could have another look at her in such a case. Send someone to find me. If I'm not at home then leave a message in the Jolly Fiddler's Tavern in Lime Kiln Lane. That should find me.' He nodded brusquely and was gone.

Septimus Prendergast's thin features showed concern, and he said apologetically, 'I'm sorry, Grainne, but he was the only one I could find who would agree to come here without being paid beforehand. There have been cases of Doctors being attacked and robbed even of their bag in this quarter of the city.'

'Don't worry.' She smiled wearily. 'I'm grateful for your help.' Her smile faded as she regarded Maggie Nolan. 'If she's no better after having these pills, then

60

I'm going to take her to the Infirmary.' She frowned as another problem occurred to her. 'But how I'll get her there, God only knows. I doubt that we'll find a cabman willing to carry her.'

'I'll speak to Tommy Tracey about it.' Prendergast answered. 'For a few shillings he'll doubtless let us take a door from its hinges to use as a stretcher for her, and lend us some of his men to bear the load.'

'Would he do that?' Grainne questioned doubtfully, and Prendergast smiled ironically.

'It is done for corpses on burial days, Grainne. I should not think he'll object to doing the same for a living woman.'

Grainne's breath caught in her throat. 'I pray to God she will live. I could not bear having to see her buried in this place.'

Maggie Nolan stirred and moaned, and Septimus Prendergast instructed, 'Come now, let us try and give her the first of these pills, while she's waking.'

As gently and tenderly as any woman, he knelt at Maggie Nolan's side and with soft words of encouragement raised her up so that Grainne could slip the lozenge between her dry cracked lips and give her a drink from a fresh bottle of porter. Afterwards, with the sick woman once more lying in unquiet sleep, the pair sat side by side on the bench looking over her, and talked quietly.

'When will you be sailing for America, Septimus?'

'I already did.' He chuckled at her expression of surprise, and explained, 'I was sent to America by my parents, but came back to this country after a year in New York.'

'But why?' Grainne could hardly believe what he was telling her. 'Why should you come back here? Everyone always says what a wonderful place America is.'

'America is the same as this country in all too many ways, Grainne. The native-born Americans resent and dislike the immigrants. In newspaper advertisements

61

when people seek servants in many many cases they stipulate that no Irish need apply. The people in the cities such as New York or Boston or Baltimore only want to use the immigrant as cheap labour, but do not want that immigrant to live in the same neighbourhood as themselves. In New York the streets are not paved with gold. I have walked ankle-deep in refuse and mud on Broadway.' He chuckled wryly. 'And pigs wander freely even through the smartest thoroughfares, as do packs of half-wild dogs. Periodically the city government employs negroes to go around shooting those dogs for fear of rabies.'

Grainne shook her head wonderingly. 'But no one ever speaks of these things.'

The young man chuckled again. 'They do not speak of the violence in New York either. Guns and pistols are so cheap that nearly every man possesses one, and men are attacked and murdered in sight of their own front doors. What's more the police are to all intents and purposes useless. Gangs of your own countrymen have formed criminal fraternities in places such as the Bowery and Hell's Kitchen, to which police appear to turn a blind eye.'

'But surely it cannot all be so bad?' Grainne protested.

'No, some things are undoubtedly better there than in this country. Provisions are cheap and plentiful, and if the immigrant has money enough to go inland from the coast he can buy land cheaply, or obtain employment, and with hard work and good luck can achieve much. But there are many thousands of immigrants who get no further than the ports where they land, and they are no better off there than the poor devils who abound in this city. My advice to you and your husband, Grainne, is to travel inland just as soon as you can, and have no truck with the runners on the dockside. They are as bad as those scoundrels who meet the ships here.'

'Where is it best to sail to in America?' Grainne wanted to hear his opinion.

His thin features furrowed in thought, and it was

some time before he answered, 'The cheapest passages are to British North America, but most who land there cross the border into the United States, because Canada and New Brunswick do not have sufficient employment to offer immigrants. So, if you have money enough, I would advise you to sail directly to one of the American ports, and then go inland. Many people land at New Orleans, but for myself I think it best to go into the Northern states. The slave states of the South do not need white labourers. Has your husband any trade or skill?'

She shook her head. 'No, his father, Daniel Shonley, was a squireen. Con was educated as a gentleman. That is, until the troubles came on the land, and then there was no money even for food, let alone schooling. But he has a good brain, and is ready to work hard, as I am myself.'

The Englishman smiled warmly at her. 'A strong back and a willing heart can achieve much, Grainne. And allied with intelligence such as you and your husband both possess in abundance, then I would hazard that you'll make your fortunes in America.'

'Jesus, but I hope so,' she exclaimed. Then she asked in puzzlement, 'But why did you not make your fortune there, Septimus?'

His smile turned rueful. 'Alas, Grainne, I do not have a strong back. I am a physical weakling, and though I have education and intelligence I am not trained in any profession. And I cannot bear to spend my days as an ink-stained clerk in some counting house, or being a teacher to snot-nosed infants.' With that, he burst out laughing. 'I think all I am fitted for is giving advice to would-be immigrants.'

Grainne joined in his laughter, feeling a warm and ever-increasing liking for him, then asked, 'But how do you now live, Septimus? How do you obtain money?'

He winked like a mischievous urchin. 'That's my secret, Grainne.'

Before any more words could be exchanged the

door burst open and two of Tommy Tracey's henchmen came stamping into the room.

'Hold your noise here!' one of them shouted, 'and stand against your bunks.'

When the people in the long narrow room only gaped in surprise, the man slammed the cudgel he carried upon the table top. 'Blast your fokkin' eyes! Do as I tell yez!' he bellowed furiously. 'Or youse 'ull be feelin' this acrost your fokkin' heads.'

'Do as he says.' Septimus whispered urgently in Grainne's ear, and went to stand by his own bunk.

The two bully-boys paced along the rows of nervous men, women and children, and only the thumping of their heavy boots on the bare boards and the squalling of the farmer's wife's youngest child broke the fearful silence.

'You? What's yer name?' The bully-boy poked his cudgel into the chest of a shabby middle-aged man standing alone. 'Spake up, blast ye, what's yer fokkin' name?'

The man swallowed nervously. 'Eamon Scullion, sor.'

'Scullion, is it?' the bully-boy growled, and the man nodded nervously.

'Indade it is, sor. Eamon Scullion is me name.'

'You never paid for last night's lodging, Scullion.' The bully-boy's cudgel jabbed hard into the man's chest, causing him to wince in pain. 'Why not? Trying to con Mr Tracey, are ye? Trying to cheat him?'

'Honest to God, no!' the man asserted wildly. 'Sure, I'm just waiting for me brother to come with me money, that's all. He's a bit late arriving, but he'll be here directly.'

The bully-boy bared his big yellow teeth ferociously. 'Well, whiles youm waiting for him, you'll be staying wit me and me mate.' His big hand grabbed the middle-aged man's coat collar, and he brutally dragged him to the door and through it, despite the man's struggles and protests.

64

Then the second bully-boy turned to the frightened onlookers. 'Listen well, youse lot,' he told them threateningly, 'If that bastard's brother don't bring the money to pay for his lodgings, then that bastard is going to end up on a fokkin' shite-heap with both of his legs broke. And that's no lie. So don't any o' youse try giving leg-bail for your lodgings here, or you'll be tasting the same medicine as that cunt me mate's just took from here.'

He slammed out of the room, leaving a silence as the occupants looked at each other with apprehensive foreboding. Septimus Prendergast caught Grainne's eye and smiled reassuringly at her. She tried to return his smile, but inwardly could only pray, 'Please come back quickly, Con. For pity's sake, come back quickly.'

Chapter Seven

London

As Charlotte Mahoney had surmised her husband had telegraphed the news of Con's arrival in London to his brother's house, and early the next morning, Sean, Mairead and Martin made the journey from Portsmouth.

James Mahoney was at the London Bridge railway station to meet them and brought them back to Somers Town by cab. Again, the man displayed his sensitivity by leaving the reunited family to themselves, so that their memories of happiness and heartbreak could be shared without any constraining influence.

The twins, Sean and Mairead, were now sixteen years old and both had their mother's fair colouring. Con's heart filled as he saw how handsome and manly Sean had grown, while Mairead had inherited her mother's slender sweetness of face and figure. Martin, aged ten, was like Con himself with his dark hair and swarthy good looks.

The hours passed with a dreamlike swiftness and all too soon for Con it was time for the younger members of the family to go to their beds. Afterwards, he sat with James Mahoney and his mother in the lamp-lit drawing room, sipping wine and talking together in easy comradeship.

After a time, James Mahoney tentatively broached the subject of Con's remaining in London. 'If you and your wife so wished to do so, Con, then I would use my utmost endeavours to procure you a suitable situation here. Although we leave for India shortly, I can still make the necessary introductions, and help you to find suitable accommodation for yourself and your wife. I know that it would make your mother the happiest of women if you were to agree to my proposals, and she could sail to India knowing that you had embarked on a career that would in the fullness of time bring you a financial surety for the rest of your days.' Mahoney ended, then grinned disarmingly, and added, 'At least you would very soon come to know that not all of we Englishmen have forked tails and horns.'

Con's grin was somewhat shame-faced, but he did not resent this gentle teasing. 'Believe me, James, I do most sincerely thank you for your kindness, but I cannot stay now in this country. That is not because I bear any enmity still towards the Englishmen, as such,' he hastened to add. 'Indeed, I never have done so. It is only their government that I resent. And judging from what I have seen during my very brief time here in England, I do truly believe that the lower classes of the English people have every right to resent that government also.'

James Mahoney nodded gravely. 'I concur most heartily with what you say, Con. I am a loyal Englishman, who bears true allegiance to the Queen, but my blood boils when I consider the plight of so many of my fellow subjects.' He paused, and sighed resignedly, then spreading his hands in supplication asked, 'But does not the Bible tell us *the poor ye shall always have with you*? I have no panacea to offer as a solution for the poor of this country. And I'll venture to suggest that this same problem, which exists all over the world, has no easy solution. One can also see terrible poverty in the Americas, Con. I have been there myself, and can vouch for that.'

'I do not doubt you, James,' Con told him with impassioned sincerity, 'But for myself, America represents a future that I cannot expect to find in this

67

country. It represents a challenge and an opportunity to better myself, my wife and the children we hope for. It is a new land, and is not chained down by the weight of tradition. It is not dominated by a landed aristocracy. No man is king by right there. All men are equal. It is a true democracy, where a man is valued for what he is, not for whatever station in life he was born into.'

James Mahoney's smile was tinged with sadness, and he thought, 'Poor young Con. Your idealism will suffer a most dreadful shock when you reach America, I fear.' Aloud he replied, 'In all truthfulness, I cannot share your views concerning America, Con, but from the bottom of my heart I wish you good fortune in your designs.' He chuckled warmly. 'And if all else fails then you could of course join us in India and become a nabob.'

'I may well take you up on that offer if I find that the streets of New York are not really paved with gold.' Con grinned, and on a note of shared laughter they bade their good nights.

Chapter Eight

Liverpool

Another day and night had passed and Maggie Nolan's condition had continued to deteriorate, despite the blue lozenges and the drinks of porter. At midday Grainne made her decision.

'I'm going to take Maggie to the Infirmary, Denis.'

Callaghan was, as usual, the worse for drink, and at first his bloodshot eyes only stared blankly.

'Do you understand what I'm telling you?' Grainne demanded sharply, and repeated, 'I'm taking Maggie to the Infirmary.'

'Infirmary?' He rubbed his stubbled chin, then objected sullenly, 'What's the good o' taking her to that bloody place? Sure, isn't she better off here with her friends, where she can be looked after properly?'

'No, she's not better off here,' Grainne declared sharply. 'I can't even keep her properly clean here, and she can't rest what with all the coming and going in this room at all hours. She's just getting weaker all the time.'

He scowled, and said with a mulish obstinacy, 'I'll not be having my Maggie took to no bleedin' Infirmary. They only go in them places to die, and then the bloody surgeons cuts their bodies up to see what's inside them.'

'Don't talk so silly,' Grainne snapped impatiently, and the man's drink-inflamed temper flared instantly.

'Don't you be talking to me in that tone, girl. I don't

give a bollocks who you think you might be. Iffen youse talks to me in that tone, then I'll be giving ye the back o' me hand. ' He tried to push himself up into a standing position from the bench he was slumped on, but before he could stretch to full height, swayed violently and sagged back onto the seat once more. For a few moments his features distorted and twisted hideously, then he burst into howling sobs and fell face forwards across the table, his head pillowed on his arms.

'Oh dear God spare me!' Grainne cried out angrily, and then felt ashamed of her anger as she heard his choked pleas.

'Don't take my Maggie from me, Grainne. Don't put her into no Infirmary. She'll die for sure iffen you put her in there. She'll die for sure. I know she will. I know it. Don't take my wee girl there, Grainne. For the love o' God, don't take her to that place. She'll die iffen she goes in there. She'll die for sure.'

Pity for him overwhelmed her and she ran round the table to sit beside him, putting her arm around his heaving shoulders in a vain attempt to comfort him. 'There now, there now, don't take on so, Denis,' she soothed. 'Maggie will get better in the Infirmary, you'll see. Don't take on so.' She hugged his shoulders and rose. 'Now you wait here with Maggie, while I go and make arrangements.' She instructed briskly, 'Stay here with her now.' Then with a final pat on his shoulder she left him and went downstairs.

In the entrance hall there was only a stunted female dressed in the remnants of gaudy finery with a battered feather bonnet over her frizzed hair, standing in the doorway looking out into the street.

'Do you know where I might find Mr Tracey?' Grainne asked.

The stunted little figure turned, and Grainne saw that she was a very young girl, with a badly swollen, bruised eye. The undamaged eye was hostile as it looked Grainne up and down.

'You his new tail?' The girl's tone was as hostile as her gaze. 'I heard tell as how he'd found a fresh fancy-piece, fokkin' bastard, that he is.'

Grainne took no offence at the imputations the girl was making. Instead she merely replied, 'No, I've nothing to do with Mr Tracey. Me and my friends are only lodging here until we can take ship. My husband's with me. Now, do you know where I might find Tracey?'

'The bastard's getting lushed in his fokkin' jerry-shop, down near the corner there. Treating every bastard piece o' shite in the town to drink, exceptin' me. The fokkin' bastard!'

Drawing her shawl close about her face Grainne went out into the street and down towards the corner the girl had indicated.

The day was sunny and the humidity intensified the stench of the enclosed courts of high ramshackle houses and the piled heaps of filth, causing Grainne to grimace in disgust and breath through her mouth in a vain effort to avoid the worst of the poisonous odours. That same heat had also brought the denizens of the slum to the windows and doorways and out onto the street itself in search of a breath of air.

It was the children swarming in the gutters, rolling in the dirt and refuse, fighting and squabbling like savage little animals that excited Grainne's pity. Ricket-legged, scrofulous, scald-headed, barefoot, they were ragged, dirty scraps of humanity with prematurely aged faces that all too often bore the tell-tale signs of brutal beatings, like the worn-out, underfed faces of their mothers.

Grainne had almost reached the drinking den where she hoped to find Tommy Tracey, when a man blocked her way. She side-stepped to go past him, but he also moved sideways. Grainne stared with repulsion at his grimy, unshaven face with its thick-layered pits and pustules. He grinned at her with blackened stubs of teeth and even at a pace distance she could smell the fetid breath rank with stale beer and tobacco and decay. She possessed considerable courage, and told him angrily, 'Let me pass.'

Stocky-bodied, his battered tall hat crammed low on his long matted hair, his clothing ragged and verminous, he was a fearsome spectacle. Grainne's heart thudded and her breath caught in her throat, but she stood her ground, and tried to keep any expression of fear from her face. Again she stepped sideways, and again he followed suit.

Grainne glanced to each side of her, but none of the faces watching this confrontation displayed any sympathy or desire to help, only avid curiosity, and on some an open enjoyment of this free show.

'Will you let me pass?' Grainne again demanded angrily.

The man made no reply but only stood there grinning, his arms hanging loosely by his sides, his body swaying slightly. For a third time Grainne moved to pass him, and for a third time he blocked her passage. Now raucous laughter and lewd gibes began to sound from the ever increasing audience.

Grainne's fiery temper overlaid her fear, and she moved forwards determinedly. 'Get out of my way!'

His arms came up and he tried to grab her, she dodged and jumped to his left, tripped and went down onto her knees. Before she could recover he had grabbed her from behind, his hands cruelly mauling her breasts, his slobbering mouth coming down on her neck. The watchers jeered and cat-called and roared with delight, and Grainne fought desperately to break free, but his strength was such that he managed to drag her backwards, causing her to lose her balance and putting her at a grave disadvantage in her struggle.

Grunting loudly he succeeded in forcing her into an entry which led to an enclosed court. Grainne screamed and twisted, her crooked fingers scrabbling at his face and eyes. He shouted a curse and punched her viciously on the jaw, and sparks exploded in her sight and her senses reeled. His fingers hooked into her bodice and he tore the buttons open, ripping her chemise also so that her firm shapely breasts were exposed. Crazed with lust and grunting like a rutting boar he grabbed for her breasts and in wild desperation she clawed at his eyes again.

Then the crowd clamouring around the pair was suddenly burst asunder as Tommy Tracey and some of his henchmen bludgeoned their way through. A cudgel smashed across the side of the attacker's head, and his eyes rolled upwards as he went slamming into the wall, then another smashing blow dropped him to his knees.

Meanwhile Grainne drew further back along the entry of the court, her breath hissing like a wildcat as she readied herself to fight on.

'Get this bastard into the court,' Tracey ordered, and his men dragged the groaning, bleeding man past Grainne, into the small enclosed courtyard, where they began to kick and batter him unmercifully, until his screams became choking whimpers, and his head and face resembled a lump of freshly butchered meat.

'Break the fokker's legs before ye leave him,' Tracey instructed, then told Grainne roughly, 'You cover up, and get on back to my place, you stupid bitch. You was askin' for trouble walking down the street by yourself.'

'Why so?' Grainne demanded. She was so charged with adrenalin from her struggle that all fear had left her. 'I didn't so much as look at that bastard.'

'Youse didn't have to look at him. Youse are dressed too respectable. Anybody could see that ye weren't one of us, so o' course that bowsie tried to make free wi' ye.'

When Grainne only glared wildly at him, Tommy Tracey snorted contemptuously. 'Youse had better catch yourself on, girlie. This is Liverpool, not some gobshite village back in Paddy land. Ye have to watch your fokkin Ps and Qs here, and cover your back at all times. Otherwise ye soon find a knife in it.'

While he spoke Grainne managed to peg her bodice closed, and wrapped her shawl around her upper body. Reaction was now setting in, and she was beginning to feel rubbery-legged and nauseous. When Tommy Tracey took her arm and led her out from the entry she went dociley enough, but felt her face crimsoning with embarrassment as the crowd's eyes devoured her hungrily. However, the presence of Tommy Tracey and the fact that she was under his protection ensured that no gibes were shouted, and the people remained curiously mute as she and the huge man with her passed through them.

Back at the lodging house Tracey told her, 'Youse are lookin' a bit sick, girl. Sit down there for a couple o' minutes.'

Grainne was now feeling sick and her body was trembling. She was glad to slump down onto a bench in the small entrance room while she recovered from the ordeal to which she had been subjected.

Tracey sat down behind his table and ignored Grainne, while he dealt with his henchmen, who now came in to see him.

Grainne could hear their exchanges, and marvelled at the casual manner with which they dealt with the maiming of a fellow human being.

'Where did ye leave him?' Tracey wanted to know.

'On the shite-heap in Brennan's Court.'

'Did you break his legs?'

'Yeah.'

'Good! Leave the bastard where he is until it gets dark. Then take him up to Scotland Road and chuck him in the gutter there. Let the fokkin crushers find him. They're sure to be wantin' him for a couple o' vamps at least. He's bound to cop for a laggin'.' Tracey's big brown fang-like teeth showed in a ferocious grin. 'And if his luck keeps on running like it did today, the bastard 'ull probably end up getting topped.'

The other men roared with laughter.

Grainne had understood Tommy Tracey's thieves' cant or slang sufficiently well to gather that her attacker was to be left where the police could find him, that the police were looking for him in connection with two robberies at least, and that he was certain to eventually receive either a long sentence of penal servitude or at worst, he could be hung. She suddenly shivered, and for a moment or two experienced a sense of guilt that she should have been the instrument that had brought her attacker to such a fate. Then her native commonsense reasserted its control, and she was able to accept that whatever happened to the man was richly deserved. He had brought it on himself, and now he could no longer subject any other defenceless woman or girl to rape and outrage.

She realised also that she owed Tommy Tracey a debt of gratitude for having saved her, and now, when things had quietened somewhat, she told him, 'I want to thank you, Mr Tracey, for coming to help me.'

He nodded brusquely. 'Just remember in future, girl, don't you be chancing yourself out there agen by yourself.' Again he grinned ferociously. 'Well anyways, not until you looks more like the judies who lives here. Once you look like one o' them, youse 'ull be grateful if any man jumps on your bones.'

His henchmen roared at this sally, but Grainne felt her throat and face flushing. Although a married woman with some experience of life, she was stilll influenced by the rigid Catholic upbringing of her childhood in the West of Ireland and although she could be amused by salty, even sometimes cruel humour, she could never entirely rid herself of a nagging sense of sin for being so.

Tommy Tracey noted her heightened colour, and for a brief instant there came into his eyes a softening, which as quickly disappeared. He scowled and told Grainne bluntly, 'Youse were lucky we come out into the street when we did. Otherwise that bowsie would have had ye. But it does no harm to remind those scum out there how Tommy Tracey's boys can do the business. I won't stand for any bastard interfering wi' my lodgers and these bowsies hereabouts knows that well enough. It's just that every now and agen we has to remind 'um what happens to them who crosses me.'

Grainne was much calmer now, and the shock of being attacked had lessened considerably. She broached the subject of Maggie Nolan, and her need to get the woman to the Infirmary.

'Youse 'ull have to take her to the Dispensary in the Vauxhall Road. It lies between here and the docks. Not so far really. I've a handcart you can use to carry her there. It'll cost you a shillin'.'

Grainne paid him the coin, and Tracey told her, 'The cart's out the back.' Then jerking his head at his henchmen he cried, 'Come on, lads. The Dublin boat is due any time.' And the room emptied.

Chapter Nine

The large building was surrounded by high spiked railings and although not an old construction, bore a neglected appearance, which complemented the groups of ragged, down at heel people clustering at the porter's lodge by the main gate. Unlike most gatherings in this strident city the groups at the gate were comparatively quiet and subdued, allowing themselves to be marshalled and ordered by the officious Gate Porter without protest or argument.

Grainne and Denis Callaghan were hot and sweaty as they pushed the handcart up to the gate with Maggie Nolan half-sitting, half-lying on its dirty boarding. Grainne looked at the people already waiting and for a moment doubted the wisdom of bringing her friend here to this place. Every face she looked at bore the hideous eruptions of disease, and the constant barrage of hacking coughs demonstrated the prevalence of consumption and other chest problems.

While Denis Callaghan kept the hand-cart steady, Grainne went to speak to the people patiently queuing. 'Is this where we have to apply for admission?' she asked an emaciated, consumptive-looking woman who nursed a sickly baby in her arms and had several tow-headed, bare-foot children hanging on to her skirts.

'That's right, my duck,' the woman nodded. 'They'll be opening for business soon.'

Even as she spoke the porter came bustling out from his lodge. His peaked cap and dark blue frockcoat had

77

a military appearance, and his manner was that of a drill sergeant. 'Come on then,' he bawled. 'Let's be having youse. Look lively, and you wi' the crutches there, keep your bloody mouth closed.'

The queue shuffled forwards towards the gate, and the porter shouted, 'Have yer tickets ready. I arn't got time to waste.'

'What tickets does he mean?' Grainne asked the woman, but she had already turned her back and did not hear the question.

Denis Callaghan shouted irritably, 'Grainne, will ye come and gi' me a hand here. We're losing our bloody place.'

Grainne hurried back to him, and together they pushed the handcart to the rear of the queue, and slowly moved it along towards the gate.

Grainne became increasingly concerned as she neared the gate and saw that each person handed the Porter a scrap of paper, which he briefly scanned before nodding permission for the giver to pass on into the main building.

'Do you see there, Denis? What's that piece of paper that they're handing in?'

Callaghan, miserable and badly hung-over, only snarled irritably, 'How the fuckin' hell should I be knowing what it is? I'm only the soddin' monkey here. T'is you that's the organ grinder.' He jerked his head towards their predecessors in the queue. 'Will ye look at this load o' wrecks. By Jasus, it's the wrong thing ye're doing here, Grainne. Putting my Maggie in among this lot. If she wasn't dying before, she will be afore very long living wi' these pitiful bowsies!'

Grainne's previous doubt flooded back to torment her. 'Am I doing the right thing here?' she asked herself. 'But what other choice have I got? I can't leave Maggie lying in those lodgings. She's just getting weaker all the time there. And that doctor was worse than useless. It was only throwing money away to bring him to see her.'

'Hey, you wi' the private carriage? Do youse want to come in, or what?' The burly Porter's voice broke Grainne's reverie, and she went to him. 'It's my friend,' she told him. 'She's taken a fever, and I've had the doctor to her, but it's done no good. I want to get her admitted here, where she can be looked after properly. We're in lodgings you see, down by the Scotland Road. And the place we're in is only doing her harm.'

'Where's your ticket, girl?' The man held out his meaty hand, and Grainne shook her head.

'I'm sorry, mister, I don't know what ticket it is that you mean.'

The man's broad features scowled. 'Are youse trying to come the cunt wi' me, Paddy?'

'No I'm not!' Grainne exclaimed indignantly. 'And I'll thank you not to use such language towards me neither. I'm a respectable married woman, not some whore.'

The man's eyes slowly travelled from her feet to her head, noting that her dress and shawl were neat, and that she wore bootees, that her glossy hair was neatly plaited and bound around her head, and her face and neck looked clean. 'Beg pardon,' he grunted. 'It's just that we get mostly the bloody dregs here, missis. And a lot of 'um tries to take liberties wi' us. Specially the paddies.' He paused, and his eyes flicked towards the handcart where Maggie Nolan slumped comatose. 'How long have you been here in the Pool?'

'Only a few days. We landed from Cork not a week since.' Grainne told him.

'Well, missis, I'll tell you how it works here.' The man explained, not unsympathetically, 'This is the North Liverpool Dispensary, there's a South Dispensary as well. It's supported partly by charity and part by the parish. Now to gain admittance you need either a ticket from the Vestry, which you can't get because you've no rightful settlement in the parish, being immigrants. Or you can go to one o' the subscribers for a ticket.'

'Who are the subscribers?' Grainne wanted to know.

'They'm the ladies and gentlemen who gives funds to the dispensary for charity.'

'But I've got some money, and I'm ready to pay for my friend to be treated here,' Grainne informed him.

'It arn't run that way, missis.' The porter seemed almost regretful. 'There was a time when I could ha' slipped your friend through, for a consideration, o'course. But the House Surgeon we got here now is a real strict man, and he insists that we only takes in them who got nothing, and they've got to be deserving cases. He reckons that if you've money enough to pay for treatment, then you must get that treatment outside from your own doctors, and leave the beds here for the really needful.'

'Come on, Grainne, let's bugger off from here.' Denis Callaghan's disgruntled voice came from behind her, but this only made Grainne more stubbornly determined to get Maggie Nolan admitted to the hospital.

'As I said already, I tried the doctor, and he did no good, and I haven't money enough to get my friend decent quarters where I could care for her properly. That's why she needs to be admitted here. Can you give me the name and address of one of these subscribers, so that I can apply to them for a ticket?'

The porter hesitated for a moment, then his eyes caught sight of an elegantly dressed man coming towards the gate, and he sprang stiffly to attention, his hand snapping up to the peak of his cap in salute.

'Dr Galbraith, sir, could I have a word wi' you, please?'

The elegant gentleman was wearing a high-buttoned, cut-away, swallow-tailed brown coat and narrow brown-checked trousers, with a high collar and dazzling white cravat. His brown side-whiskers reached almost to his clean-shaven chin and his tall shiny top hat was cocked at a rakish angle on his thick wavy brown hair. He was very handsome in a slightly raffish way, and his dark eyes twinkled as if he was enjoying some secret joke.

He came up to the porter and smiled admiringly at

Grainne.

'Yes, Matthews, what is it?' His voice was husky, and pleasant to the ear.

'It's this young woman, sir.' The porter went on to explain Grainne's problem, Dr Malcom Galbraith hearing the man out in silence. Then smiling he asked Grainne, 'What is your name, my dear?'

'Mrs Grainne Shonley, sir,' she told him.

He went on to ask her more questions concerning her past and present circumstances, and extracted the full details of Maggie's illness. Once satisfied, he smiled warmly at Grainne. 'Very well, Mrs Shonley. I will take responsibility for your friend's admittance here.' He bowed charmingly as she thanked him. 'Please, Mrs Shonley, say no more. It is my pleasure. Will you see to the admission, Matthews.' With a final warm smile to Grainne his elegant figure sauntered on into the main building.

'Many thanks to you also, Mr Matthews. Please, take this.' Grainne pushed some coins into the man's hand.

'You was lucky that Dr Galbraith come along when he did, missis. It's saved you a deal o' running about trying to get a ticket. He's the House Surgeon's Chief Assistant.'

'He seems a real gentleman,' Grainne remarked, and the Porter winked meaningfully.

'Oh, he's that alright, missis. And he's got a rare eye for a pretty face. Why else do you think you got the ticket from him so easy?'

Grainne could not help but flush. Then laughing, she said, 'Well, no matter why he gave it me, I'm still very grateful for having it.'

The ward was long and high with white-washed walls and ceiling. It contained three rows of box-beds which stretched its entire length. Nearly every bed contained an occupant and some contained two. On one wall in big black lettering was inscribed:

81

Naked came I out of my mother's womb
and naked shall I return thither;
the Lord gave, and the Lord hath taken away;
blessed be the name of the Lord.

As if to illustrate these sentiments, as Grainne and Denis aided by two porters carried Maggie into the ward, some Irish women were keening loudly around a bed on which lay a man who had just died.

A fat, grubby woman wearing a stained white apron which looked badly in need of washing, and an equally dirty mob-cap came bustling up to the newcomers.

'Put her in there,' she ordered pointing to a vacant bed in the centre row.

When Grainne saw the bed sheets she frowned unhappily, and taxed the nurse. 'They're dirty. Cannot they be changed?'

The eyes were small and pig-like in the woman's flabby, mealy face. 'Laundering costs money, missis, and this is a pauper hospital, not a watering spa for the gentry.'

In Grainne's nostrils the stench of the ward seemed only marginally sweeter than the slum she had brought Maggie out of, and now doubts as to the wisdom of what she was doing multiplied.

'She'll come to no harm in that bed, missis,' the fat nurse affirmed. ' 'Tis a lucky bed, that 'un. Both o' them who last used it walked out of here completely made well agen. You might even ha' seen the last 'un. A widow-woman, she was. Her son's took her from here but a couple o' minutes since.'

'What was she suffering from?' Grainne was intrigued enough to ask.

The fat woman screwed up her face in concentration. 'Let me see now, if I recollects proper, her had the Scotch Itch, and the Intermittent Fever. Here for three weeks, she were. And went out not a couple o' minutes since, as bright and frisky as a new-born lamb.' The woman's voice throbbed with satisfaction.

Across the crowded ward the Irish women's keening rose higher and higher, and the fat nurse bawled at them. 'Iffen youse lot don't quiet yourselves I'll ha' the bleedin' boilin' o' youse chucked outta here!'

Grainne thought briefly about the Scotch Itch – a virulent suppurating rash which could cover the entire skin of a sufferer – and handed the nurse a two shilling piece. 'Look, here's a florin for yourself. Can you try and get fresh bedding for my friend?'

The coin instantly disappeared, and the woman's few remaining teeth showed as she smiled ingratiatingly. 'Now don't you be fretting about your friend, missis. Liza Davis, which is me, arn't the sort o' woman who'd neglect to look arter a decent sort o' patient. We get a lot o' the bloody riff-raff in here, missis, and that's no lie. But I can see plain that youm a better class o' person altogether.' She glanced about her, then satisfied that no one was watching, brought her head close to Grainne's ear and whispered breathily. 'You look arter me, missis, and I'll see to it that your friend won't be wanting for nothing.'

Grainne performed a series of mental sums in her head, and promised, 'There'll be a florin a day for you, Mrs Davis, if you look well to my friend.'

The woman nodded. 'That's agreed, missis. Now you must go and you may set your mind at rest. I'll change the bedding the fust chance I gets.'

'When will that be, Mrs Davis?' Grainne pressed.

'Why, within the hour,' the nurse assured expansively. 'I'll have to get him and his womenfolk shifted first.' She indicated the dead Irishman and the wailing mourners, and with that Grainne was forced to rest content.

'When can we visit my friend?'

'Come tomorrow afternoon, missis. If the porter at the gate tries to stop you, then tell him that youm a particular friend o' mine.' She nodded her head sharply, causing her many chins to wobble. 'D'you get what I mean?'

Grainne leaned over Maggie Nolan and spoke to her, but the sick woman remained comatose, and knowing that at this time she could do nothing more to aid her, with a heavy heart Grainne walked out of the ward, and from the Dispensary, with a glum-faced Denis Callaghan trailing after her.

Chapter Ten

Con Shonley left London with conflicting emotions. Naturally his desire to be reunited with his beloved wife was predominant, but he felt a deep sense of sadness and loss at parting once again from his family.

Back in Liverpool he hurried through the bustling streets to Tracey's Hotel. In the room Grainne was asleep, lying on her side, her hands tucked under her cheek, looking heart-breakingly young and defenceless. He kissed her tenderly into wakefulness, and as soon as she opened her eyes and smiled in delight, his love for her welled up in him so intensely that he was near to tears.

The room was as usual crowded and noisy, but oblivious to everything except each other the two young people sat and talked as they held hands. Con made no comment as Grainne told him all that had occurred during his absence, but swore savagely beneath his breath as she related the incident of her attack in the street. When she had finished, he told her about his reunion with his family, and also about James Mahoney's offer to aid them should they wish to go to London.

'What do you think, honey? Would you like to go there?' he asked.

Grainne pondered the question for some minutes, then shrugged. 'To be honest, sweetheart, it's a small peaceful place that I'd prefer to live in, not another city. Septimus tells me that in America if we go inland we can buy land cheaply.'

Her husband laughed wryly. 'How much is cheaply? If we don't sail soon we'll not have enough even for the passage money. How long do you think it will be before Maggie's well enough to travel?'

She shrugged pensively. 'I don't know, Con. She's really ill, poor soul. It could be weeks yet.'

'And Denis? Where's he at?'

Again she could only shrug. 'God only knows, for I don't. We came back here after leaving Maggie this afternoon, and no sooner had we got back, than Denis was off out again. I'd gone down to the privy, and when I came back up, he was gone.' She shook her head, puzzled. 'But what he's using for money, I can't tell you. I've only been giving him the few shillings for drink.'

Con frowned, and bending low pulled out the two chests of their baggage from beneath the bunk. 'There it is. That's where the money is coming from.' He indicated the broken padlock on Denis and Maggie's chest. He opened the lid and found that all the clothing that they had bought the couple, plus Maggie's few cheap trinkets had all gone, and the chest was virtually empty.

'Oh Con!' Grainne sighed sadly. 'He's been taking it to pawn or sell. What a terrible shame for Maggie. He's even taken her few bits of jewelry, and they weren't worth more than a few coppers at the outside.'

Con was more saddened than angry at the discovery. Denis Callaghan had been a very dear friend to him, and when all else had failed him, Denis Callaghan had not. 'He's a bloody fool, Grainne,' Con told her quietly, 'and the drink has him fast-gripped these days. That's why he's behaving this way. It's the fault of the drink. When he's sober, he's the best man I know.' He closed the lid and pushed the chest back under the bunk.

'Maybe when we sail he'll be better, Con.' Grainne tried to comfort her husband. 'Perhaps it's only with him being so worried about Maggie, that he's behaving this way.'

'And perhaps pigs will be flying before the month is up, Grainne.' For the first time a note of anger entered Con's voice. 'I love the man, but when he acts like this, I could kill him. He knows well enough that I've only sufficient money to get us all to America and hopefully keep us there until we can find work, yet he's throwing money away on the drink from morn 'til night. Jesus Christ! We all like a drink now and again, but he's acting like a bloody idjit. For two pins I'd leave him here in Liverpool, and only take the three of us on to America.'

Grainne said nothing, knowing that it was only anger talking. Con Shonley's sense of loyalty was too strong for him ever to desert a friend, even if that friend was behaving as badly as Denis Callaghan was now doing.

Eventually the young man's mood passed, and he was able to grin shamefacedly and admit, 'I'm talking nonsense, of course. I'd never be able to bring myself to desert him, bloody nuisance though he is.'

He leant to kiss Grainne's lips again, and she felt a rush of longing course through her; a desire to have her husband's arms around her and his strong body crushing against her own.

'I wish we could be by ourselves, honey,' he whispered in her ear. 'I'm so hungry for your loving.'

The delicious lassitude of sexual desire stole over her body. She wanted to lie back on the narrow bunk and surrender to his rampant need, and feel him filling her with his love. The mood was rudely broken by a dispute erupting at the end of the room between a man and his wife.

'You bastard, I'll larn you!'

'Oh will you now? Oh will you? Just try, you bleeder! Just try!'

The couple began to fight, and the rest of the people in the room rushed to separate them as their flailing bodies and arms threatened to upset the table and benches.

Grainne giggled and whispered, 'I think we'll have to wait until we get to America, Con.'

He grinned and hugged her. 'Ah well, if past experience is anything to go by, then it will be well worth the wait. But it's time's like this that I can appreciate Saint Paul.'

Grainne laughed at his sally and laid her head against his shoulder. 'When you're with me, Con, I'm feared of nothing. All I want from life is to be with you.'

'Well that's exactly what you're going to be getting, sweetheart. Me, for the rest of your life,' he whispered fervently, 'because I love you more than life itself, honey. In fact, you are my life, because if I were ever to lose you, I could no longer continue to live.'

'You'll never lose me, Con,' she told him with a passionate sincerity. 'You'll never lose me.'

Fully clothed, they lay enfolded in each others arms on the narrow bunk and eventually, despite the noisy bustle of the crowded room, drifted into sleep.

'Con! Grainne! Wake up! For the love o' God, will ye wake up?'

They were roused by a sober Denis Callaghan soon after dawn and Grainne could not hide her surprise. 'Didn't you go drinking last night, Denis?'

He shook his head. 'I did not. I went walking instead, to clear me head so that I could think straight. Which I haven't done for these many days past.' He seated himself on the bench next to their bunk. 'I want to tell you that I'm sorry for the way I've been behaving lately.' He regarded them anxiously. 'Can you forgive me for it?'

'Of course we can,' Grainne answered for both of them.

The relief showed visibly on Denis's plump face. 'That's good! I couldn't bear to part on bad terms wi' you both. You're my dearest friends in this whole world.'

'What's this talk of parting from us, Denis?' Con asked with concern. 'We're going to wait until Maggie gets better. We're not leaving without you.'

Denis looked down at the floor, as if he was not able to meet their eyes, and his hands nervously twined and untwined as he told them, 'Well, that's what I wanted to tell you.' He hesitated, and seemed stuck for words.

'Tell us what, Denis?' Grainne urged gently. 'Come now, friends should not hold secrets from each other. What is it that you want to tell us?'

He coughed nervously, once, twice, then still staring at the floor, words tumbled from his lips. 'I'm going back home. Back to Skibereen. I don't want to go to America, or anywhere else. I know now that I can only be happy in my own country.'

'But why? Why have you changed your mind so suddenly?' Con was genuinely puzzled. 'You seemed so happy to be going to America. is it anything that we've done, that's caused you to change your mind like this?'

He shook his tousled head, and now looked squarely at them. 'No, of course it's nothing that you've done. How could it be so? You're my best friends, and I love you both dearly. It's just me. I can't bear the thought of leaving Ireland, now that it's come to it.'

'But there's nothing there for you, Denis,' Con protested. 'All you left behind was famine. Why go back to that?'

'Because it's home.' There were tears in Callaghan's red-rimmed eyes. 'It's the only place where I'll ever be happy.'

'You can't say that until you've lived in other places,' Con argued. 'After a while a man can come to regard anywhere as home.'

'Some men, maybe, but me, never!' Denis stated emphatically.

'But how will you live there? What will you do for your bread?' Con demanded.

Callaghan's toothless mouth rounded in a brave attempt at his old infectious grin. 'Sure now, Con, there's still a call for good burial men over there, isn't that so? I'll go back and work for Doctor Donovan agen.'

'If you do that the chances of you surviving more than a few weeks are bloody minimal.' Con was beginning to sound angry. 'It was only by the grace of God that you and I lived through it as we did the last time. Look how many of the men died who worked with us. Pretty well all of them.'

'That's as maybe,' Callaghan answered with a touch of sullenness, 'but I'll take my chance wi' that, Con. Because I'd sooner die in Ireland, than live in exile in America or England or anywheres else in this bloody world. Me mind is made up. I'm going back home.'

'And what about Maggie?' Grainne intervened, 'What's going to happen to her?'

'I'll wait here until she's better. Then ask her to come back home with me.'

'And supposing she doesn't want to go back, but wants to come on to America with us?' Grainne pressed.

Callaghan sighed raggedly, and wiped his eyes with the edge of his grubby hand. He started to speak, then gulped, coughed, and began again. 'I love my Maggie, bad as I am to her wi' the drinkin' and wastin' that I do. But I really love her, and that's the truth. If she wants to go with you to America, then I'll give her my blessings, but to tell true, I'm hoping that she'll want to come back home with me. The only reason she was coming to America was because I talked her into it. In the bottom of her heart she never wanted to leave Ireland. It was me who kept on to her until she agreed to come with us,' his voice broke as the tears fell freely from his eyes, and he choked out, 'and look what I've brought the poor wee girl to. She's laying up there in that bloody hospital, and could be dying for all I know.' Sobs tore from his throat, and he could no longer speak.

'Oh Denis, don't blame yourself for it.' Grainne rose swiftly from the bunk and cradled the sobbing man's head against her breast. 'There, there now, man dear. Don't blame yourself. Don't take on so. Maggie will soon get better, you'll see,' she soothed. 'She'll soon be well again. Don't cry now. Don't cry.' She looked up and caught Con's eye, and could only grimace sympathetically.

Con rose from the bunk and patted the sobbing man's shoulder. 'Bear up, Denis. I'm sure Maggie will be alright. And if she decides to go back home with you, well, I'll see to it that you'll have sufficient money to get yourselves back there and to keep you going for a while until you get settled.'

Denis Callaghan's fingers sought and found his friend's hands and he clung to them as a small child clings to its mother's hands when in distress. Slowly his heart-rending sobs quietened and came to an end.

Chapter Eleven

It was two days later that Maggie Nolan died. Grainne, Con and Denis Callaghan walked into the big ward during afternoon visiting time to find her shrouded corpse in the box-bed.

Liza Davis, the fat nurse bustled over to them as they stood in stunned silence around the still form of their friend. 'She went near on three hours since. Very peaceful too.' The woman spoke in hushed, reverent tones and her fat, mealy face bore a practised expression of sympathy. 'I was with her at the end, and I sent for Father Mulcahy to give her the Last Rites. The porters wanted to shift her out to the dead house, but I udden't allow them to touch the poor soul. I made 'um fetch screens instead and I laid her out meself. Just see how nice and peaceful she looks.'

She pulled the shroud down from Maggie's face, and it was now that Grainne started to weep as she saw the thin waxlike features, and remembered Maggie as she had first seen her, back in Skibereen at Mulrooney's lodging house dancing a jig, and full of joyous vitality.

Denis Callaghan was white faced and shaking, yet it was he who appeared to recover from this terrible shock before Con and Grainne. 'Can you give me some money, Con?' he asked huskily, and his friend immediately handed him several sovereigns. 'Here y'are, Lady.' Callaghan gave Liza Davis a sovereign. 'My thanks to ye for doing the right thing by my Maggie.' He turned to Con. 'I'm going to take Maggie back home with me, and lay her to rest in her own soil.'

He spoke again to Liza Davis. 'Can youse get me a coffin to put her in?'

'Certainly I can. I'll arrange for it directly.' The fat woman sensed further profit to be made. 'What did you say you intended doing about burial, mister?'

'I'm going to take her home to Skibereen, and lay her to rest there.' Denis Callaghan was very calm and matter-of-fact. Grainne wondered at his self-control and found herself admiring the strength he was now displaying.

'Then you'll be needing a cart to get her to the docks, mister?' Liza Davis held out her hand. 'If you'd like to pay me a couple of sovereigns to cover the coffin and cart, I'll see to that. My brother is first mate on the *Nimrod* ferryboat. It's in dock now and sails for Cork on the next tide. I can fix the passage with him for you. And the money can cover that as well.'

Callaghan nodded, and gave her the money. 'My thanks to ye, missis.' He took Grainne's arm. 'Say goodbye to Maggie now, my honey, and try to remember her as she used to be, not as she is now.'

Grainne leaned and kissed the cold cheek of her friend. Con followed suit and then led Grainne out from the ward. Denis Callaghan came with the couple as far as the main gate. There he embraced them both. 'God Bless and protect ye,' he whispered huskily, 'and don't you be forgetting Denis Callaghan.'

'We'll write to you, care of the post master at Skibereen, just as soon as we get settled in America,' Con promised, and his own voice was husky with emotion, tears shining in his eyes.

Grainne could not hold back her grief, and sobbed bitterly as Con led her away from the gate.

Denis Callaghan stood and watched them until they were gone from his sight, then wiping the tears from his own eyes he went back inside the hospital to mourn his dead.

Chapter Twelve

Early one morning, a week after Maggie Nolan's death, Grainne was standing with a bucket in the long queue at the water standcock in the court adjoining Tracey's Hotel, when Con came in search of her. Grinning excitedly he held two long pieces of paper before her eyes. 'We've got them at last. From Tapscott's.'

Grainne experienced a rush of thankfulness. Finally after daily badgerings by both herself and Con, Tommy Tracey had got the sailing tickets from the broker for them.

'When do we sail, Con?' she questioned eagerly.

'On the twenty-fourth, three days from today.'

'Thank God for that,' she breathed in heartfelt relief. 'I think another week here would have done for me. If only poor Maggie could have been with us.'

Con sobered, and sighed regretfully. 'I know, honey, I know. But there's nothing to be done about that, is there? The poor girl has gone from us, and we can only pray for her soul. I just wish Denis was coming with us. I'm feared that he'll not last long back in Skibereen.'

For a couple of moments they both stayed silent, touched by the sadness of fresh bereavement. Then Grainne shook her head sharply as if to rid herself of the burden of her thought, and told Con, 'We mustn't dwell on what might have been, sweetheart. Maggie wouldn't have wanted us to spend our lives grieving for her. She loved laughter too much for that.'

'You're right,' Con accepted, and made a visible effort to dispel his own sadness. 'Only think of it, Grainne, this time next Saturday, we'll be on our way to New York.'

'How much did the tickets cost?' she asked.

'Nine pounds for the two of us, including steerage

94

naturally. Tracey said that there were cheaper passages at three pounds ten shillings, but they were to Canada, and the boats are very bad on that run. He says that our boat, the *Florida*, is one of the best sailing packets, and among the fastest. But we'll needs talk about what we'll be needing in the way of provisions for the voyage. They do issue some food to the passengers, but Tracey reckons it's wisest to buy your own and take it with you. And we'll be needing bedding as well as stuff for when we land in America. Tracey reckons we can get better bargains here than over there.'

'It sounds as if you and Tracey are bosom friends these days,' Grainne observed with a touch of irony.

Con shrugged his broad shoulders. 'I know he's a rogue, honey, but I owe him much, don't I? He saved you from that bastard who set upon you, and like Septimus tells us, there are a lot worse rogues fleecing the immigrants in Liverpool than Tommy Tracey.'

A raucous cheer from the queuers announced the arrival of water through the standcock and Grainne smiled thankfully. 'Everything is beginning to go well for us, Con,' she said gaily. 'Even the water's come early today.'

'I'll see you later,' Con told her. 'I'm going to get a list of what we'll be needing for the voyage from Tracey. He's got his own provision shop, and says he'll give me a fair price.'

Grainne bit her lip thoughtfully, then told herself, 'Ah well, maybe it's a question of better the devil we know,' and accepted Con's plans without demur.

As Grainne waited for her turn at the standcock, her thoughts went to Septimus Prendergast. he had been absent from the lodging house for the last two days and nights and she wondered now if anything untoward had happened to him. He was something of a mystery to Grainne, and she often wondered what it was he did to obtain money, of which he always seemed to have a sufficient supply. She had asked him once if his parents supported him, and he had laughed and assured her that the only money his parents would ever make over

95

to him, would be the price of his funeral.

'I hope he comes back before we leave,' she thought now. 'I'd like to wish him goodbye because he's been a good friend to me while I've been here.'

At last it was her turn at the standcock, and she filled her bucket with the discoloured, musty-smelling water and carried its heavy weight back up to her room where, to her surprise she saw Septimus Prendergast seated at the table, his thin sallow features badly swollen and bruised, as if he had been brawling.

He smiled at her shocked face, and pointed a finger at his teeth. 'Never fear, Grainne, my molars are still intact, so the eventual return of my good looks is assured.'

'What happened to you, Septimus? Have you been fighting?' she wanted to know.

He laughed softly. 'I'm no pugilist, Grainne. I was trying to avoid the fight. It was the other fellow who persisted in punching my head. Anyway, no matter to that. I've just been speaking with your husband. He tells me that you are sailing on the *Florida* packet next Saturday.'

She confirmed that they were, and told him, 'I'm glad to have seen you before we sailed, Septimus. I wanted to thank you for your goodness to me while I've been here.'

Still smiling, he told her lightly, 'It is me who should be thanking you, Grainne. You have been a constant reminder to me that there exists another sort of life in this wicked world, other than the life I lead. You remind me always that decency and goodness can still be met with, even here in these vile slums.'

They were interrupted by the return of Con Shonley with his list of necessary articles and the three of them sat down to scan it.

'Well Septimus, you've sailed to America before. What to you think to this list?' Con wanted to know.

The Englishman ran his long-nailed fingers down the paper, and nodded. 'It seems very reasonable. You'll be needing the pots and pans, if only to keep your cooked food in. As for the cooking itself, it's better that you bribe the ship's cook. He'll prepare everything for you then. Bedding is also a necessity. It can be damned cold at sea. I would think that it might be wise to buy a couple of those new waterproof capes for yourselves as well.' He nodded once more and passed the list back to Con Shonley. 'I declare, Con, that Mr Thomas Tracey must have a soft spot in his heart for you both. He's only put down useful and necessary articles and foodstuffs. Some of the things that are sold to the immigrants are absolutely useless. The poor simple fools are persuaded to load themselves with all sorts of unnecessary rubbish.' He smiled and joked, 'I'm beginning to think that you must have some sort of a hold over Tracey. He's not trying to rook you of all you possess, as is his normal wont with his lodgers.'

'I think it's Grainne he has the soft spot for,' Con smiled fondly at her, 'and who could blame him for that?'

'No one in full possession of their faculties!' Prendergast asserted roundly. Then from inside his black frockcoat he produced a bottle. 'Come my friends, I've some very fine French brandy here, and I want to drink to your continued good fortune. Will you join me?'

'Gladly.' Con answered. 'I believe that we have some tumblers in our chest, have we not, Grainne?'

While she found the tumblers, Grainne spoke to Prendergast. 'Will you be coming to see us off, Septimus?'

He shook his head regretfully. 'Sadly, that cannot be, my dear friends. I have some pressing business matters to attend to in Manchester, which necessitates my leaving here this very night. So I'm afraid that this will be our parting glass. But who knows what the future may hold? Perhaps we shall meet again some day.' He filled the three tumblers with the golden liquid and lifted his glass in salute to them both, 'I wish you God speed, and good fortune, and may you find all that you seek for in your New World.'

As Grainne raised her glass to her lips she was assailed with the peculiar feeling that she had experienced this scene before, and suddenly knew without any doubt that she would someday meet this Englishman again.

Chapter Thirteen

The Government Medical Inspector's Office was a hut near to the docks which opened from ten o'clock in the morning to four o'clock in the afternoon. On Friday morning Grainne and Con, went to the public bath and changed into fresh clothing after cleansing their bodies. Then they made their way to the 'Doctor Shop', as the Medical Office was called by the locals.

On arriving there they found a large crowd numbering more than a thousand men, women and children, waiting for the inspection to begin. The crowd was predominantly Irish, many of the men wearing the caubeens, short blue cloaks and knee breeches of Irish countrymen, and several of the groups that Grainne passed were speaking in Erse.

'I don't know how Denis could claim he was homesick,' she remarked jokingly to her husband. 'It looks like we're taking the whole of Ireland with us.'

'Mrs Shonley? Mrs Shonley?' A voice called from the crowd and Grainne turned to see the plump farmer's wife surrounded by her numerous brood of rosy-cheeked children.

'Are you also sailing tomorrow, Mrs Carter?' Grainne asked, and the pink, motherly face beamed delightedly.

'Indeed we are, my dear. We sail on the *Florida*.'

'We'll be shipmates then, Mrs Carter. I'm glad of that.' Grainne was pleased that she would be having the company of the woman, and in her turn Mrs Carter also expressed her pleasure at the prospect.

While waiting for the door of the Medical Office to open Grainne studied the crowd around her. For the most part they were shabby and down at heel, but here and there she saw more prosperous looking groups. There were only a few people in actual rags, and she pointed this out to Con. 'When we came over from Cork there were a lot more ragged ones with us, than there are here, Con.'

'I shouldn't think that they had the price of the passage, honey, more's the pity for them. They'll be stuck here now.'

The door opened and the crowd cheered good-naturedly. Grainne frowned as she watched the people surging to enter the office. 'We'll be hours before we can get examined.'

'Ne'er mind, at least it's fine weather today,' Mrs Carter said comfortably, 'and to speak plain, I'd a sight sooner be here than asitting in that lodgings. I can't abear all the dirty people.' She sniffed expressively and looked around her with a slightly jaundiced eye. 'Mind you, my dear, there's more nor a few strangers to soap and water right here, arn't there just.'

Grainne readily agreed. Most of the crowd smelled strongly, and although she could appreciate the difficulties of keeping clothes and bodies clean while in transit through this city with little money to spare, yet she felt that at least people could make some effort. She could actually see the lice crawling upon the shirt collar of one man standing near her, and she dreaded to think what the cramped steerage cabins of the ship would be like if there were many more like him aboard.

Con shared her opinion. 'I hope that the medical examination turns some of these back,' he muttered. 'I don't mind a bit of honest dirt, but some of these people here disgust me, they're so filthy looking.'

Mrs Carter's husband joined them, carrying a bag full of hot baked potatoes. The woman beamed at Con and Grainne saying warmly, 'Come now, have a bite o'

99

breakfast with us. There's plenty for all of us here.' She would accept no refusal, and from her own bag produced salt, cheese, and a small knife with which she cut open the big steaming potatoes and inserted slices of cheese which melted, mingling deliciously with the floury-white meat.

Con called over a ginger-beer seller and bought several bottles which he distributed, as his contribution to this alfresco meal. As Grainne ate and drank she experienced a tremendous uplift of her spirits, and for the first time since Maggie Nolan's death felt happy.

She watched the crowd entering the 'Doctor Shop' and was surprised at the speed with which they went through the front door and poured out through a side door. When she pointed this fact out to Con, he smiled. 'Well, at least we won't have to wait here for as long as we feared.'

When their own turn came Grainne went in first. The room was merely a bare hallway, and on one side was a small window behind which two doctors were standing. As each immigrant presented him or herself at the window the doctor merely said, 'Give me your ticket. What is your name? How do you feel? ... Open your mouth, and let me see your tongue ... Alright.' Then he stamped the ticket and returned it to the immigrant.

Behind Grainne, Con chuckled wryly. 'This is a farce, honey. No wonder there is so much fever on board the immigrant ships, and so many of the poor souls die at sea.'

Directly in front of Grainne was the man with the lice crawling on his collar and Grainne saw the doctor's eyes fix on those lice as the man presented his ticket. She waited for the doctor to turn the man back, to tell him to cleanse himself, or to get disinfested, but the doctor only yawned with boredom and asked the usual questions, before stamping and returning the ticket.

When her own turn at the window came she was tempted to challenge the doctor, to ask him how he could permit such an obvious hazard to the health and

100

well-being of other passengers, but realised the futility of such an action. 'I'd only be wasting my breath. These men don't care what happens to immigrants. Nor does anyone else care from what I've seen so far.'

Her earlier high spirits were somewhat subdued as she walked away from the 'Doctor Shop' with Con. Sensing this he tried to cheer her and suggested, 'Look honey, it being our last night here, let's go out and enjoy ourselves for once.'

'Can we afford it?' She felt constrained to ask, although the idea of an evening of enjoyment greatly appealed to her.

He grinned down at her. 'No, we can't. But that's just why we'll do it. It's more fun spending what we can't afford.'

Her high spirits burgeoned anew and squeezing his arm, her laughter rang out so infectiously that people nearby heard it and smiled too. 'Where shall we go?' she asked excitedly.

A bill-poster was hard at work on a blank section of wall with a small crowd watching him, and Con's attention was caught by the large garishly coloured bill he was plastering up.

'Look there, honey.' He drew Grainne's attention to the bill.

It depicted five handsome, elegantly-dressed negroes, sitting on straight-backed chairs playing banjos, accordion, tambourine and bones. Above their heads was the legendary 'Royal Amphitheatre', and beneath their feet in larger letters 'The Ethiopian Serenaders'.

'That's where we'll go,' Con stated.

> *I came from ole Kentucky*
> *A long time ago*
> *Where I first learn to wheel about*
> *And jump Jim Crow.*
> *Wheel about, turn about, and do jes so,*
> *Eb'ry time I wheel about, I jump Jim Crow …*

The five Ethiopian Serenaders sang the words of the rollicking tune, and all around the packed theatre hands clapped out the tempo.

> *I landed first at Liverpool*
> *Dat place of ships and docks ...*

The audience cheered at the mention of the city.

> *I strutted down Lord Street*
> *And as'd the price of stocks.*
> *Wheel about, turn about, and do jes so,*
> *Eb'ry time I wheel about, I jump Jim Crow ...*

Seated up in the gallery Grainne's eyes shone with pleasure, and her foot tapped in time with the music.

> *I us'd to take him fiddle,*
> *Eb'ry morn and afternoon*
> *And charm the old buzzard*
> *And dance to the Racoon.'*

Down in the pit among the crush, sailors and their girls began to dance, stamping their feet and bellowing at the tops of their voices.

> *'I paid my fare den up to town*
> *On de coach to cut a dash,*
> *De axletree soon gave way*
> *And spilt us wid a smash.*
> *Wheel about, turn about and do jes so,*
> *Eb'ry time I wheel about, I jump Jim Crow ...'*

'Are you enjoying it, honey?' Con placed his mouth close to Grainne's ear to ask.

She smiled radiantly and nodded. 'I think it's wonderful.'

Her gaze wandered, taking in all the ornate splendour of the plush surroundings: the gilt, and the glittering chandeliers, the elegant gentlemen in evening dress with bejewelled ladies in the boxes, the colourful crush of sailors and their women in the pit, the serried ranks of respectable tradesmen, ships' officers and shopkeepers in the gallery, many with their wives and children. The over-heated air smelled of oranges and perfumes, of pomades and tobacco, beer and brandy, soap and sweat.

Grainne looked back at the stage with its backdrop of plantation slaves picking cotton and a colonnaded white mansion, and wondered if she would see such a scene when she reached America. She could see that the five entertainers were not real negroes, but were white men; their hands, faces and necks coloured with a chocolate brown greasepaint, and black wigs covering their own hair. They wore the full finery of evening dress: black cut-away coats and pantaloons, dazzlingly white shirtfronts and waistcoats with high-winged collars and black stocks around their throats and shiny patent leather dancing pumps on their feet.

> *'Dem urchins what sing my song*
> *Had better mind dar looks,*
> *For anyhow dey can't be crows,*
> *You see d'ar only rooks.*
> *Wheel about, turn about, and do jes so,*
> *Eb'ry time I wheel about, I jump Jim*
> *Crooooowwww . . .'*

The song came to an end to a roaring of applause and a thunderous stamping of feet, and as the Ethiopian Serenaders got to their feet, bowing low, the curtain came down for the interval.

'Shall I fetch you something to drink, honey?'

Grainne shook her head. 'No, I'm fine thanks, but you go and have something.' When he hesitated she pushed him gently saying, 'Go on now. I know you're thirsty.'

He smiled and kissed her lightly on the lips. 'I'll not be long. Are you sure you don't want me to bring you something back with me?'

Again she shook her head. 'No, really, I'm fine as I am.'

The gallery rail was directly in front of the bench she

was sitting on. Grainne leaned forward, and resting her forearms along the coping gazed with keen interest at the occupants of the Boxes. She admired the fine clothes and jewellery, and could not help feeling a touch envious of how beautiful some of the young women appeared in their finery. One young woman, in particular, intrigued Grainne. She had blonde hair, parted in the centre, swept back and swathed in a long gilded net. Her red satin gown was low-cut, displaying the powdered tops of her rounded breasts and smooth shoulders and in her hand she carried a jewelled fan which she used coquettishly and with charm as the three young men clustered around her vied for her attention.

'I see that là belle Adelaide is fascinating you, Mrs Shonley.'

Grainne started in shock as the man seated himself in Con's vacant seat.

'Forgive me for startling you. I trust that you now remember me?' It was the handsome doctor from the Dispensary, Malcom Galbraith. He removed his top hat and asked, 'There, Mrs Shonley, do you now recall my face?'

Flustered, she told him, 'Oh yes, I do remember now, sir.'

'I'm sorry about your friend, Mrs Shonley. We did our best for her, but sadly to no avail.'

'It was God's will, sir,' Grainne said quietly.

Galbraith grimaced wryly. 'I'm not entirely sure that the gentleman in question takes a deal of interest in the poor of Liverpool, Mrs Shonley, nor in the immigrants who flood into this city.' He saw Grainne's shocked expression, and chuckled. 'Forgive me, Mrs Shonley; I was forgetting my manners. I must confess to being inclined towards atheism myself, and this tends to make me somewhat careless as to the tenderness of others' religious beliefs.' He changed the subject abruptly asking, 'When do you sail for America, Mrs Shonley?'

'Tomorrow, sir, on the *Florida* packet.'

'What a pity! Liverpool can ill afford to lose such a

beautiful woman.'

Grainne found that her reaction to this compliment was uncertain. She was half-pleased to receive a compliment from such a handsome man, yet at the same time partly angry that he should be so forward towards a respectable, married woman.

Galbraith, indicating the beautiful blonde-haired young woman in the box said, 'Adelaide is considered to be the reigning beauty of Liverpool at this present time, Mrs Shonley.' His brown eyes twinkled at her as though he was laughing inwardly, and inviting Grainne to share his amusement. 'But alas!' he continued, 'I fear that she'll not be here for much longer. I have it on very good authority that she has been invited to take up residence in London.' His twinkling eyes studied the beautiful blonde for a moment or two, then he sighed regretfully, and turned again to Grainne saying, 'I do declare, Mrs Shonley, that I can never understand why our reverend brethren are always stating with such certainty that the wages of sin is death. It's patently nonsense in the case of Adelaide; she's positively blooming, ain't she just?' He winked and added drolly, 'I most certainly intend to tax the Reverend Coolidge with uttering blatant falsehoods when he next repeats that assertion in my hearing, and I shan't give a damn if he is in or out of the pulpit.'

Grainne could not repress a smile. 'You are a wicked man, I fear, Dr Galbraith.'

'Indeed I am not, Mrs Shonley. My soul is purer than the driven snow. Now, regretfully, I must leave you, my lovely lady, for I have a most pressing appointment at the bar of this establishment.' He rose and bowed politely. 'I wish you good fortune in America, Mrs Shonley.'

'Who was that?' asked Con, returning just as Galbraith was walking away.

'His name is Dr Galbraith. It was him who gave Maggie entrance to the Dispensary.'

Con remained standing, watching the doctor passing through the crowd. 'What did he want with you?' he asked, frowning.

'He wanted me to run away with him,' Grainne teased, and laughed aloud when she saw her young husband's startled reaction. 'I do believe that you're jealous!'

He grinned at his own discomfiture. 'I do believe that I am,' he admitted, 'but that's understandable, isn't it? After all, I'm with the most beautiful woman in Liverpool, arn't I, and I don't want to share her company with anybody.'

She reached up to take his arm and draw him down beside her, telling him fondly, 'You must never feel jealous if I sometimes talk to other men, Con. You are my husband, and the only man that I'll ever love.'

A storm of applause announced the return of the Ethiopian Serenaders to the stage.

> 'Way down upon the Swannee Ribber
> Far far awaaayyy
> That's where my heart is turning ebberrr
> Back where the old folks stayyyy . . .'

From the pit a chorus of voices rose to join in with the Ethiopians, and Grainne smiled in pleasure at the tuneful harmony. Her eyes were drawn to the side-box where the beautiful blonde-haired girl was sitting, and she saw that the three young men had gone to be replaced by an older, prosperous looking, corpulent gentleman, who was standing behind the blonde girl's chair with a proprietorial air; his hand resting upon one of her rounded shoulders. The girl's posture struck a chord of recognition in Grainne, and for a while she puzzled over what that chord of recognition meant to her. Then she knew, the posture suggested the resigned submission of a caged animal that senses it can never be free again.

'How sad it is for her,' Grainne thought. Then, remembering the disease-ravaged prostitutes she saw constantly in the slums of the docks, admitted, 'But at least that girl is more fortunate than those pitiful creatures. She seems to be well rewarded for selling herself, judging by her clothes and jewels.'

Grainne passed no moral judgement upon the prostitute. She knew from bitter experience the agonies of hungry poverty, and the desperate plight of women left alone in the world to fend for themselves. She was honest enough to admit to herself that if she was faced with the stark alternatives of starvation or prostitution, she might well follow the path that the blonde girl was travelling down. 'I pray to God I'm never faced with that choice,' she thought, and then tried to dismiss these troubling thoughts from her mind, and immerse herself in enjoyment of the show once more.

When the programme ended and she and Con were outside on the gas-lit pavement in front of the theatre the thought of returning to the rancid slums filled Grainne with repulsion. She knew that tomorrow would find them in an overcrowded, unsavoury steerage cabin, where they would know no privacy for several weeks, and she hungered to be alone with her husband, shut off from the clamorous world around them – if only for a few hours – before setting out on the next stage of their journey.

Con Shonley was experiencing that same longing, and as if they shared a telepathic communication, he smiled tenderly at her, and told her, 'Tonight we stay at a hotel where we can have a room to ourselves, honey.'

She gladly agreed, and arm in arm they went in search of their goal.

Very soon they found a respectable hotel and took a room. Con ordered a supper to be sent up to them, and they shared a bottle of good wine.

Later, in the clean, sweet-scented bed their bodies fused in a hungry passion and they gloried in each other's flesh until, satiated, they fell asleep in close embrace.

In the dark hours of early morning Grainne woke,

and lay listening to Con's soft breathing beside her, and cuddled up to his muscular leanness. Her thoughts turned again to the blonde-haired girl of the theatre, and she wondered where that girl was now lying, and who was sharing her bed, and if she had known the fierce tenderness of a shared mutual love in the night, instead of the mere assuagement of a man's lusts.

Grainne thought of what awaited her in a few hours time, and remembered the stories she had heard of storms and shipwrecks and plague boats. 'Please God, bring us safely to America,' she prayed fervently. 'Look over us and protect us when we are at sea.'

Sleep stole over her once more, and in that sleep came dreams; strange dreams in which she seemed to be wandering through thick mists, searching for Con, and calling his name, but receiving no answers to her calls. And in the depths of her sleep she stirred restlessly, tears trickling slowly down her cheeks.

Chapter Fourteen

From long before dawn the quayside of Waterloo Dock had been a noisy, boiling maelstrom of human beings. The *Florida* was moored alongside the quay, but its master, Captain Lockyer, would not permit any of the emigrants to come aboard until his cargo of gunpowder and rail iron had been stowed safely in the holds, and so they huddled with their boxes, bundles and sacks of provisions, pots and pans, their numbers continuously augmented by fresh arrivals, being pestered by pedlars and abused by porters, sworn at, cuffed and buffeted by dockers and sailors.

In the middle of the seething throng Grainne and Con squatted on their bedding roll waiting with what patience they could muster for the order to embark. Next to them was the Carter family, and Mrs Carter kept on staring uneasily at the gangplank that led up onto the ship's deck from the quayside.

Grainne noticed the plump woman's concern, and asked her, 'What's troubling you, Mrs Carter?'

'It's that there plankwalk, Mrs Shonley. Just see how it bends so. I can't think it's safe for a heavy woman like me to goo up it.'

Grainne looked at the gangplank and saw how it sprang under the boots of the dockers who were toting crates of provisions aboard. 'It's safe enough, Mrs Carter,' she smiled, 'It needs to bend beneath the weight like that, otherwise it wouldn't retain its strength.'

Mrs Carter's motherly features were still doubtful,

but she made no comment.

Grainne found herself in a curious state of mind. Although excited that the day of sailing had finally arrived, yet her dreams of the previous night had left a residue of uneasiness in her mind, which this fine, breezy day could not dispel. And although she had been told that the three-masted ship was over a thousand tons burthen, yet to her landlubber's eyes it looked a very small vessel in which to cross the trackless wastes of the mighty Atlantic Ocean.

Mrs Carter appeared to share Grainne's doubts about the size of the vessel. 'I don't know what you thinks, Mrs Shonley, but it looks a bit on the small side to be fitting in all o' the people here, don't it?'

"Ull you give over werritin', missis,' her bluff-featured husband told her angrily, 'and stop moitherin' that poor wench. If the bloody ship warn't big enough to take us, then the bloody captain 'udden't allow us aboard, 'ud he?'

'Well! He's taking his time about that, arn't he!' His wife sniffed indignantly. 'It seems like we bin waiting here for a powerful long stretch.'

'Look there!' Con straightened his body and pointed. 'I think we'll be moving soon.'

A steam tug was nosing alongside the prow of the *Florida*. The wind took the thick black smoke belching from its tall funnel and carried it swirling through the masses on the quayside. The sooty smuts alighted on heads and bodies and Mrs Carter grumbled, 'God Almighty. It's like to smother us, arn't it.'

Captain Alfred Lockyer paced up and down the after-deck, his head throbbing agonisingly from the effects of his overnight drinking bout. Although the *Florida* was an American-owned and registered ship and Lockyer himself was an American, his First and Second Mates were British. The remainder of his crew were a hodgepodge of nationalities and, like the crews of most of the ships engaged in the emigrant trade, were mainly riff-raff, as the majority of good steady

110

seamen disliked sailing in the emigrant ships, of which all too many deserved their nickname, Coffin Ship. He knew that at this very moment the major part of his crew were drunk, but also knew that he could rely on his two bucko mates to drive them hard and make them work.

A man in a peaked cap and dark blue uniform coat came up onto the after-deck, and Captain Lockyer scowled when he saw him. It was Lieutenant Heath, one of the Emigration Officers of the port.

The *Florida* was registered for three hundred passengers, but Heath knew that when the ship sailed there would be at least five hundred passengers crammed into its steerage. Heath was also supposed to ensure that only trained seamen formed the crew, but again he was virtually powerless to ensure that the regulation would be complied with. So many emigrant vessels were leaving Liverpool each day that the officers of the Emigration Commision were under too much pressure to cope, and were forced to turn a blind eye to the abuses of the trade.

Heath saluted the Captain. 'Is everything in order, Captain Lockyer?'

'It is,' the American replied, shortly.

His first mate shouted from the main deck, 'Cargo's stowed, sir. Tug's standing by for our lines.'

'Get 'em inboard, Mr Harper, and move 'em fast.' Lockyer's thin lips twisted in disgust. The presence of the Emigration Officer at this moment could cost him valuable time, in that his crew could not exercise any undue brutality in packing the emigrants into the steerage with maximum speed.

'Aye, sir.' The First Mate's hatchet features scowled ferociously at the mass on the quayside and, cupping his hands around his mouth, he bellowed, 'Get aboard you lot, and look lively, blast your eyes!'

For a very short space of time the emigrants tried to embark in an orderly manner, then pandemonium erupted as the first mate and some of the crew members burst among the mass on the quayside, cursing and shouting, and laying about them with ropes' ends and belaying pins, snatching up bundles and sacks and heaving them over the bulwarks and taffrail, forcing men, women and children to scramble over those same obstacles.

Con and Grainne had only their chest, a roll of bedding and a couple of sacks of provisions to worry about, but the Carter family possessed an abundance of impedimenta. Mrs Carter wailed in despair, throwing up her hands, her children shrieking in fear and distress, as people trampled over them to escape the vicious swings of the ropes' ends and belaying pins wielded by the seamen.

'Con, lets throw our baggage over the side there. I'll guard it while you give the Carters a hand,' Grainne suggested, and Con nodded in agreement. By brute force he pushed his way through the struggling mass and after thrusting his baggage inboard, lifted Grainne, carrying her to the bulwark. Disregarding the standards of decorum, Grainne bunched her long skirts high and scrambled onto the deck. Then she collected the baggage and stowed it against the butt of the mainmast.

While the tumultuous embarkation was proceeding, crew members made ready to cast off the mooring lines, and made fast the tugboat's tow lines.

Lieutenant Heath frowned unhappily at the distressful scenes being enacted, and remonstrated as he saw one old woman being dragged feet first over the bulwarks by a drunken seaman, shrieking with outrage as her voluminous skirts and petticoats were pulled up to reveal her thighs and intimate parts. 'Damn it all, Captain Lockyer, cannot your crew treat these people with more respect?'

The dour New Englander scowled. 'Time's wasting, Mr Heath and that damned tugboat won't wait around for this cargo of rubbish to come aboard all dainty like. When the Harbour Master sends it to move me, then

112

move I must. Them that can't get aboard now, must take a rowboat and come out to me in midstream.' He walked to the edge of the after deck and bellowed, 'Cast off forrard! Cast Off aft!'

The mooring lines splashed into the water and the tug began to pull the *Florida* away from the quay.

There was a howling clamour from those unfortunates still stranded on the quay and one man tried to jump across the widening gap. He thudded against the ship's side and his hands scrabbled vainly for a hold on the bulwark rail, then with a choking scream he fell into the water, and splashed there wildly until a small rowing boat fished him out.

The ship was towed out of the narrow dock entrance lock and into the centre of the estuary, and its anchors were dropped to hold it in position until the turn of the tide.

A passenger, whose wife and child had been left on the quayside came charging up onto the afterdeck and began to remonstrate furiously with Captain Lockyer.

The American stared at the ranting man with silent contempt, then beckoned to the First Mate, 'Remove this man, mister.'

The burly Mate grabbed the passenger's coat collar and with an ease that displayed his immense physical strength, pitched him headlong onto the main deck. When the passenger struggled to his feet and made as if to come back at the after deck again, the First Mate grinned and brandished his belaying pin threateningly.

'Don't even think o' trying it, gob-shite,' he jeered, and the passenger swallowed hard and backed off.

'Listen to me all of you,' Lockyer shouted. 'Anybody left on the quayside can hire a boat and come out to us here. So I don't want to hear any more complaint. The next person who comes to me with such, will be put off my ship.' He paused and his hard eyes scanned his audience as if daring anyone to step forwards. 'Get this into your heads now, because I won't be repeating it.

113

I'm Captain Alfred Lockyer, and not God himself stands above me aboard this vessel. I'm the master here, and for your own sakes, you'd best not ever forget it.' Again he paused, as if daring anyone to step forward and question his statement. When no one did so, he ordered his first mate, 'Get rid of the pedlars, Mr Harper, then call the roll.'

The pedlars had pushed themselves on board with the emigrants during the scuffling embarkation, and even now were passing around the crowded deck trying to sell their wares: oranges, sweetmeats, pies, toffee, ribbons, laces and a variety of knick-knacks.

Roughly the seamen drove them into a tender which had come alongside the *Florida* bringing out the stranded passengers from the quayside. In the noise and confusion of the transfer from tender to ship some of the passengers lost pieces of luggage which fell into the murky waters of the estuary.

The passenger broker's clerk, a cadaverous, pedantic man, had also come out on the tender, carrying with him his lists of passengers' names. He came to stand at the hatchway leading down into the steerage, and handed his list to Harper. Many of the emigrants had already gone below, and the ship's Second Mate was sent with some seamen to drive them back up on deck. Once they had done that the seamen set about searching the vessel for stowaways. Rolls of bedding were hammered in case someone might be wrapped up in them. Sealed barrels large enough to contain a body were tipped upside down and a long nail-tipped pole was jabbed into dark corners, and some of the larger chests were broken open. In all five stowaways were discovered and roughly handled as they were dragged up onto the after-deck and forced to stand in a hang-dog row against the taffrail to await the tender mercies of Captain Lockyer.

He and Lieutenant Heath stood at the after-deck rail overlooking the steerage hatchway, and Lockyer nodded to his First Mate. The man's hatchet features glowered at the emigrants.

'When you hears your name called, then step up and show your ticket. When I'se passed it, you can take your baggage and go below and find a berth. Don't forget, that it's four adults to each berth. You must fit in the bloody kids where you can. Now look lively!'

He began to chant out names in a rhyming chant, and as each name was called the passengers hurried forwards, scrabbling their baggage with them as best as they could. When their tickets were verified they disappeared below. 'Samuel Kean, come and be seen ... Peter Jones, show your bones ... John Lancaster, come move faster ... Michael McCarthy, bring your party ... John Carter, follow after ... Conrad Shonley, two tickets only ...'

Grainne half-stumbled down the steep stairs into the gloom of the steerage, and looked about her with a sinking heart. A spattering of box lanterns fixed high on the stanchions were the only sources of light, and the two-tiered sleeping berths six feet squared, ran continuously down each side of the long low steerage deck, leaving only a narrow passage in the centre of the deck for the stowing of baggage.

'Con, let's take a berth near to the stairs,' she suggested. 'At least we'll get some air then.'

'We'll probably get a deal of cold sea water splashing on us as well,' he joked grimly. 'Still, I think you're right; it's probably a better place to be than further along.

She heard Mrs Carter's voice raised high in angry dispute with her husband, and called to the woman, 'Mrs Carter, come up here by us. Then the kids can share our berth.'

The deck slowly filled and before an hour had passed Grainne was thankful that she had suggested taking berths near to the hatchway.

Fights broke out as the emigrants disputed over berths and space, and the air quickly staled. All the time there was a constant cacophony of noise assaulting the ears of the passengers. The Second Mate, a hulking Welshman, rampaged up and down the steerage-deck shouting continuously, 'No smoking down here! Iffen I catch anybody smoking I'll shove his pipe up his arse, You can only smoke topside.'

Grainne went back up on deck to help Mrs Carter bring the last of her bundles down, and stood for a while to watch the captain dealing with the stowaways.

'Have you got money?' Lockyer asked the first man in the line who was a weazened-faced, derelict with a bent body and a ragged coat.

The man shook his head sullenly, and without any warning Lockyer punched him full in the face. The man cried out and fell back against the taffrail, and Lockyer's boot thudded into his groin.

The derelict emitted a high-pitched squeal and dropped to the deck where he lay writhing in agony. Lockyer kicked him several more times, until the writhing and squealing ceased and the man sprawled senseless, blood oozing from his smashed mouth and nose into a pool on the deck beneath his head.

Grainne gasped in horror, and wondered why the uniformed man standing on the after-deck did nothing to stop the brutal attack. But Lieutenant Heath knew better than to try and thwart a ship's captain on his own territory.

Beside her, Mrs Carter's plump body quivered with anger, and Grainne heard the woman shout, 'Leave that poor man alone, you great brute!'

Captain Lockyer spun on his heels, his eyes wide with surprise.

'Is that you I heard?' he demanded of Grainne, and for a moment or two she stood motionless, not wishing by denial to get her companion into any trouble.

'No, it warn't this maid at all. It was me,' Mrs Carter spoke out fearlessly, 'You should be ashamed o' yourself, serving that poor man so bad.'

'Get below, you cow,' the Captain ordered contemptuously and turned back to the next man in line, who was already fearfully proffering coins.

'Did you hear what he called me?' Mrs Carter demanded indignantly, and went to move forwards. 'He arn't agoing to speak that way to me! I don't care who he thinks he may be.'

Grainne caught hold of the woman's arm and held her back. 'You stay here,' she told her urgently. 'There's nothing you can do now to save that man. He's already taken his beating. Come on back down below with me.'

'You'd best do as she tells you.' the First Mate came up to the two women. 'Like he told you afore, the Captain is God when he's aboard here. The best thing you can do is to mind your own business, and not be troubling yer heads about scum like that. If you gives him any more o' your lip he'll most likely put you ashore, and where will you be then?'

'Think of the kids, Mrs Carter,' Grainne added her own urging. 'If you were to be put ashore, what will happen to them?'

The woman snorted angrily, but allowed Grainne to lead her back down below, where she immediately began to volubly threaten what she would do to Captain Lockyer when the ship reached New York.

Grainne quietly related to Con what had occurred, and he shrugged indifferently. 'I reckon we shall all have had our bellyfull of Lockyer before we reach New York, honey. But there's no sense in antagonizing the man against us by interfering in matters that are no concern of ours.'

'I think you're right,' Grainne agreed, 'but from what I've seen of this ship so far, I'll be very pleased when we can get off it.'

Con hugged her briefly. 'We've lived through worse than this, honey. It will soon pass.'

For the next hour or so they helped the Carters to sort through their many bundles and tend to their numerous children. Then, from the deck above came a flurry of bellowed orders and the rhythmic tramping of feet, and the sounds of men bawling in tuneful chant as they pushed the capstan bars round and round.

> *'John-ny Todd he took a not-ion*
> *For to cross the rag-ing ocean*
> *And he left his love be-hind him*
> *Weeping on the Liverpool shore.'*

Con crowed happily, 'They're raising the anchor! We're leaving, honey. We're on our way.'

There was a rush for the upper-deck and the emigrants crowded to the ship's rails to wave farewell to the land. Some were cheering, some shouting, nearly all were joyously excited, and only here and there could be seen any tears or sadness. For most of those on board, this ship was taking them from nothing but poverty and suffering.

Grainne stared up at the great brown sheets of the weather-stained canvas sails swelling out as they filled with wind and felt the deck beneath her moving like a living thing. Her heart pounded with excitement, and she clung to Con's arms and laughed exultantly, 'We're going, Con. We're going to America. At last, we're going to America.'

118

Chapter Fifteen

The elation of leaving Liverpool did not last long. Almost as soon as the *Florida* reached the open waters of the Irish Sea the weather worsened dramatically. Winds of gale force and massive swells caused the ship to heave and pitch and reel drunkenly, scudding rain lashing her decks. Captain Lockyer ordered the hatchways closed, and in the dark steerage large numbers were already prostrated because of sea-sickness. Each time the vessel lurched and juddered the screams and wails of terrified women and children added to the agonies of enforced incarceration in this already fetid prison.

The overcrowding meant that instead of four people to each cramped berth, there might be five or six struggling to lie down, and savage struggles took place as men and women fought to gain a space to rest their tortured bodies.

The stench of vomit and human waste made the already stale air intolerable to breathe but when some of the stronger men tried to raise the hatches to admit fresh air they found that the heavy shutters had been barred and lashed shut, and all they could do was to scream futile pleas and curses as they hammered with impotent fists against the thick unyielding planking.

Grainne lay in her berth with three of the Carter children crushed between her body and Con's, doing her best to comfort the frightened children, while her own head seemed to be spinning giddily and her stomach heaved with will-sapping nausea.

All through the night and most of the following day the *Florida* fought through the storm, and then, mercifully, the gale eased and the mountainous swells flattened. The hatches were opened, and Grainne thanked God as she saw the sunlight lancing down into the dark deck. Those that could made their way shakily up into the clean air and as they emerged the sailors laughed and jeered at their misery.

'That was nothing; that was just a bit of a blow.'

'Just you wait 'til we gets a proper storm.'

'You look like fokkin' bilge rats.'

'No they don't; bilge rats smells better!'

Grainne was uncaring of the jeers. All she could feel was an overwhelming thankfulness that the storm had passed, and that she had gained release from the purgatory below. She went forward and stood gazing out over the bows, the wind blowing her long hair about her face. Gazing at the white-flecked green billows she became almost hypnotized by their ever-changing patterns, while above her head the sails cracked, the rigging hummed and gulls wheeled and screamed harshly as they soared and swooped, the sunlight flashing on their white wings. Grainne became intoxicated by the wild beauty that surrounded her and suddenly understood why the sea with all its cruel treachery could yet enthrall men and enslave their very souls. She lost all count of time, and remained at her post until finally Con came in search of her.

For a time he did not intrude upon her rapt fascination, but stood quietly watching the smile that curved her lips, and blessed the fates that had given him this woman as his wife. At last, reluctantly, he went to Grainne and broke the spell that held her motionless.

She turned and smiling at him, said, 'It is truly beautiful, isn't it? No matter what happens now, I'll never regret making this voyage.'

He shook his head, and teased, 'Will you say that even if we get ship-wrecked, girl?'

She laughed gaily. 'Well, I might have to give the matter some consideration in such an event.' She looked about the deck and was surprised to see how few of the emigrants had come up from the steerage. 'Jesus, are the rest still laying down there?'

Con nodded, and his expression became grim. 'There's some that are really ill, I think, honey. And if the deck isn't cleaned and freshened, then there'll be a lot more that'll be ill afore much longer. I'm going to have a word with the Captain, and see if we can get cleaning materials from him, and some of the crew to help us clean up down there. I want to find out about the cooking facilities, and the issue of fresh water. According to our contract we're supposed to be given food, as well.'

He looked back over his shoulder at the after-deck. 'There's the Captain now. I'm going to have a word with him.'

Impelled by an unaccountable feeling, Grainne said sharply, 'No! Con, don't speak with him.'

He stared at her with incomprehension. 'Why do you say that?'

She shook her head. 'I can't tell you for I don't know myself why I did. I only know that you mustn't.'

'But that's nonsense, Grainne. You're talking silly now,' he told her. 'Do you not feel well?'

Angered at her own inability to explain her instinctive conviction, she burst out, 'I'm as well as I've ever been in my life. I just don't want you to go near that man right now.'

While he stared at her with half-angry mystification another group of passengers emerged from the hatchway. Grainne recognised them from the wait at the quayside. An elderly couple with two younger men and one young woman; judging by their clothing they were more prosperous than the majority.

One of the younger men approached Con and Grainne. 'Have ye been told anything about the water issue? And how we get our food cooked?' he asked in a

Scottish accent.

'Not yet,' Con told him. 'I was about to ask Captain Lockyer there.'

'Con, why don't you ask one of the sailors?' Grainne suggested.

He stared hard at her, then drew a deep breath and said with enforced patience, 'Because, honey, the ones up here on deck are all very busy. The only man who appears not to be, is the Captain. All he's doing is walking up and down.'

There were several crew members topside, but most of them were up in the rigging, and the three men on the deck itself were engaged in various tasks.

The Scotsman called to his group, 'Pa, ye'll need tae ask the Captain.'

The elderly man acknowledged him with a wave of his hand and went, alone, up to the after-deck.

Grainne watched his progress with a sense of foreboding, and could find no justification for that sense. 'Am I going daft?' she asked herself wonderingly. 'What's the matter with me, feeling like this?'

She stood motionless, her breath coming in short nervous gasps, and her hands clenched into fists, fearing what, she did not know, but fearing it just the same.

Con stared at her curiously, with a dawning anxiety in his eyes. 'Grainne, are you alright?' he questioned.

She nodded silently, her eyes still locked on the old Scotsman. She watched him step up onto the after-deck and stand in front of the Captain. Words were exchanged between the pair, and then Lockyer turned away from the older man and resumed his restless pacing. The Scotsman stepped to confront him, and she heard their voices raised in angry altercation. Then, abruptly, the Captain stepped up to the Scotsman. His knee suddenly shot upwards into the old man's groin, and the old man doubled up and fell to his knees in obvious agony.

Then everything seemed to explode simultaneously

in Grainne's eyes. The hulking Second Mate slid down the rigging, and the First Mate appeared through the stern hatch. The sailors on deck left their tasks and ran aft.

The two younger Scotsmen also ran aft with Con after them, and after a moment's hesitation, Grainne followed.

Confronted by the crewmen, the two Scotsmen and Con stood on the after-deck, and while one of the Scots tended the injured man, the other demanded furiously, 'What in Hell's name did ye dae that for?'

The elderly Scotswoman, her face twisted in fear and distress, wringing her hands came, crying out, 'Graham! Graham, come away now. For God's sake come away!'

The man ignored her, and stepped towards the Captain with raised hands. 'I asked ye why ye did that, ye bastard ye?'

Instantly the Second Mate jolted the oncoming man backwards with a swing of his massively muscled arm across his chest.

'Keep your distance, Jock!' he growled warningly. 'You can say what you got to say from there.'

His freckled face pale with anger, the Scotsman again demanded furiously, 'Why did ya dae that to my Pa, you Yankee bastard?'

The New Englander's pale eyes reddened in his narrow, clean-shaven face, and a muscle began to twitch in his cheek.

'Mr Harper,' he hissed, 'put this scum in irons until he learns to keep a civil tongue in his head.'

'Aye, Sir.' The First Mate instantly sprang at the angry Scotsman and wrestled him down onto the deck. Then with the aid of two of the sailors dragged him shouting and struggling through the stern hatch.

'Listen well, the rest o' you,' Lockyer roared. 'I'm the Captain o' this ship and you're only a damned cargo, and I hold no speech with cargoes. If you've any questions, then ask my crew.' He turned to the Second

Mate. 'Mr Morgan, shift this offal.'

'Come away, Con,' Grainne begged her husband, who looked as if he was ready to hit the American. 'For the love o' God, come away.'

Seeing that she was genuinely afraid, Con Shonley allowed himself to be pulled away from the after-deck. His face was working with anger, and he told Grainne furiously, 'As soon as we get to New York, I'm going to have words with that bloody Captain. The man is not fit to command any vessel.'

They went back to the bows where a small knot of passengers stood huddled miserably together. 'When are they going to give us an issue of water and rations?' A Dublin man asked, and Con jerked his thumb at the elderly Scotsman who was being helped back down into the steerage by his family; the two women sobbing bitterly, and the remaining son white faced and worried.

'That gentleman you see there has just asked the Captain the very same question.' Con jerked out the words. 'If you and your friends are ready to stand by me, then I'm ready to go and teach that Yankee bastard and his bully-boys a lesson they'll not forget in a hurry.'

'Be Jase, I'm your man,' the Dubliner blustered. 'Jimmy Docherty is not feared of any bloody sailor boy, I'll tell ye.'

'Hold your stupid tongue, Jim Docherty!' Another man, short and thickset, dressed in a pea jacket and old peaked cap, with a face as weathered as old mahogany snapped curtly, then asked Con, 'Have youse ever been to sea before, mister?'

Con shook his head. 'No, I've not.'

'Well I have, many times,' the man asserted, 'and I can tell youse all, that the Captain was spaking nothing but the truth when he told yez that he was like God aboard here. That fella is lucky that he's only bin put in irons. Iffen the Captain wanted he could have charged the stupid bowsy with mutiny, and had him tried for

124

that when we reach New York, and the man would be lucky to escape having his bloody neck stretched. The Captain can do as he likes aboard his own ship.'

'So what can we do to obtain fair treatment?' Con demanded.

'Nothing!' The ex-sailor said shortly. 'Nothing at all, except to kape a civil tongue in your head, and obey orders. Iffen that Yankee bastard goes too far, then you can always lay complaint agen him when we reach New York. But to spake the truth, ye'd only be wasting your time doing that. Excepting that the bugger commits actual murder afore plenty o' witnesses. If he did that then ye might stand a chance o' laying him by the heels, but apart from that happening, then there's little ye can do about him.'

'This ship is a floating disgrace,' another man put in disgruntedly, and the ex-sailor laughed grimly, and told them, 'I've been a crewman on emigrant ships, and believe me, there's plenty worse than this 'un sailing this sea.'

Now that he had told the group that he was an ex-sailor a barrage of questions assailed him. He grinned and held up his hand.

'Hold on a minute will ye, and I'll try to give yez an idea o' the layout here.' He indicated the crude wooden cubicles on the forrad-deck alongside the bulwarks. 'There's the privies. Try not to use them in heavy weather, unless you want your arse soaking. Down amidships there, behind the main mast, are the passengers' galleys. You do whatever cooking you need in them. That's if it ain't raining or blowing half a gale. The fires get put out afore ye can boil a kettle then. The water butts are kept forrad as well, usually under the fo'c'sle. Ye'll need to bring your own cans to collect your rations, and remember, you must use your water ration for drinking and cooking, both.'

'How's about washing?' he was asked, and answered by pointing at the heaving seas. 'Get a bucket on a line and draw all ye want. But it can make your skin real sore, the old briny can. And there's no use trying to raise any sort of a lather with it. So don't waste your soap in trying.'

As the man continued to answer questions the tension engendered by the Captain's assault on the old Scotsman lessened and Grainne saw with relief that Con's normally equable temper was returning.

A short time later the Second Mate announced that there would be an issue of fresh water within the hour, and that the amidships' galley fires would be lit for the use of the passengers. He also told them that next morning they would be receiving their first contracted issue of provisions: wheat flour, ship's biscuit, rice, oatmeal, molasses, pork, vinegar and tea; and that for those who desired it, there was rum and tobacco available for purchase from himself. Emboldened by the Welshman's apparent good temper, Grainne asked him about the cleansing of the steerage, which now stank vilely.

The man stroked his thick black side-whiskers and leered suggestively at Grainne. 'You needn't worry about how it stinks, *cariad*. You can share my berth.'

'I'm a married woman,' she told him curtly. 'I only share berths with my husband.'

The Mate shrugged his meaty shoulders. 'Suit yourself. There's plenty on board who'll be only too pleased to be opening their legs afore we gets to America.'

'What about the cleaning of the steerage, mister?' Grainne persisted. 'There's vomit and filth all over it, and it smells.'

The man's heavy features grinned mockingly. 'Clean it yourself, then. But I'll tell you now, that pigs likes to wallow in their own filth. You'll not be finding many to help you, I'll lay odds to that.'

To Grainne's disgust she found that he had spoken truly. She went all through the steerage-deck asking for people to come and help her cleanse it, and with a few exceptions was met with indifference, and in some cases scornful rebuff. She made her way back to her own berth and complained bitterly to Con about the lack of response, but all he could tell her was, 'It's every man for himself on board here, honey. You saw the state some of these people were in when they came on board. They were filthy then, and they'll remain filthy here, and there's nothing you or I can do about it, except do our best to keep ourselves as clean as possible.' He sniffed the foul air, and shrugged. 'We'll get hardened to this pretty quick. I've smelled worse before and lived.'

Although his cavalier attitude angered her, Grainne was forced to admit that he only spoke the truth. There was nothing she could do to force people who were happy to live in filth to be clean. At least she could be thankful that Mrs Carter shared her own views on dirt. Drawing the sea water from the side with a long line and bucket, and using a scrubbing brush and rags to loosen and wash away the caked filth from the decking and berths, they managed to create a small oasis of cleanliness around their berth.

Chapter Sixteen

The weather stayed fine for a couple of days and with a surprising speed the emigrants adapted to their life on board. Those who had money to spare bribed the ship's cook to prepare their meals in his galley. Others spent their money on rum and tobacco and there was dancing and singing on deck and in the steerage.

Living in such close proximity there were numerous opportunities for sexual play, and already the sailors and ship's officers had begun inviting willing, and in some cases unwilling, girls and women to share their cabins and fo'c'sle. As there had been no attempt to regulate the distribution of steerage berths, and women and men who were strangers to each other were forced to share berths, lying under the same blankets, frequently during the dark hours of night there would ring out screams as some of the men tried to force themselves on the women beside them. A sizeable number of woman were quite ready to accept these advances however, and on several occasions Grainne saw couples copulating openly in the darker corners of the steerage.

She was no prude, but the blatant disregard of moral conventions that took place on board filled Grainne with disgust, and she pitied with all her heart those women and girls who were sailing without the protection of relatives, or friends, because even the most unattractive of these unfortunates were harassed ceaselessly by sex-starved men.

Grainne spent all the time she could up on the deck,

and never tired of standing looking out over the bows. At sunset on the fifth day of their journey, Grainne was in her usual position at the bows of the ship, enthralled by the glory of towering clouds coloured in magnificent kaleidoscopic hues of scarlet, purple and gold. Lost in her own thoughts she gradually became aware of someone near her sobbing. She turned to find a young girl crouching against the bulwark, with her shawl pressed to her face, and her hunched shoulders shaking.

'What's the matter, honey?' Grainne knelt by the girl's side. 'What is it?'

Gently she drew the girl's hands down so that she could see her face. 'Come now, you tell me what the matter is,' Grainne coaxed softly, and continued to coax until the girl, hiccupping and weeping, poured out her woes.

While she talked Grainne regarded her pityingly. Squat-bodied, her face pitted with the scars of old smallpox, her hair matted and greasy, the girl was an unappealing spectacle. Her name was Theresa Dillon. She had been born in Cork, she told Grainne, and was now sailing alone to join her only living relative; an elder sister who lived in Boston. She was sharing a berth with a widower man, and two of his children. The man got drunk every night, and then, when the children were asleep he kept trying to force Theresa to have sex with him.

'I've never known a man's body.' She hiccupped between her sobs. 'I'm a good-living girl; you can ask Father O'Brady at St Jude's. I go to Mass regular and make my confession. I'm not a bad girl, I'm not.'

'Has the man managed to have his way with you yet, Theresa?' Grainne asked, and the girl wailed out in grief and buried her face once more in her shawl.

'There now, there, don't upset yourself so. I'll look after you,' Grainne comforted, and as she felt the girl's body shaking in anguish, her pity became laced with a terrible anger at the man who had caused it. Feeling that she must know the full extent of what the girl had endured, because she intended to go to the Captain and make a complaint against the girl's persecutor, Grainne gently pressed, 'I know it's very hard for you, my dear. But you'll have to tell me all, if I'm to help you.'

The girl's tear-filled eyes blinked woefully at Grainne, and she hiccupped, 'Will you help me, missis? Will you?'

Grainne nodded forcefully. 'I will. You need have no doubt on that score. I'm going to help you, Theresa.'

'Last night he hurt me bad,' the girl choked out, and with her hand shyly indicated her intimate parts. 'He hurt me here. You know, here, where men make babies.'

Although she hated to badger the girl, Grainne realised that if she was to go to the Captain, then there must be no ambiguity about the charges she was going to lay before him.

'I'm sorry to keep on asking you, Theresa, but I have to know exactly what he did to you.'

'He near choked me, so he did,' the girl wailed heartbrokenly. 'He squeezed me neck with his hands 'til I thought I was going to die. And then he did it to me. He put his thing inside me, and hurt me something cruel, so he did. And when he'd finished, he told me that if I kept quiet about what he'd done, then he'd marry me once we got to America, but if I breathed a word to any living soul about what he'd done to me, then he'd catch me one dark night, and pitch me into the sea.'

Grainne's anger was a white-hot flame, and she would have risen and run to the Captain that very instant, but Theresa Dillon clung desperately to her and begged over and over again, 'Don't leave me, missis, please don't leave me. Stay here wi' me for a bit. Please God stay here wi' me!'

Sensing that the girl was on the edge of hysteria, Grainne cradled her in her arms. 'All right, dear, we'll stay here for a while, until you're calmer. I won't leave you, I promise I won't.'

Time passed and darkness fell. The wind strengthened and the sea roughened, so that the ship began pitching and heaving, but still Grainne stayed cuddling the weeping girl, and trying to soothe her as best she could.

On the steerage-deck men, women and children were dancing and singing to the music of an accordion and fiddle. People were sitting in their berths sharing pannikins of rum and smoking in complete disregard of the warnings they had been given. Mothers nursed their children, fathers mock-sparred with their sons and in some dark corners men and women were close-locked in sexual embrace, watched by wide-eyed children and sniggering adults. The sailors not on watch were prowling the steerage deck searching for company, and other men and women were either eating, sleeping, talking, playing cards, or just simply sitting or lying waiting for the hours to pass.

A young sailor carrying a lighted lantern made his way down the steerage, his eyes switching constantly from side to side. The woman he was was seeking was sitting on the edge of her berth, and behind her, her fat-bellied husband lay snoring loudly. The young sailor reached the woman's berth, and smiled at her, then jerked his head and went on. After a quick check that her husband was sleeping soundly, the woman rose and followed. On the opposite berth a man nudged his wife in the ribs, and chuckled, 'I see Bridie Mulvenny's off to get that itch of her's scratched agen.'

His wife snorted contemptuously. 'She's nothing but a wee whore, that one. It 'ud serve her right if poor Tommy there caught her at it. Bad cess to the slut, that's what I say, and Tommy such a dacent fella, as well.'

At the stern-end of the steerage-deck was a cubicle partitioned by planking, which was used to store lamp oil and paint. The sailor entered and placed the lantern on the floor at his feet. The woman joined him there, and without a word being passed he pushed her against the deckhead and kissed her passionately as his hands fumbled to loosen and open her clothing.

On the berth the sleeping man stirred, and grunted loudly, and the man on the opposite berth called to him, 'Tommy? Tommy, are ye awake?'

The sleeper rolled over and peered blearily across the passageway, then licked his dry lips with his furred tongue and belched resoundingly, before pushing himself to a sitting position and bringing his booted feet onto the decking.

'Jase, I've a mouth that tastes like a cow's arse,' he half-groaned. 'Have you a wee drop about ye?'

'Certainly I have.' His neighbour handed him a tin mug with rum in it. 'Take a swig o' this, Tommy.'

'God bless ye!' The fat man took a long swallow, and exhaled in noisy satisfaction, 'Jase, that's better.' He peered suspiciously about him, eyes straining to pierce the fuggy gloom. 'Where's my missis? Is she around anywheres?'

'She's probably gone up on deck to use the privy,' the other man told him, but his wife's thin lips twisted spitefully, and she said, 'No, I don't reckon she's on deck. Didn't I see her go down that way not a minute since.'

She pointed to the stern end of the steerage. She deliberately ignored her husband's warning frown, but the fat man saw it, and suddenly erupted, 'Is that fokkin bitch putting herself about agen? By Jase, I'll break her fokkin neck for her if she is. I'll fokkin kill the whore!'

He jumped to his feet and went lumbering down towards the stern.

His neighbour turned on his wife savagely, 'Why did ye have to tell him that, ye evil slut, ye?'

She sniffed and tossed back her head with righteous indignation. 'She deserves to be catched at it, bloody whore that she is. She's a disgrace to all us dacent women, so she is. A bloody disgrace. I hope Tommy leathers her well and truly.'

'And I hope that trouble-making tongue o' yours fokkin chokes ye,' her husband declared fervently.

In the cubicle the lovers were leaning against the wooden partition. The sailor's trousers were dropped to his ankles and the woman's skirts bunched up around her hips. The young man grunted continuously as his lean hips pounded against her, and she gasped and moaned with pleasure, and bit at his neck, her hooked fingers clawing at his back and shoulders.

'Bastards! Fokkin' bastards!'

The husband launched himself at the writhing bodies, his boot sending the lighted lantern smashing against the kegs of lamp-oil, paint, and a pile of picked oakum. The lantern's glass shattered and it rolled across the deck as the ship pitched and heaved, its flaming oil igniting the tarry oakum. Within seconds flames had taken hold on the oil-saturated deck and partitions.

Oblivious to the flames the husband and sailor fought like wild beasts, and the woman, screaming hysterically, tried to force a way past the battling men. Her long skirts trailed over the flames, and took fire. Shrieking in terror she reeled out of the cubicle and stumbled into the main steerage.

After an initial second or two of blank amazement, men bawled out, women screamed, and panic erupted. One man, more quick witted than his neighbours, tried to trip the flaming woman so that he might roll her and smother the flames, but in her blind terror she fought against him, and staggered on along the deck like a living torch.

'Fire! Fire! Fire!'

The cry triggered pandemonium and within seconds the steerage deck had become a brawling, stampeding, mindless riot as men, women and children fought like mad animals to escape the fast moving tongues of flame.

The flaming woman had staggered half-way along the deck before she fell across a berth. The berth's palliasse had split and the dry straw which filled it bulged out unshielded so that the filling flared up instantly, creating a fresh focus of fire. Many children and the weaker-bodied women had been knocked down and trampled in the stampede to the only exit from the steerage, and others tripped and fell across their bodies, creating heaps of shrieking, struggling obstacles, whose hands grabbed and held those who would cross over them.

The Second Mate, a Welshman, Morgan, was the Officer of the Watch, and held the deck. He heard the screams and shouts, and reacted instantly. Running forwards to the fo'c'sle he turned out the off-duty sailors, and they ran to man the deck pumps, and break out the hoses, axes and buckets from the deck-locker. The first emigrants to escape from below reached the upper deck and ran wildly backwards and forwards, bawling and screaming, and impeding the sailors.

In his cabin, Captain Lockyer lay senseless on his bunk, his one leg dangling over the guard-board, the brandy bottle he had emptied, rolling from side to side on the deck as the ship heaved and plunged through the high-rolling waves.

Harper, the First Mate, heard the noise and smelled smoke in his berth above the stern. Naked he sat up in his bunk, and beside him the naked girl woke up, complaining pettishly, 'Not agen, you'll make me fokkin' sore.'

'Shurrup,' he growled, and listened, then cursed and hurriedly drew on his clothes and boots.

'What's the marrer wi' you?' the girl challenged aggressively, and he shouted savagely, 'We're on fire, you thick bitch!' Slamming out onto the upper deck, he left her gaping mouthed, staring after him.

Grainne fought to find Con, but was powerless to maintain her place by the steerage-hatch as the terrified passengers boiled up its narrow stairs. She fought desperately to control her own fear, and tried to reason her best course of action, while Theresa Dillon clung to her skirts and wailed continuously.

The upper deck was chaos; men, women and children blundering blindly about in the darkness. The howling of the strengthening wind and the pitching boards beneath their feet disorientating them even more than they already were, and adding immeasurably to their terror.

The First Mate swore horribly as he saw the prone body of his Captain. Then he bludgeoned his way through the maelstrom on deck to find Morgan. When he did, he grabbed the huge Welshman and shouted, 'It's the steerage on fire, is it?'

Even as he questioned, a series of muffled thuds shook the deck beneath his feet and answered his question.

'That'll be the barrels o' lamp-oil,' he realised.

'We can't get to the hoses below,' Morgan told him. 'These fokkin' bastards are blocking our way.'

Harper glanced at the mass of bodies fighting their way out of the steerage-hatch. For a brief moment he debated the chances of cutting through the stern-decking with axes and attacking the fire through the holes, but realised that time was against him. His heart sank as he computed how long it might take for the flames to eat their way through to the lower holds, and the barrels of gun-powder stored there.

'Taffy, make a boat ready. Me and you had better be shifting a bit quick, else that fokkin' powder down in the holds is going to blow us all to smithereens. We've got no chance of throwing it overboard before the fire gets to it.'

Grainne was existing in a living nightmare, moving around the deck, grabbing dark, bellowing, shapes to try to find Con's face. By now the smoke was starting to pour out of the port-holes at the stern, and already the tar was bubbling in the seams of the stern-decking.

135

Hundreds of people were now on the upper deck, some calling for God, others on their knees praying, children insane with terror, shrieking and squealing, men and woman behaving like demented beings, and always the seas getting rougher and the wind gusting ever more strongly.

'Con! Con! Con! Con!' Grainne screamed over and over again. 'Con! Con! Con!'

A body slammed against her and sent her tumbling into the scuppers, and as she tried to rise, a running man tripped over her and fell on top of her, pinning her beneath his weight, and crushing the air from her lungs.

Harper, aware of the calibre of his crew, knew that at any moment they were liable to throw off any restraints of discipline. He made his way back to the stern cabin. Captain Lockyer was still sprawled in a drunken coma, and Harper grinned savagely. 'This is your last trip, you Yankee bastard.'

Then he rapidly ransacked the cabin, cramming into a canvas bag anything of value that he could find: money, jewellery, the Captain's watch, his sextant and compass, and the man's pistols.

He hurried back to find Morgan, and thrust the bag at him. 'Stow this as well. Is the boat ready?'

Morgan indicated the dark shapes of a few hand-picked crew members standing by the davits. 'We're ready when you are. There's water and biscuit stowed, and a keg o' rum.'

Harper was thinking with comparative coolness now. Eventually, he knew, there would be a Board-of-Trade Enquiry into this disaster. He thought it inevitable that there would be some survivors from such a large number of passengers, and to cover himself he must now make sure that as many of these terrified people as possible saw him exerting himself to the utmost to save the ship and them.

'You stay here, and be ready to lower away the second I come back to you,' he instructed the massive

Welshman. Then he ran back to the stern cabin to fetch the distress rockets and maroons.

The helmsman was still at the ship's wheel, and Harper shouted, 'Don't leave your post until I tell you so.'

The rockets soared high in a shower of sparks and exploded with great flashes of light.

The crew trying to fight the flames reacted instantly. 'Abandon ship! Abandon ship!'

They hurled themselves at the boats slung on the davits, and hurled execrations to the skies as they found those same boats piled with useless lumber, and clawed at that lumber and threw it around them frantically. The passengers saw the crew trying to lower the boats, and heard the cries to abandon ship, and there began a mad battle as each tried to save themselves and their dear ones.

With a roar the flames burst through the stern-decking and began to lick up the tarred rigging towards the booms and sails. Now, for the first time the upper-deck was lit up, and Grainne was able to see about her instead of blundering through darkness. In swirling, choking smoke and showers of fiery sparks she fought her way about the deck searching for Con, and always she dragged with her Theresa Dillon.

The crowds around the davits fought with the crew and each other to gain places in the boats, and people were pushed screaming into the sea. The davit blocks and tackles had been sadly neglected, and some stuck immovably, while men slashed with their knives at the jammed ropes, and boats fell and tipping over, cast scores more people into the sea. As the flames took hold spreading along the upper deck and aloft, passengers mad with fear jumped over the side and in the garish flickering of the fire screaming, splashing, drowning bodies were thick in the heaving waters.

Grainne thought she glimpsed Con in a vicious struggle at one of the davits, and shrieking his name she fought like a wildcat to get to him. Theresa Dillon abandoned her grip on Grainne's skirt as the fierce fight enveloped them and ran back screaming. Though Grainne succeeded in reaching the davit post, she was caught by a wild blow on the side of her head. As she spun round she hit the rail and toppled over the side to fall into the sea. The icy water closed above her head, and terror drove her to fight desperately upwards. Her long, thick skirts saved her, because as she had fallen they had ballooned to catch and trap air within their folds. Now, that trapped air brought her up to the surface. Terror-stricken, she flailed her arms and fought to breathe.

Up on the deck, under the direction of Harper, the First Mate, cooler heads among the crew and passengers were tossing anything that would float over the sides. Some of these objects crashed onto the people already in the water, crushing heads and breaking bones, but Grainne's luck held and a big cork float splashed down within reach of her flailing arms. She clung to it grimly and by a supreme exertion of strength succeeded in getting her body across it. Instinct drove her to get as far away as she could from the ship's side, and kicking with her legs and paddling with her hands she managed to get into clearer waters.

For a few seconds she rested, retching and gasping, and as the waves lifted her she could see the ship – now flaming almost along its entire length – and on its decks and bowsprit she glimpsed the figures of helplessly trapped men, women and children.

The boats that had been successfully lowered were now trying to distance themselves from the ship, their occupants knowing of the gun-powder stored in its holds. One of the boats, only half-full, neared Grainne and she paddled and kicked frantically to try and intercept its passage. She could hear the splashing of its oars and the voices of those rowing, and she shouted weakly for help. Then she felt like weeping in relief as the oarsmen ceased rowing and faces peered at her, the ruddy glare of the fire shining on them. Strong hands gripped her arms and heaved her into the rocking boat, and she lay upon its boards, too spent even to thank her rescuers. The oars dipped once more into the water and they travelled on – for what seemed to Grainne's disorientated senses an eternity of time and then there came a tremendous roaring blast and the *Florida* seemed to rise from the surface of the sea, and to fall apart in a mighty ball of flaming smoke. Split seconds later Grainne felt the force of the explosion hit the rowing-boat and set it bobbing wildly. And then the shattered vessel sank with a steaming hiss and all was darkness once again, and the only sounds that Grainne could hear were the loud creaking of the rowlocks, the laboured breathing of the people surrounding her, and the howling of the wind.

After the explosion, at the rudder of the boat, Harper shouted a command and the oarsmen ceased rowing, and only sculled sufficiently to keep the prow turned into the wind, so that the boat could ride the heavy swell safely.

'Taffy, broach that rum and give everybody a good sup on it. Then we'll head back and see if we can pick up anybody else,' the First Mate ordered.

The rich, strong spirit burned its way into Grainne's soaked, half-frozen body, and Morgan fished out a big piece of canvas sheeting from under the thwarts and wrapped it around the shivering girl. 'Keep this tight about you, *cariad*;' he told her with a rough gentleness, 'it'll keep the wind off.' He patted her head as if she were a child. 'Don't fret now, lovely girl, this is a busy stretch o' channel, this is. We'll be picked up tomorrow, no doubt.'

He poured more rum into the tumbler and made her drink it down in several gasping gulps.

Harper took the boat to where he judged the *Florida* had sunk, but in the darkness, howling wind and rough seas they could find only stray pieces of floating wreckage, and two dead bodies.

'It's no use.' The First Mate called off the search.

'We'll keep her into wind 'til morning, then set a course for a landfall. Squeeze together as best you can to keep warm. Me and Taffy here will see to the boat.'

He distributed more large measures of rum, and huddled in a tight clump of bodies – Grainne, praying that Con had managed somehow to survive, drifted into an alcohol induced semi-consciousness.

Chapter Seventeen

Dawn rose on a calm sea and a fresh breeze. Grainne awoke stiff and sore and cold. The dreadful memories of the night rushed in on her, and terrible anxieties about Con's fate gnawed at her ferociously. She looked at the unshaven, brutish faces of the men in the boat, and inwardly cursed the fortune that had brought her to such a pass.

'Sleep well, did you, *cariad*?' The Welshman, Morgan, was at the tiller. During the night he and Harper had rigged a makeshift mast and sail and now the small craft was wallowing over the green swells without the need for oarsmen.

Grainne nodded, but made no verbal reply. Around her the remainder of the survivors stirred and roused themselves. Grainne counted seven of them, all men, and all appearing to be crew from the *Florida*. Harper dealt out water and ship's biscuit, and gave everyone a ration of rum. The boat was fairly dry, as being only half loaded it rode high in the water, and shipped no waves.

While they were eating and drinking the First Mate told them, 'We're running east-south-east. That should bring us a landfall on the Irish coast, if we don't get a ship sighting afore then. If the weather stays like this, then we shouldn't run into any problems.'

There came a series of grunted acknowledgements, and Grainne marvelled at how matter-of-factly these men were treating this situation. She raised her head and stared around her, hoping against hope that she might see other boat-loads of survivors from the *Florida*. There was nothing but the shifting wastes of the sea, and Harper told her, not unkindly, ' 'Tis not likely we'll be seeing any of the other boats, girl. The wind and currents will have separated all of 'um pretty widely. Did you have any kin aboard?'

'Yes,' Grainne bit her lips as the sharp visual image of Con filled her mind, and tears came to her eyes, 'my husband.'

The First Mate nodded understandingly. 'I expect you'll be worrying yourself sick about him, missis. 'Tis only right and proper that you should. But don't you go giving up hope now. There's always a deal more survives than is reckoned on, at first. A fair number o' the boats got away. I sent three of 'um off meself. So there's a good chance he might be on one o' them, and there's always a few who manages to get on hatch covers and planking, and that.'

'But what chance would they have?' Grainne asked, doubtfully.

'You'd be surprised, girl,' Harper told her bluffly. 'This is a real busy channel, wi' plenty o' traffic. Anybody has got a good chance o' being picked up.'

Grainne looked miserably at the emptiness around her, and wondered how it could possibly be described as busy.

'Here, take this.' The First Mate pressed another pannikin of rum onto her. 'Now you get this down you, girl. It'll raise your spirit, and put fresh heart into you. Your man 'ull turn up safe and sound, just you see if he won't.'

His rough kindliness was in such contrast to how he had behaved on board, that Grainne found it hard to believe he was the same man. During the hours that followed all the other men in the boat did what they could to make her more comfortable, and spared her any embarrassment when she needed to perform her natural functions. In return she did her best to be cheery with them, and keep her hope high that she would be reunited with Con.

At one stage she asked Harper, 'When we reach land, how will I be able to find out if my husband has survived?'

The First Mate's hatchet features frowned thoughtfully. 'Well now, that might pose a bit of a problem, missis. Normally in these cases, and we gets a fair amount on 'um, then the lists of survivors is sent back to the home port and to the port o' sailing. So in our case, there'll be a list posted in Tapscott's Offices down in the Regent Road. Mind you, it can take an awful long time to get the full lists made, because it depends on where the survivors fetches up at. I mean, we could get picked up by a vessel sailing for Hamburg, or the Brazils, or the West of Africa, and then it could be months afore our names got posted.' He smiled and told her with a rough gentleness, 'So you see, missis, you can live in hope, even if months pass wi' no news o' your man.'

Despite her woes Grainne warmed towards him, and suddenly castigated herself, 'Stop behaving like a weakling. These men have all endured what I've endured, and they must have loved ones who will be thinking of them as I think of Con. I must do as this man tells me. Live in hope, and make an effort to keep my spirits up.'

Aloud she said, 'I want to thank you all for saving my life. I'd never have managed to stay on that float if you hadn't picked me up. I shall forever be grateful to you.'

A fleeting shadow of shame darkened the First Mate's eyes as he heard her, and he replied gruffly, 'There's no call for thanks, missis, we only done our duty.'

He fell silent for some seconds, and then seemed about to say something more, but before he could do so, one of the men shouted, 'Sail! There's a sail!' He was pointing over their stern, and at first Grainne could not see anything, although another man shouted, 'I see it. Three master by the looks on it, heading due-east I reckon.'

Morgan brought the row-boat onto a different tack,

aiming to cross the other ship's course, and Harper busied himself in setting up a couple of distress rockets, one of which he fired as soon as he could.

Grainne watched it soaring and prayed silently, 'Please see it. Please stop and pick us up. Please God let me find my Con. Let me find him. I beg you, let me find him.'

With an agonising slowness the row-boat wallowed on and now Grainne could see clearly the pale sails of the other vessel. No one spoke, all eyes were locked on those distant sails, and Harper fired the second rocket. At first it appeared that that also had not been seen, but then the keen-eyed man who had first sighted the ship bellowed joyously, 'She's changing course! She's seen the rocket! She's changing course"

Excited cheers burst from all throats, including Grainne's, and laughing and shouting, and hugging each other in gleeful relief they watched with thankful eyes as the sails slowly came nearer and nearer.

It was a Dutch cargoboat, bound for Glasgow from Baltimore. The crew treated the survivors with a wonderful kindness, giving up their own bunks, and plying them with wine, brandy and Hollands gin. The Captain even sorted out a dress for Grainne, and one of the crew gave her a fine woollen shawl and shoes small enough to fit her, but they could not give news of any survivors from the *Florida*, and had not sighted any other ships for more than a week.

Their comparatively quick rescue buoyed Grainne's hopes that Con might have also survived, and she began to feel, if not cheerful, at least reasonably confident that things would eventually turn out well. 'After all,' she reasoned to herself, 'if I survived, and I'm only a weak woman, then surely a man as strong and brave as my Con will have survived too. I'll find him again, I know I will.'

The cargoboat was a slow sailer, and it was more than a week later when it reached the port of Glasgow. The night before it docked there, Harper, the First Mate, drew Grainne to one side.

During the period on board this ship she and the rest of the survivors had become friends, and now she knew some of the hardships that the sailors were forced to endure to earn their meagre livelihood. While she could not condone, she could understand why their harsh life made them behave as brutally at times as they did.

'What will you do now, Grainne?' Harper wanted to know.

'I shall go back to Liverpool, and try to find out what's become of my Con,' she told him. 'And you, what will you and the others do?' she asked in return.

He smiled grimly. 'Ship out again. What else can a sailorman do? I'll have to go back to the Pool when we dock, and make my report to Tapscott's office. Morgan will be coming with me. I don't know what the rest o' the lads are doing, yet. They might try their luck in Glasgow.'

'Won't you feel nervous of going to sea again, after what happened to us?' Grainne asked curiously, and he laughed long and loud before telling her, 'That's my third wreck, Grainne. I been following the sea since I was half the height of a marlinspike. It's all I knows. Any sailorman worth his salt expects to get scuttled some way or other a few times in his life. That's part o' the fun, that is.'

'I wouldn't call it fun,' Grainne said sadly. 'More like a nightmare, it's been to me.'

He patted her shoulder with a rough sympathy. 'I hopes it all goes well for you, Grainne, and that you finds your man agen.' He fell silent, as if searching for words, and then went on with an air of embarrassment, 'What I was going to say, Grainne, was ... well ... don't go thinking the wrong thing, will you ... but I wants you to come to Liverpool wi' me and Morgan.' He waved one work-scarred hand in a gesture of dismissal. 'Not for anything other than friendship, you understand. Only I 'udden't feel comfortable in my mind

145

iffen I left you to fend for yourself. You can come wi' me and Morgan, and we can see you fixed in Liverpool afore we ships out agen. I knows that you got no kin you can turn to there, so I reckon it 'ud be the best course for you to sail. To come down wi' us, and let us see you fixed up.'

His kindness moved Grainne deeply, and it was some moments before she was able to tell him, 'I'd be very grateful for that, Mr Harper, but I couldn't allow myself to be any sort of burden to you.'

He grinned and winked. 'Don't fret on that score, girl. I've money enough at present.'

'No,' Grainne shook her head, 'no, I'm more than grateful to you for being so kind, but it wouldn't be right.'

He displayed a shade of irritation. 'Don't talk saft! You've not even got money for the journey, have you? And it's certain sure that you won't find any laying about the bloody streets in Glasgow, or anywheres else for that matter. If it makes you feel any better, then whatever I spends in getting you to Liverpool, and leaving you fixed there for a while, you can pay me back.'

Tempted though she was to accept his offer, Grainne was still not able to easily accept. 'But how can I promise to pay you back, Mr Harper? You might sail off and never return to Liverpool, or I might be gone from there whenever you did return.'

'You can always leave a letter care of the Post Office for me. Don't you think that sailormen never have anyone writing to 'um, girl? We gets letters the same as anybody else, so don't give me any more excuses. Say you'll come wi' me and Morgan.'

Knowing as she did that after landing on the morrow she would be in desperate straits, alone and penniless, Grainne at last gave in, and with a deep sense of gratitude accepted Harper's offer.

'But I swear that someday I'll pay you back every penny,' she vowed from her heart, 'Every single penny.'

146

Chapter Eighteen

After their arrival at Liverpool, Harper and Morgan went directly to the offices of the brokers, Tapscott's, in the Regent Road opposite the dock where Grainne had first landed. As she trudged along the bustling roadway Grainne remembered the day she had first walked that road, and how excited and full of hope she had been. For a few moments tears blurred her eyes, but she dashed them away with her hands and refused to give way to despair.

They reached the tall building of St George, and Grainne read the ornate sign, *Tapscott's American Emigration Office*, and asked Will Harper, 'Do you think it possible that some of the passengers might have got here before us?'

He shrugged his broad shoulders. 'They could have, if they got picked up by a fast ship, that was bound for the Pool.' Then he asked her, ''Ull you do something for me, Grainne? 'Ull you make an affidavit that me and Morgan here did all we could to save the ship and the passengers?'

She nodded, inwardly wondering why he should need to ask her to do this. Then she remembered the half-filled row-boat and the fact that every man in it had been a crew member. Doubt entered her mind, but against that doubt she was forced to acknowledge the fact that she owed her own life to these men.

The Broker's clerk, that same cadaverous man that Grainne had seen on board the *Florida*, greeted the trio coldly, acting towards them as if they were an unwelcome intrusion into his ordered life.

'You're the fourth lot to come back here,' he informed them. 'What you think we can do for you, God only knows.'

'Do you have the names of the others who've come back?' Grainne asked him eagerly. 'Is my husband, Conrad Shonley among them?'

He searched among the papers in his desk, and found the lists of passengers.

'What was his name again?'

'Conrad Shonley.' Grainne's voice was tremulous, and her hands nervously twisted the front of her skirts.

'No, he's not here,' the clerk told her, 'but there's some of them that were so badly hurt, we haven't been able to get names from them yet.'

Her heart sank. Then she asked, 'Where are they now; the people who've survived?'

'The ones who were badly burned are at the Infirmary, as for the rest I can't tell you. They took the refunds of passage money and that was that.' He paused and looked at another list. 'If you want to sail, we've a ship in dock at the moment, The *Rappahannock*; Captain Cushing. She leaves tomorrow for New York. I can give you a ticket, and you'll have compensation money totalling twenty-five shillings for the loss of your goods aboard the *Florida*.'

'Twenty-five shillings?' Grainne could not believe what she was hearing.

'That's right. The ship owners are being very generous in my opinion. Most o' the passengers didn't have twenty-five pence in their pockets when they boarded the *Florida*.'

For a moment Grainne was tempted to tell this clerk what he could do with his compensation money, but she knew that she could not afford to reject the offer. 'I'll take my refund and the compensation money.'

He nodded brusquely, and told the two mates, 'I hear that Captain Miskelly is seeking a crew for the *Scotia*. He sails for Baltimore on the morning tide ... It would be in your best interests to go down and see him straight away. But first the three of you had best go to the offices of the Emigration Commissioners, and make your affidavits about what occurred on the *Florida* to Lieutenant Heath. When you've done that, young woman, and have brought me a note from Lieutenant Heath to that effect, then I'll pay you your refund and compensation money. Good day to you.'

He ushered them from the office and slammed the door abruptly.

Grainne felt a terrible sense of depression as they walked towards the Waterloo Road, and to cheer her, Will Harper suggested, 'Look, once you've made your affidavits and collected your money, then you can go to the Infirmary and ask them whose been taken there and if they saw anything of your man.'

She nodded agreement, and tried to force her depression away by telling herself that there was bound to be someone in the Infirmary who would have seen Con.

After they had made their affidavits at the Emigration Commissioners Will Harper told Grainne, 'Look, girl. Me and Morgan are going to have to leave you now, and go looking for Captain Miskelly. So I don't know how long we'll be, or if I'll be able to get back and see you before we sail.' He took two sovereigns from his pocket. 'Take this. I'm sorry I've not more to give you. When you've done what you want at the Infirmary, then go to Brunswick Street, it lies behind the Goree Piazza. Ask there for Ellen Chester, and when you find her tell her that I sent you, and that she's to fix you up with a place to stay.'

Grainne nodded, then handed him back the coins. 'I shan't be needing this now, because I'll have my refund money.'

He was reluctant to accept the money, but she insisted so forcefully that in the end he gave way.

'Right then, I'll be saying goodbye, girl. You take care of yourself now.'

She took his proferred hand and shook it warmly. 'And you. And thank you for all you've done for me.'

'Goodbye, *cariad*.' The big Welshman's hand buried her own, and she stood watching the two men walk away with their swaggering gait and was assailed by a desolate loneliness. Rough and hard men though they were, they had proven to be her friends, and she knew that she would never forget either of them as long as she lived. A lump came to her throat as they passed from her view, and she muttered, 'Oh Con, will I ever find you?

Chapter Nineteen

Grainne climbed up the steep rising Brownlow Hill on top of which stood the imposing structures of the Workhouse and further back the Infirmary. She walked towards the latter building's great pillared and porticoed front with conflicting emotions. Hoping that some survivor might be able to tell her of Con, yet at the same time dreading what they might tell. The Infirmary was surrounded by a low wall topped with ornate iron railings and along that wall were ranged pie, fruit and sweetmeat sellers calling their wares to the people visiting the hospital.

As she neared the gatehouse a group of workmen wearing aprons came trotting past her, carrying on their shoulders a stretcher on which a bloodstained man lay, crying out piteously. A sudden visual image of Con, lying bloodstained and screaming out in pain came into Grainne's mind, and she was forced to stop and drag deep gulps of air into her lungs so badly did that image affect her.

When she had recovered she went on, and explained the purpose of her errand to the gate porter. He directed her on into the hospital and she traversed the wide corridors looking for the ward he had named. A door opened onto one of the corridors and a group of young men came through it shouting and laughing and tussling light-heartedly with each other. They were dressed like gentlemen and Grainne moved aside to let them pass.

'By God! Is it really you, Mrs Shonley?'

Her eyes widened in surprise as she saw Malcom Galbraith standing before her.

'Dr Galbraith?'

His handsome face still mirroring his own surprise at

151

seeing her there, he asked, 'Did you not sail on the *Florida* packet?'

She nodded. 'I did. I was one of the lucky ones.'

'Indeed you were, Mrs Shonley. I've just been watching one poor woman from that ship having both legs amputated. There's more than a dozen of the survivors in here at present. Most of them with bad burns.' He frowned suddenly. 'Your husband, Mrs Shonley? Did he survive?'

She spread her hands helplessly and tears rose to her eyes. 'I don't know, sir. That's why I've come here; to ask the survivors if they saw him.'

'Are you coming, Galbraith?' One of the young men shouted from the end of the corridor.

'No. You go on, I'll join you later,' Malcom Galbraith shouted back, and said to Grainne, 'I'll take you to the wards where the people from the *Florida* are. I must warn you that some of them are not pleasant to look upon and smell badly.'

'I'll be all right,' Grainne told him, 'and I thank you for helping me like this.'

He smiled briefly, then took her arm and led her down the corridor. A middle-aged man wearing a frock coat which was encrusted with blood and badly stained, came towards them, and Malcom Galbraith whispered, 'It's Simon Sinclair. It's he who did the amputations that I watched just now; a brilliant surgeon. Do you know he took only a minute and twenty-three seconds to complete both thighs. It is by his invitation that I'm here at the Infirmary. I shall ask him to aid us in searching for your husband.'

He stopped the other man and briefly explained why Grainne was there, and Sinclair told her sympathetically, 'I am sorry to hear of your sad misfortune, Mrs Shonley. Come, I'll take you directly to the patients.'

The vile smell that Grainne remembered from her visits to the Dispensary filled her nostrils as she entered the ward. But she was uncaring of it, as her eyes swept across the box-beds. Her heart fell as she scanned the greyish white, pain-drawn features. Con was not among the men there. She went from bed to bed as Sinclair pointed out the *Florida* survivors to her. But none of them could remember seeing anyone of Con's description, and Grainne herself acknowledged that the quest she had embarked upon was almost futile; so greatly were the odds stacked against her.

Sinclair conducted her to another ward where two women and a child lay, but they could not help her either. Grainne swallowed hard to dispel the lump in her throat, and fought against giving way to tears of bitter disappointment.

'Are these all the survivors?' she asked Sinclair, and he frowned and looked as if he were trying to make a decision which he found distasteful.

'Is there anyone else from the *Florida* here, Dr Sinclair?' she pressed anxiously.

Still he stood silent, as if he found it difficult to reply. Then, he sighed heavily, and told her, 'Yes, Mrs Shonley. There is one other here; a man. We don't know his name.'

'Then let me see him,' she begged.

Sinclar gnawed his lower lip, and was obviously very troubled in his mind.

'Why do you not want to let me see this man?' Grainne demanded to know, aggressive in her determination to search out all possible news of Con.

The doctor stared hard at her for some seconds, as if trying to will her not to press him, but realising that she would not be thwarted by anything he could do or say, he nodded in reluctant agreement.

'Very well, Mrs Shonley, you shall see him. But I must warn you that you will only be wasting your time.'

'Why?' she wanted to know.

'Because, Mrs Shonley, the poor fellow was so badly burned about his face and head, that he is unrecognisable. It is a miracle that he still lives. He has lost his sight, and I fear his reason, also. When I speak to him he makes no acknowledgement of my presence.'

'Perhaps he cannot hear you, Sinclair.' Galbraith's

interest had been aroused. 'After all, there was a most tremendous explosion, we're told. Could not the blast have deafened him by breaking his ear-drums.'

The other man shook his head. 'Both tympanic membranes are undamaged. No, I fear that the poor devil has lost his reason. And if he should live, which I doubt, then he will be good for nothing.'

He conducted them to a small room at the extreme end of the corridor. At its closed door he paused and asked Grainne, 'Are you sure you want to see this man, Mrs Shonley. All you will be looking at is a faceless figure.'

Grainne took a deep breath and nodded.

Inside, the stench in the confined space made her physically nauseous, and she was forced to swallow hard several times before she could go to the side of the box-bed. The motionless figure lying before her was swathed in bandages from his head to his waist, including his arms and hands. There were just two small openings where nose and mouth should be.

'How well can he take nourishments?' Galbraith questioned.

'We give milk and brandy, and milk and tincture of opium by tube and bladder directly into the stomach,' Sinclair informed them.

Grainne stared with fearful fascination at the motionless figure, trying by sheer force of will to visualize who this man was. All was silent; only the raspings of the injured man's ragged breathing could be heard. It was Grainne who finally broke that silence.

'Is there any way that you could tell what his age might be, sir?'

Sinclair shrugged his narrow shoulders. 'From the waist down he suffered only minor injuries. His body is that of a young and muscular man, standing two yards high, I would judge, and he has black hair, judging from the hairs on his lower body and legs.'

'Might I see his lower body?' Grainne requested.

The Doctor looked shocked briefly, then he half-smiled. 'To be sure you may, Mrs Shonley. It may help you to recognise if it is your husband, and if it is not, then that poor fellow will not be embarrassed at being so displayed.'

Grainne flushed, but angrily told herself, 'Don't be so bloody silly. You have the right to see if you can recognise Con.'

Sinclair lifted back the coarse sheet and looked at the legs and lower body. Con had had no scars or other uniquely distinguishing marks on his lower body, and he had been uncircumsized as this man was. The muscularity matched Con's, and the feet were small and narrow as Con's had been.

Grainne was racked with a bitter inner turmoil. She admitted that she could not say with certainty that this man was her husband, but she could not say with certainty that he was not. And what was most terrible, because she loved him so much, she did not know whether she would prefer him to be dead and at peace, or to be this dreadfully maimed human being.

'Well?' Sinclair asked gently, 'Can you say if it is your husband?'

Grainne shook her head, and burst into heart-rending sobs.

'Come, Mrs Shonley, control yourself,' Sinclair told her not unkindly. 'Tears will do nothing to help here.'

'I'm sorry.' Grainne choked out her apology.

'Do not be,' Malcom Galbraith said warmly, and frowned towards his medical colleague. 'Tears ease grieving souls.' He came to her and took one of her hands between his own. 'Shed your tears, my dear, and let your soul find ease through them.'

'Look, Galbraith, I must go. I have urgent business elsewhere,' Sinclair told the younger man. 'I am sorry we did not meet in better circumstances, Mrs Shonley.' He bowed curtly and left them.

Grainne dried her eyes and tried to smile at Malcom Galbraith. 'I'm sorry for behaving as I have ...' she began, but he interrupted.

'Do not say one word more of apology, Mrs Shonley.

There is no necessity for it. It is only fitting that a lady should give way to her emotions at times like this.' He waited until she had fully composed herself once more, then went on, 'And now, what do you intend?'

Grainne's eyes went to the figure on the bed. 'I intend, Doctor Galbraith, to continue searching for my husband.' She spoke very quietly, but her utter determination radiated from her like an aura. 'I cannot tell if this is Con, or no, but I shall return here every day and I pray that God will somehow give me the truth of it.'

Her green eyes were huge and solemn as she gazed up at Galbraith, and he found his heart beginning to pound faster as he saw how beautiful she was. At that moment, there surged through him a mingling of lust and protectiveness towards her.

He coughed, to allow himself time to bring his own rampaging emotions under control, then asked, 'Might I enquire where you intend living, Mrs Shonley?' He hesitated a moment, then continued, 'And forgive my asking for I intend no offence by it I do assure you, but how will you live? I assume that you lost all your possessions when the *Florida* was lost?'

'I have some money, Doctor. Tapscott's refunded my own fare, and also gave me twenty five shillings of compensation for the loss of my possessions. That will last me until I can find work to support myself.'

Among his social peers Malcom Galbraith had a reputation for being a notorious womaniser, and that reputation was richly deserved. He was by nature a generous and kind-hearted man, but he was also a victim of his own passionate desires, and when driven by them the baser side of his nature came to the forefront. Now, as he looked into Grainne's limpid eyes, his sympathy for her was strongly interlaced with his awareness of her sexual attractions, and his increasingly strengthening desires to possess her. But he knew that with this woman, he would need to tread very, very delicately, and to exercise the utmost guile and patience.

'Mrs Shonley, I know that we are barely acquainted with each other,' he said diffidently, 'but I would very much like to aid you in any way that I can. You are alone and friendless in a land that is strange to you, but I would not wish you to feel that you dwell among strangers. I want you to give me your solemn promise, that if and when you need help, you will come directly to me.' He saw a questioning look come into her eyes, and hastened to mollify any suspicions or doubts she might have about his motives for offering to help her.

'I pray you do not doubt my sincerity in offering you help, Mrs Shonley. Once, many years ago, I found myself in a somewhat similar predicament. A comparative stranger offered me her help on that occasion, and her kindess to me sustained me through the grief that I was shortly to meet with. God willing, your search for your husband will end happily, but I want you only to know that I stand ready to be your friend if you have need of me. So will you promise that you will keep me informed of your progress in this matter?'

Feeling that to refuse would be churlish, Grainne nodded and smiled. 'Very well, Dr Galbraith, I so promise, and I thank you for your kind interest.'

'Do you return to the town now, Mrs Shonley?' he asked.

'Yes. I have to find Brunswick Street and speak with a woman who lives there.'

Galbraith looked momentarily shocked. 'Brunswick Street?'

Grainne nodded. 'Yes, I've been told that it lies close to the Goree Piazza.'

'It has an unsavoury reputation, Mrs Shonley. There are many bawdy-houses there, and it is much frequented by criminals. I believe that they call it "Tiger Bay".'

'"Tiger Bay"?' Grainne could not help but smile at the name. 'Why that, Dr Galbraith?'

He returned her smile. 'I would think that it is called by that name because of the ferocity of its inhabitants, so take care! And do not forget the promise you have given me. I shall be expecting to see you often to hear what is happening with you. I have rooms at Number Fourteen, Rodney Street. A message sent there will always find me.'

Chapter Twenty

Brunswick Street did not look much different to any of the other dockland streets that Grainne had been through. Narrow, lined by tall, ramshackle, smoke-grimed buildings, behind the street there were courts of close-packed houses, lots of pubs and shops catering for the poorer sections of the community, and swarms of children hooting and running amongst the passing traffic.

She went into a dingy provision shop and asked the shopman if he knew of an Ellen Chester.

'Try The Grapes,' he told her shortly. 'That's where all the whores call in when trade's slack.'

His words gave Grainne pause for thought, and for a while she stood outside his shop wondering if she was acting wisely. Then she shrugged mentally. 'It can do no harm for me to find Ellen Chester now that I've come here.'

The Grapes proved to be a garishly tiled gin palace, and again Grainne hesitated before entering. Inside there was one long room with a tall counter running along its entire length and, apart from a few wall benches, no other furnishings, except for the barrels lining the wall behind the counter, each one elaborately scrolled with the title of its contents: best Hollands, the Old Geneva and the Cream of Creams, among others.

Several barmaids were behind the tall counter, wearing low-cut dresses, their faces heavily rouged, and their hair worn in a variety of styles. A couple of burly, brawl-scarred barmen stood around the bar too. Only a few customers lined the bar, and these were mostly women and sailors. Grainne's fresh clean beauty attracted some admiring looks and lewd invitations from the men, along with resentful glares from their partners but she ignored them, and kept her shawl drawn close around her head as she asked one of the barmaids if she knew of Ellen Chester.

'That's her over there.' The barmaid gestured to a wall-bench midway across the room on which a woman was sitting alone, with a glass of gin in her hands, from which she sipped at frequent invervals. Grainne looked with interest at Ellen Chester. Unlike the other women in the bar, Ellen was dressed in sombre black, and her hair was plaited and coiled around her bare head. Her pale face bore no sign of rouge or paint, and the only jewellery that she wore was a brooch of white coral on the front of her high-necked bodice. She looked to be in her early thirties, but Grainne knew that a woman of the slums invariably looked much older than her actual years, so perhaps Ellen Chester was younger than she appeared to be.

When Grainne approached her Ellen Chester looked up suspiciously, and Grainne was struck by the beauty of her dark eyes, and the cleanliness of her face, neck and hands. Grainne seated herself by the side of the other woman.

'Will Harper told me to come to see you. He said that you might be able to help me find somewhere to live.'

The other woman studied Grainne closely, then took another sip of gin, before saying, 'You'd best tell me the full story of how you come to know Will.' Her voice lacked the stridency of slum-women's voices, and had a lilting intonation which denoted her Welsh origins.

Grainne told her the full story of the loss of the *Florida*, and her search for her husband, and Ellen Chester heard her out in silence, only sipping reflectively from the glass in her hand, and keeping her dark eyes fixed on the floor.

The silence continued when Grainne had finished her story, and she began to wonder if the other woman wasn't rather strange in some way. She shifted restlessly on the hard bench, and then Ellen Chester said simply, 'You're having a bad time of it, *merch fach*.'

'There are many having worse,' Grainne replied quietly. 'At least I still have hope.'

'I lost that years since,' Ellen Chester stated matter of factly, and drained the last drops from her glass. 'Come.' She rose to her feet and moved towards the door with an easy grace, and Grainne rose to follow her.

In the street the two women walked in silence, amd Grainne found herself wondering why she was going with this strange woman so trustingly. They came to a slops dealer's shabby shop and Ellen Chester told her, 'I've the room above.'

They entered a doorway at the side of the shop which opened onto a dark narrow staircase at the top of which was a tiny landing and the door to Ellen Chester's room.

Grainne was surprised to see how large the room was, and how comfortably furnished and clean it appeared. In one corner was a large four-poster bed. Before the fire stood two stuffed armchairs. Pictures had been hung on the walls, on the mantelpiece there was a collection of crock ornaments, and above it a large rosewood framed mirror. The chintz curtains were spotlessly clean, and the wooden floor highly polished with several small rugs scattered about its surface. A small table, three straight-backed chairs, a dressing table, a large wardrobe and a Welsh dresser with a plentiful display of crockery and domestic implements, made up the rest of the furnishings and although to Grainne's mind the room was over-filled by all these articles, yet the overall effect was of a cosy domesticity.

'Sit there, *merch fach*.' Ellen Chester indicated one of the stuffed armchairs, and Grainne obediently perched on its edge.

The Welshwoman took a bottle of brandy and two glasses from the dresser, then came to sit on the other armchair facing Grainne. She filled the two glasses with brandy and handed one to Grainne. 'Here, you look to be needing this.'

Grainne ruefully admitted to herself that indeed she did need something to steady nerves, overstrained by the events of the day, and gratefully sipped the fiery spirit.

'Now, beginning with your name, tell me about your life, *merch fach*,' the woman instructed, smiling for the first time, disclosing even, white teeth, and for the first time Grainne realised just how physically attractive this strange, taciturn woman was.

Although normally a reticent and private person herself, for some unaccountable reason Grainne felt no qualms about telling her story to her new acquaintance, and immediately began: 'My name is Grainne Shonley, and I was born near the town of Skibereen twenty years since ...' She went on to tell of her childhood, and how she had gone to England in the service of a titled Lady when she was just fifteen, and at the age of nineteen returned to Ireland; a country then ravaged by famine and disease. She had found that her father had deserted her mother, her brothers and sisters, and that her mother had taken up with her husband's brother, a drunken, violent man. But no matter how hard Grainne had tried to persuade her mother to break with him, the woman had refused. Then Grainne had met and fallen in love with Conrad Shonley. She spoke openly of his involvement with the farcical Young Ireland rebellion, and of her own rejection of any cause or loyalties, except to her husband. When she spoke of the recent tragedy of the *Florida* and her fears for Con's fate, Grainne's eyes filled with tears and her voice faltered, but she forced herself to finish her story, and then fell silent.

'And this man in the Infirmary, do you really think him to be your husband?' Ellen Chester.

Grainne shook her head confusedly. 'My instinct tells me that he is, yet my mind tells me that he cannot

161

be. But if he were dead, then I'm sure that I would sense it. I can't help but believe that he still lives. But if he is not that poor man in the Infirmary, then where is he? Will Harper told me that sometimes it is many months before all survivors of shipwrecks can be listed. So all I can do is to wait here in Liverpool until those lists are completed. And of course, I've the hope that the man in the Infirmary will someday be able to tell me who he is.'

'And what if he did turn out to be your husband? Could you still love and care for him no matter how hideously scarred he would be?'

Grainne pondered very deeply before making any reply to this question, and when she did answer it was as though she were discussing that answer with herself: 'I loved Con for his nature as much as for his good looks, and I would hope that him being so sadly maimed would not alter the love I bear him. But to live with him being blind and horrible to look at, whether I could bear him to touch me, and to make love to me, I just don't know. But what I do know, is that if that man does turn out to be Con, then I'll look after him and care for him for the rest of my days, and if he wishes me to be his wife and to share his bed, then I will try to do so.'

'But suppose you were to meet another man, who was handsome and loved you, what would happen then?' Ellen Chester asked softly.

'I could never love another man as I love, Con,' Grainne stated vehemently. 'While Con lives, I'll be faithful to him, and the way I feel now, if he were proven to have died, then I will be faithful to his memory.'

'You sound very certain of that,' Ellen Chester observed.

'I *am* certain,' Grainne said with force.

The Welshwoman sighed heavily. 'You're still very young, *merch fach*, and have much to learn about life. I was as you are once, you know.' Sadness clouded her fine dark eyes. 'It seems so very, very far away now. Sometimes I wonder if it was all a dream.' Bitterness came into her voice. 'And at all times I wish this present life was a dream, and that I could wake up from it, and find myself back in my past, a young girl once more, with my life stretching before me.' She fell silent, and sat staring into the ashes of the grate with a brooding air.

The silence lengthened interminably, but Grainne was content to dwell in it. Her own thoughts filled her mind to the exclusion of all else and, try though she might to think of other things, her thoughts reverted constantly to the burned man in the Infirmary.

Nearly an hour passed, and then Ellen Chester stirred, and smiled towards Grainne, 'Forgive me. I fall into these fits of melancholy at times, but it's passed now. So let us think about you, Grainne. Now, how much money do you have?'

'A little under five pounds,' Grainne told her.

'That won't last for very long, my dear. Do you or Con have any kinfolk that can help you?'

'No,' Grainne grimaced ruefully. 'I could not ask my mother, not as long as she is with uncle. But even if she were not with him, it's her who would be needing my help. And Con's mother has gone to India with her new husband. I'm hoping to find work of some sort that will enable me to support myself.'

'If the man who lies in the Infirmary is your husband, then you will be needing to support him also, will you not? Because from what you have told me, he will be only fit to become a beggar, or enter the Workhouse,' the Welshwoman pointed out.

Grainne had no answer to offer, and could only shake her head and say, 'That is a bridge I'll have to cross when I reach it, for at this moment I've no idea what I would do.'

'Do you know what I do to earn my bread?' Ellen Chester challenged, and Grainne flushed with embarrassment, on which the other woman continued dryly,

'Judging from your colour, I think you have already guessed. But I'll tell you anyway; I'm a prostitute.' She smiled wryly. 'There was a time, not so very long ago, Grainne, when I regarded prostitutes as evil, depraved creatures, who were not fit to touch even the hems of my skirts. I shuddered at their depravity, and agreed whole-heartedly with those moral, righteous people who said that prostitutes should be whipped, driven from the streets, and locked away until they had repented and reformed.' She chuckled mirthlessly. 'I rode in my husband's carriage and looked down at those wicked women, and I wanted to scourge them myself! I considered their very existence to be an abomination; an affront to all good, decent women like myself.'

She bent forwards and picked up the brandy bottle from the floor at her feet. She refilled her own glass and despite Grainne's protest, poured more into her's also.

'Drink it down, *merch fach*, it won't harm you.' She lifted her glass in salute and took a large swallow, gusting out a sigh of satisfaction. Then she leaned back against the cushion of her chair, and told Grainne with an amused air, 'I was married to a man of property, Grainne. A son of the Manse, who had originally intended to follow his father into Holy Orders, but had decided instead that to be a successful man of business would suit him better. I was beautiful when I was a young girl, and he loved me. We had children, money and position in our community, and for many years I thought that I was happy.' She suddenly fixed Grainne with her dark eyes and asked, 'Did you ever read the story about the queen who had everything that her heart could desire, and was forbidden by her husband one thing only?'

Grainne, held enthralled by the soft lilting voice, shook her head silently.

'Well,' Ellen Chester continued, with a smile hovering about her full well-shaped lips, 'the only thing that her husband the king, forbade her to do, was to bunch her skirts high and wade through the filth of the midden. If she ever did that, he warned her, he would banish her forever to a cold, barren, desolate pinnacle of rock, and she would never see him or her children again. For many years they lived happily, but always the queen was drawn to the midden, and for some reason unaccountable to herself, she began to crave to do that very thing that was forbidden to her, even though, gently and delicately nurtured as she was, the midden filled her with a violent sense of repulsion and disgust.' Again she fell silent, and resumed her brooding staring into the ashes of the grate.

Grainne waited for the continuance of the story, and finally asked, 'What happened to the queen in the end?'

Ellen Chester laughed aloud, but there was no joy in that sound. 'The Queen is now dwelling on the pinnacle of rock, Grainne.'

And Grainne was left in no doubt that she had just heard Ellen Chester's own story.

The night was drawing on and the room was dark. Ellen Chester struck a lucifer match and lit an oil lamp. In its pale yellow glow her face appeared to be that of the young girl she had once been, and Grainne thought her very beautiful.

As if she could read Grainne's thoughts, the Welshwoman said softly, 'Yes, I still possess some remnants of beauty, do I not?' There was no suggestion of any boast in her voice, merely a statement of fact. 'You may stay here with me for tonight, if you wish, *merch fach*. The bed is large enough for four such as we.'

Grainne did not answer. She found herself suddenly assailed by doubts about what she was doing here with this woman. Grainne could not find it in her heart to condemn Ellen Chester for being a prostitute, but the thought of sharing her bed, the bed on which she probably entertained her clients, made Grainne mildly repulsed.

In the dark eyes regarding her lurked a sardonic amusement. 'You have no need to fear this bed, *merch fach*. The sheets are fresh on today. And you may rest easy on another score; I am not one of those women who has unnatural desire for my own sex.'

Grainne coloured hotly, but she did not attempt to make any flustering apologies. Instead she said evenly, 'I have only ever shared a bed with my blood kin, and my husband, Mrs Chester. It is strange for me to be contemplating sharing your bed. I mean you no insult.'

The other woman nodded. 'If you prefer you may sleep in the armchair, or on the floor. I can give you a blanket and a pillow.'

'Yes, perhaps for this night that might be better for us both,' Grainne agreed.

'What ever you wish,' Ellen Chester said indifferently, and Grainne felt deeply disturbed by what she considered her own churlish reception of this woman's hospitality.

In an effort to make some amends she told the Welshwoman, 'I am very grateful for your giving me shelter like this, Mrs Chester. Please do not take my preference as anything other than what it is. We are strangers to each other, and I am grateful to you for trusting me enough to give me this shelter, it's just that I have never ...'

'Enough, *merch fach*!' Ellen Chester sharply ended Grainne's increasingly floundering attempts to explain herself. 'You need say nothing more. Here.' She handed Grainne a blanket and a pillow from the bed. 'Settle yourself where you please. We'll talk some more tomorrow, but now I must sleep.'

She took off her gown and undershift and for a moment was naked before Grainne. Her body was shapely and fullbreasted, and was smooth, unblemished and pale in the lamplight. Then she pulled a night shift down over her head, blew out the lamp and got into bed.

'*Nos Dar, merch fach.* Good night, dear girl,' she said, then turning away from Grainne, she pulled the blankets over herself.

'Good night, Mrs Chester, and thank you,' Grainne replied. She wrapped the blanket around herself and curled up in one of the large armchairs. For a time her thoughts wandered aimlessly, and Septimus Prendergast's face etched itself in her mind.

'I wonder if he has returned yet from Manchester?'

For a brief moment she toyed with the idea of going to Tom Tracey's hotel in search of the young Englishman. Then she rejected that idea. 'No, I'll not do that. My trouble is my own, and it's up to me to deal with it. Besides there's nothing he could do to aid me. The poor soul has troubles enough of his own from what little I knew of him.'

Now the full realisation of her utter weariness overcame her, and within scant minutes she was deeply asleep.

Chapter Twenty-One

'Grainne? Grainne, it's time to wake up.' Ellen Chester's voice brought Grainne out of a confusing jumble of dreams, and she opened her eyes drowsily to see the Welshwoman, fully dressed, leaning over her.

For a second or two Grainne was uncertain of where she was, then full recollection flooded back, and she sat upright and knuckled her eyes. 'Jesus, I slept heavy last night! What time is it?'

The Welshwoman went to the fireplace and lifted a man's hunter watch from the mantelpiece. 'Just gone eight o'clock. I've the use of a wash house at the rear of the shop, so if you'll come with me I'll show you where it is. Do you have a towel and soap?'

'Yes, they're here.' Grainne showed the contents of her small canvas bag in which she kept the toilette articles she had been given by the sailors on the Dutch ship. 'I've toothpowder, brushes and more in here.'

She followed the other woman down the dark, narrow staircase and out into the street. The way to the rear of their building was a narrow, rubbish-filled, covered entry which stank of urine and excreta, but even amongst this filth a couple of derelicts were curled, snoring in drunken slumber.

'Pay no mind to them.' Ellen Chester stepped over the prone bodies. 'They've been using this entry for nearly a year now. They're harmless enough, and if you speak sharply to them they won't pester you too much for drink money.'

The wash-house was a small lean-to in a minute yard

surrounded by high, blank walls.

'I'm very lucky here,' Ellen Chester remarked without any trace of irony, 'because there is only myself that comes into this yard. I can draw my water and leave it safely in the wash-house. The last house I lived in, any water was stolen the moment you took your eyes from it.'

From a wooden barrel she drew a bucket of water and lifted it into the shallow stone trough. Then she leaned against the door-jamb and watched Grainne make her toilette.

As Grainne was brushing her long hair Ellen Chester told her, 'You're a very beautiful girl, Grainne. I know men who would pay a small fortune to have you as their mistress.'

Shocked by the statement, Grainne ceased from brushing and stared challengingly at the other woman and asked, 'What do you mean by saying that?'

'Nothing more than what I said,' Ellen Chester explained good temperedly. 'Do not begin to think I'm any sort of procuress, *merch fach*, because I'm not.'

Grainne studied the woman's features until she was satisfied that she spoke truly, then shrugged and said shamefacedly, 'I'm sorry, Mrs Chester. I seem to be always causing you offence, and really I've no intention of doing so. It's just that ...'

'It's just that you are alone in a strange city, and cannot help but suspect the worst of people, having seen what you've seen in these mean streets,' the Welshwoman answered for her. 'And I don't blame you for it, *merch fach*. You are right to be suspicious. A young woman who is as beautiful as you will always attract the predators.' She paused, as if considering something in her mind, then drew a sharp breath. 'I want you to listen very carefully to me, Grainne, and do not take anything I say amiss. Because I am only offering you advice. Advice that is based on my own experiences here in Liverpool.' Again she paused, but this time as if awaiting some reaction from Grainne.

Grainne nodded to her. 'Please go on, I'll not take what you tell me amiss.'

'Very well, then.' The Welshwoman nodded in her turn. 'I told you last night that I am a prostitute. I am indeed that, but I do exercise considerable discretion in that calling. I only sleep with men that use me with some degree of kindness. I only accept those who come to me with a recommendation from someone I know already. Men like Will Harper, for example. He stays with me when he docks here in Liverpool, and we dwell together as man and wife. It is the same with my other men. They entrust me with their money when they have their pay, and in return I try to ensure that when that money is spent they still have sufficient money for their sea going gear, and their tobacco and snuff when they sign on their next ship. As far as it can be said that a woman like me can hold a good name, then I hold one among the men I sleep with.

I keep away from the dancing houses and the singing pubs, and I don't consort with the riff-raff of the city any more than I can help doing so. I've never given a penny piece to any cash-carrier or any ponce. Look well at me, Grainne. If you were to meet me in the street, would you take me for what I am, a judy, a tail?'

Grainne shook her head. 'No, the way you were dressed last night I would have taken you for a respectable widow woman.'

Ellen Chester smiled. 'Exactly so, and that is why I have been able to earn sufficient for my needs during these last years, and still have my health.' A fleeting sadness passed over her face. 'Many poor women I have known who came to this calling after me are already lying in their graves, and many, many more are hidden around the dock alleys, only stirring abroad by night, too afraid to show themselves by day because they are so ravaged by disease that even the lowest of men would not go with them if they saw them in the light. And so they only walk in the darkness, and will allow any sort of perversion to be committed against them, because they have no other choice. It is either that, or starve to death.'

'Mrs Chester, I know that you mean well by telling me these things,' Grainne tried to choose her words with great care, 'but I have no intention of ever selling myself to men. I intend to find work and support myself.'

The other woman smiled sadly, and her eyes held all the wisdom of bitter, hard-bought experience. 'Believe me, *cariad*, when I say that I hope with all my heart that you will be able to do just that.'

When Grainne had finished they went to an eating-house and had bread and butter, and hot sweet coffee for their breakfast.

'What will you do today?' Mrs Chester wanted to know.

'I shall find a room, and then visit the Infirmary, and then look for work,' Grainne informed her smilingly, her spirits high now that she had rested well.

'You can stay with me for a while, if you want,' the other woman told her. 'The next of my men will not be here for a week or more.'

'But I don't want to impose on your kindness, Mrs Chester,' Grainne protested. 'You've been very good to let me stay last night.'

'I like you.' Ellen Chester smiled. 'And I become very lonely at times, when all my men are away. I should enjoy having your company. And in the meantime I will help you to find a room for yourself. There is only one thing I would ask of you, and that is to call me Ellen.'

For a few moments Grainne could not answer. Then she said softly, 'Do you know, when I was a very wee girl, my Mammy was always telling me that,"God tempers the wind to the shorn lamb". It's only now that I'm beginning to understand what that old saying really means. Ever since the wreck, everybody I've met has offered me so much kindness, that it helps me to bear with my own troubles.'

A ragged, dirty old hag came into the eating-house

and moved along the row of booths holding out her cupped hands, and mouthing incoherent pleas. Deaf to the shouts of the proprietor who was in the middle of serving a customer, the old hag reached the booth where Grainne and Mrs Chester were seated. On impulse Grainne reached inside her bodice to the small leather pouch between her breasts, and taking out a sovereign, pressed it into the old hag's hands. The red-rimmed, eyes blinked unbelievingly at the gold coin and then she stared at Grainne with a gaping toothless jaw.

Grainne smiled reassuringly at her. 'That's all right. I know what I've given you. That's all right.'

The proprietor came whooping round the counter, and with a surprising speed the old hag scuttled out of the door.

Aware of Ellen Chester's questioning gaze, Grainne shrugged her shoulders. 'I thought it was time I tried to pass on a bit of the kindness I have received. The poor old thing looked as if she were starving.'

'Well she might be.' Ellen Chester said cynically. 'But it's not food that she'll be spending your sovereign on. She'll be as drunk as a lord until that's all gone.'

'Well,' Grainne smiled unconcernedly, 'If she's that, then at least she won't be feeling her miseries for a time, will she?'

The other woman frowned at her. 'You acted like a fool giving her so much. You've little enough yourself! Then her face softened. 'But at least, you acted like a kind fool.'

172

Chapter Twenty-Two

It was the first day of the fourth week in September and several days had elapsed since Malcom Galbraith had extracted Grainne's promise to keep in touch with him, but he had neither seen or heard from her during that time.

He sat now moodily toying with his late breakfast of devilled kidneys, his thoughts filled with Grainne Shonley. Malcom Galbraith was not accustomed to being so ignored by the women that he desired and it piqued him.

'Gally, what's the matter? Why are you so glum this morning?' The young girl sitting across the breakfast table asked him anxiously.

Galbraith looked at his current mistress with sudden acute distaste. 'Bloody dollymop,' he thought sourly, comparing her pert painted features and tawdry finery with the unadorned, natural beauty of Grainne Shonley.

'Are you angry with me, darlin'? What have I done?' The girl's nasal Liverpudlian intonations rasped on the young man's nerves.

'How could I have ever wanted to thread this slut's needle?' he asked himself wonderingly. Then with a casual cruelty told her. 'I am uncertain about our association, Catherine. I feel we are growing apart from each other.'

'You weren't feeling that last night!' The girl's gutter-devil was rousing as she sensed what was to come. 'Aren't I good enough for you now, or summat?

You couldn't get enough o' me last night, could you. What's brought this on now?'

Galbraith sighed impatiently. 'It's no use your caterwauling, Catherine. It won't serve with me. Our relationship is ended, and there is no more to be said about it.' He slammed his knife and fork down on the table. 'So hold your tongue!'

She stared at him with mingled anger and despair. 'But why, Gally, what's I done to be treated this way?'

He rose to his feet and tossed some money onto the table. 'Here, take this. I'll settle the bill on my way out.'

Disregarding her pleas he took his hat and gloves and went from the room. Downstairs in the foyer of the small, discreet hotel, he settled the bill and went out into the street, where he was immediately hailed by a young man passing by.

'Now then, Malcom, been having yet another night on the tiles?'

Galbraith grinned at him, recognising a friend who was one of the assistant surgeons at the Infirmary. 'Hello David, where do you go to?'

The young man grimaced in fun, 'To the Infirmary, where else?'

'Then I'll walk up there with you. I want to have a word with Simon Sinclair.' Galbraith told him, and they set off in the direction of Brownlow Hill.

'I take it you were with what's-her-name last night.' David's boyish features were envious. 'I don't know how you do it, Malcom.'

Galbraith grinned disparagingly. 'Money helps, my boy. All the dollymops love a gentleman, particularly when he's free with his rhino.' Cruelty entered his eyes. 'I've just given Catherine the heave-ho. She was becoming very tiresome. Even had the cheek to mention marriage during the course of last night.'

His companion laughed, and questioned with a hint of mockery.'Why is it, Malcom, that these shopgirls and barmaids always want to marry you? Are you sure that it is not yourself that makes the proposal to them, in order to have your wicked way with the poor innocents.'

The gibe was nearer to the truth than Malcom Galbraith cared to acknowledge, and stung enough for him to react savagely. 'I don't need to promise marriage to get what I want from slumrats.'

His friend was delighted with this reaction, and baited further. 'Oh come, Malcom, Catherine could hardly be described as a slumrat, could she now? Admittedly, like so many of your other conquests, she is unmistakeably from the lower orders, but at least she makes some attempt to wash her face and neck, does she not? And she uses a knife and fork to eat her meals.'

Galbraith was forced to smile himself, and he quipped, 'She might wash those parts that can be seen, David, but like the rest of her class, she neglects the hidden areas. Now do give over ragging a fellow, will you!

The other man laughed triumphantly, and then asked. 'Why do you go to the Infirmary?'

'I'm interested in a case there; the fellow from the *Florida* who was badly burned about the head and upper body.'

'Oh yes, I know of him. Sinclair cannot understand how the poor devil still lives. He told me yesterday that the chap cannot possibly last many more days.' Then the young man grinned broadly. 'But is it he, or that good-looking Irishwoman who comes to visit him everyday, that really interests you, Malcom?'

By now Galbraith's customary good humour had reasserted itself, and he admitted light-heartedly, 'Well, in all truth, I must confess to having some degree of interest in the woman.'

'By God, but she really is a beauty,' enthused David, 'but I'd hardly think, she will prove an easy conquest, not even for the redoubtable Dr Galbraith. She gave one of our fellows a roasting and sent him packing in double quick time when he tried to charm her into meeting with him.'

'You should know by now, that apparent virtue in a woman only serves to make me more determined to win her favours, David.' Galbraith smiled. 'After all, it's only the hard won victories that are worth achieving.'

In the small room the bandaged man lay motionless, and Grainne stood looking down at him.

During the past five days her daily routine had not varied. She rose early and breakfasted with Ellen Chester. Then set out for Tapscott's offices in the Regent Road to see if they had received any news of further survivors from the *Florida*. She then made the rounds of the offices of the city's many newspapers, namely the *Mercury*, the *Courier*, the *Mail* and the *Journal* to enquire if any reports of survivors had been sent to them. Every negative answer struck her like a physical blow, yet paradoxically only served to stiffen her resolve not to lose hope.

Once these rounds were completed she would then trudge up to the Infirmary. Upon admittance she would hurry to the small room, and then stand watching the motionless, bandaged figure, praying for some sign of animation. For long periods she would talk to the man as if he were indeed her beloved Con; speaking of any happening they had shared, dredging the depths of her memories for any minor recollection that might finally bring some sort of response. Sometimes she would merely keep on repeating softly, 'It's me, Con. It's Grainne. Speak to me, honey. Please speak to me. Give me some sort of sign that you can hear me, and that you know who I am. Please Con, please try, please …

Dr Simon Sinclair was very absorbed in dissecting the brain of a recently hung criminal so when Malcom Galbraith came into his cluttered surgery, he paid only scant attention to the younger man's greeting.

'A moment, I pray you.' After a few deft slices with the scalpel Sinclair grunted with satisfaction, laid it

176

aside and turned to the younger man. 'Now then, what brings you here, Galbraith?'

He frowned in puzzlement as he listened, and when the young man had finished speaking commented, 'This is a damned strange thing to ask of me, Galbraith. Why on earth should you want the fellow transferred to the North Dispensary? Is it because you've run short of subjects for dissection?' He joked grimly. 'I would not have thought there to be any shortage of unclaimed cadavers at your establishment.'

Galbraith assumed a diffident air. 'You force me to confess, sir. It is precisely for the reason you mention that I would like to have the man transferred. I've never had the chance to study at first hand such a severe burns case.'

Sinclair's narrow features were doubtful. 'You surprise me Galbraith. Do not we have an abundance of fires in this city?'

'That is so,' Galbraith accepted readily, 'but we do not have an abundance of cases such as this one, who continues to live when by all reckonings, he should be dead long since.'

'Yes, certainly the man is exceptionally tenacious,' Sinclair agreed. His eyes strayed towards the partially dissected brain lying on the earthenware dish on his desk. His fingers itched to take up his scalpel again and, eager to get rid of his uninvited visitor, he clucked his tongue impatiently, and told him, 'Oh very well, Galbraith. Take the fellow if you want him. He'll not last above another couple of days in my opinion. So the North Dispensary must take responsibility for his burial.'

'Naturally, I shall see to that, Sinclair. Many thanks to you. I'll leave you to your work.'

Sinclair was already leaning over the specimen in the dish, and only nodded absently as Galbraith wished him good day.'

'Denis was a great gas that night, wasn't he, Con? Do you

remember when he stood on that wall and tried to make a speech, and then fell backwards into Granny Mullins' ash tip, and she set her wee dog on him? He was shouting blue murder and trying to get back over the wall with the wee dog hanging onto his britches, and Granny Mullins beating him with her frying pan. Do you remember that night, Con? Do you remember how you and me were near helpless with laughter?'

Malcom Galbraith stood at the partially opened door of the small room listening to Grainne's soft voice, and for a brief instant wondered who she was talking to. Then he gently pushed on the door and coughed to draw her attention.

She swung round startled, and the colour rose to her cheeks in embarrassment at being caught talking to a senseless man.

Galbraith smiled at her, and came to the bed. 'I wondered whom you were talking with, Mrs Shonley.'

'It must seem a great foolishness to you, Dr Galbraith. Me talking to a man who doesn't even seem to be hearing me, let alone giving me an answer,' Grainne said defensively.

'But not at all, Mrs Shonley.' Galbraith's voice was warm and his handsome features radiated sympathetic understanding. 'Let me tell you, that we doctors understand very little about the workings of the human mind. It may well be that your talking to this poor fellow could eventually bring forth some response from him.'

'Do you really believe so?' she questioned eagerly.

'Really,' he nodded.

Her gratification shone in her great green eyes, and Malcom Galbraith knew that he would not be able to rest until he had succeeded in possessing this woman. He found that his desire for her had strengthened until it was threatening to become an obsession.

'And what if it does become so?' he asked himself now, and answered without any hesitation, 'Then let it, for I don't give a damn. I want this woman, and I'll have her someday, that I swear to.'

Aloud, he told her. 'I have news which should please you mightily, Mrs Shonley. I am having this man transferred to the North Dispensary, where I can give him my personal attention.'

The reaction he expected was not forthcoming. Instead, to his surprise, Grainne's face was instantly filled with doubt. Her memories of the North Dispensary were unhappy ones. Maggie Nolan had died there.

'Are you not pleased to hear this news?' he asked.

'Why must he be transferred from here?' Grainne asked unhappily.

Galbraith's thoughts raced, and he told her with a great show of confidence, 'Because, my dear, I feel he will be better served by being under my personal attention. There are certain treatments which I believe will benefit him greatly. You see, in confidence between you and I, the doctors here are more concerned with surgery than with the treatment of severe burn cases. That is no reflection on their professional competence, you understand, but I have specialised in the treatment of scalds and burns ever since my student days. It is my particular interest. I truly believe that in the whole of the North country I am the best man for treating such cases as this poor fellow.'

'But will I be able to spend time with him there?' Grainne wanted to know. 'And will he be in a room to himself, as he is here?'

Galbraith smiled sadly. 'My dear, the only reason that he has been left in this room by himself, is that he is expected to die at any time. The doctors here cannot understand how he has managed to cling to life for this length of time, as it is.'

'No, he must not die!' Grainne burst out. 'He cannot die! He cannot go to his grave without anyone knowing who he is!' In her mind she was almost shrieking. 'I must know who he is. I must know. I must know. He cannot die until I know who he is!'

'Now you must listen very carefully to what I say, my dear,' Galbraith told her kindly, 'and then you will understand why it is in his best interests to be transferred. If he remains here, and continues to live, then he will only receive the same treatment as all the other patients here. There will be no one to guard his interests, or to ensure that he gets the best of everything that is available.'

'*I* will guard his interests,' offered Grainne.

Galbraith only smiled and shook his head. 'Regretfully, Grainne, you cannot do so. The only reason that you have been allowed such access to him, is because of my intercessions on your behalf. As far as the world is concerned, you have no relation to this man. Therefore you have no rights, and have no say in what is done with him.'

He lapsed into silence, watching her keenly to see what effect his words were having on her.

Grainne tried desperately to marshal her thoughts. She accepted that there was no rational objection that could be made to the transfer, but instinctively she feared it. She understood that because the Dispensary was where Maggie Nolan had died, then that could be the major reason for her fear. Buried in the depths of her being she sensed another reason for her fearing the transfer, but try as she might could not recognise what that reason was.

Galbraith watched her in silence for some considerable time, then judged that the moment had arrived for him to apply a little more pressure.

'I had not wished to tell you this, Grainne, but I think that in all fairness to you, I must. Objections have been raised by some of the families of other patients against you having so much access time allowed to you. They have taken the trouble to find out that this man is unknown to you, and they demand either that they be allowed equal access to their own loved ones, or you should only be given the same times of access as they.' He shook his head with apparent regret. 'In all fairness, I must concede there is some justice in what they say. Naturally I have spoken on your behalf, but the hospital guardians have decided that there is no justification for continuing to allow you so much freedom.'

Grainne was forced to accept that she was powerless to do anything other than allow Galbraith to do as he wished. 'Very well, Dr Galbraith. Forgive me for behaving so stupidly. When will you transfer him?'

Satisfied that he had won his object, Malcom Galbraith smiled charmingly. 'Within a day or so, Grainne. And please, I shall want you to work very closely with me in restoring this poor fellow to health and vigour once again, so from now on, I shall be Malcom and you shall be Grainne. I want you to continue to talk to him, as you've been doing. There is always the possibility that your voice will, some day, trigger a reaction in his mind. And now I must leave you.' He took her hand briefly. 'Don't despair, Grainne. Despite what the world says, you and I together will save this fellow; I'm sure of it.'

When he had gone Grainne stood looking down at the bandaged head lying on the soiled pillow, trying to understand why, despite Malcom Galbraith's kindness, she should still be feeling uneasy in her mind.

'Can you tell me, Con?' she whispered to the man in the bed. 'Can you tell me why I should be feeling so uneasy in my mind.' She smiled sadly and reached out to gently rest her hand on the man's bandaged arm. 'Are you really my Con?' she whispered. 'Are you?'

And the arm beneath her fingers moved.

Chapter Twenty-Three

'He is my Con, Ellen. I know he is!' Grainne stated.

'But you say that it was only the one time that he reacted to your voice, *cariad*, and then it was only a movement of his arm,' reasoned the older woman. 'Don't think that I'm trying to dash your hopes, but I don't want to see you carried away by something that was a mere coincidence.'

The two women were sitting in Ellen Chester's room in the dusk. No lamp was lit and to Grainne the other woman was only a darker shadow with pale, indistinct features.

'It was not a coincidence, Ellen. Con heard me, and answered in the only way he could.' Grainne spoke with a firm conviction, and Ellen Chester accepted that no matter what she might say, the younger woman wanted so badly to believe that she had found her husband, that any attempt to caution her was doomed to fail.

'Very well then, *cariad*. You have found your husband. Now what will you do?'

'I shall care for him, of course!' Grainne's tone showed how incredulous she was that such a question should be asked of her.

'Where?' Ellen Chester was deliberately acting as the devil's advocate in an attempt to illustrate the difficulties facing Grainne.

'I shall find a room for us.'

'And how will you pay for that room?'

'I shall work and earn money, naturally.'

'What sort of work?'

'Any sort that I can find.'

'And who will care for him while you're at that work?'

'I can pay someone to watch him for me.'

The older woman clucked her tongue against the roof of her mouth.

'Why do you do that?' Grainne demanded.

'Because, *cariad*, you are talking like a fool.'

'How so?'

'Any respectable work that you could get hereabouts, would not pay sufficient to support yourself with any degree of decency, let alone support a helpless man as well. If you go into service, you might be allowed out for one afternoon and evening a week. So you'll be seeing next to nothing of your man, and the wages you will earn as a servant will not be enough to have him cared for properly. Believe me, Grainne, I know from my own experience how hard it is to merely survive in this city for any woman who is alone, and to care for a helpless man as well is an impossibility.'

Ellen Chester paused, then leaned forwards in her chair and took Grainne's hand. 'Shall I tell you why there are so many thousands of prostitutes walking these streets, Grainne? They are selling their bodies because they have no other choice but to do that, or starve. I have known women to slave night and day for a pittance in order to keep decent and respectable, but eventually, even the most determined and strongest have been forced to surrender.'

Grainne made no reply at first, as she mulled over what Ellen Chester had told her, and momentarily her heart quailed at the thought of what was facing her. She was absolutely convinced now that the man in the Infirmary was indeed her husband, and that conviction was matched by her determination that she was going to care for him for the rest of his days.

She knew that if he lived, he would not be allowed to remain in the Dispensary indefinitely. Once his wounds had healed sufficiently then he would be expected to vacate his bed. The pressure on the

Dispensary was such, that patients were discharged as quickly as possible, in order to make room for the hordes who daily clamoured for admittance to its wards. Then Con's only alternatives would be to beg in the streets, or to enter the grim Workhouse, and remain there until he died.

'We couldn't even be together in there,' Grainne thought sadly, 'because men and women are kept separate.'

There was also another thought which had begun to intrude in Grainne's mind with an unpleasantly increasing frequency. And that was that it was really her fault that this terrible tragedy had struck Con, and she voiced it now to Ellen: 'If I had not insisted that we go to America, then this would never have happened to him. He told me that James Mahoney had offered to help him in London, and I said that I wanted to go to America as we had first planned.'

Ellen Chester now squeezed hard on Grainne's fingers, and told her urgently, 'You must not blame yourself for what has happened, *cariad*. It was not your fault. What is, is what was meant to be. We are all of us only the pawns of fate. That I truly believe.'

Grainne stared with wide eyes. 'Do you really believe that, Ellen? Can it be possible that all that happens to us in our lives is predestined?'

The woman nodded firmly. 'I do.'

'If I could believe that, then I might draw some comfort from it,' Grainne whispered, and Ellen Chester smiled sardonically.

'Why do you think I believe it implicitly, *cariad*? It is my sole source of comfort …'

They remained in a companionable silence for an hour or more, both immersed in their own thoughts.

It was Ellen Chester who broke the silence. 'One of my men is due to dock tomorrow, Grainne, so you won't be able to stay here for a few days.'

The news, although expected, still came as a shock to Grainne.

'But you've no need to worry,' the older woman continued. 'I've found a room for you a little further along the street. You can sleep there until he sails again. The rent is four shillings a week.'

Grainne computed her resources. She had two sovereigns and a few odd coppers left to her. 'That's very good of you, Ellen. It seems cheap enough if I am to be the only tenant.'

'You will be,' the Welshwoman assured her. 'All the rooms in the house are let to single tenants.' She appeared to hesitate, before going on, 'It's mostly judies who rent them, Grainne. They need single rooms to take their customers to. But I've made sure that there's a lock on your door, and a key that fits it, so you'll be safe enough. And also, you'll have a place to bring your husband to.'

Grainne could not understand why the other woman had said this. 'To bring Con to?' she repeated. 'But he will be in the Dispensary for some time. I've already told you that. He should be transferred tomorrow or the day after.'

'This Dr Galbraith, has he made any sort of advances towards you?' Ellen Chester's voice was carefully neutral.

'No. He is a perfect gentleman,' Grainne asserted.

In the darkness the Welshwoman's mouth curved in a pitying smile, but still she kept any inflection from her voice.

'I'm pleased to hear that, *cariad*. But take care that you don't trust too blindly. Could I come with you to the Infirmary tomorrow and visit your husband?'

'But of course you can.' Grainne welcomed the offer with a genuine pleasure.

'Very well. And we'll also make the rounds of some of the registry offices to see what employment they can offer you, if you'd like that.'

'Yes, I would, very much.' Grainne assented warmly, and her heart filled with something akin to love for this strange woman who had befriended her.

185

Chapter Twenty-Four

'Rest your hands on his arm,' Grainne instructed Ellen Chester, and when the women had obeyed, she put her head close to the bandaged head of the motionless man and asked urgently.

'Can you hear me, Con? Do you understand what I'm saying to you? Move your arm if you can.'

There was no reaction from the man, only the rasping of his breathing.

'Why does his breathing sound so harsh and noisy?' Ellen Chester wanted to know.

'Dr Galbraith says that the heat of the fire damaged the insides of his throat and lungs,' Grainne informed her, then lifting her finger to her lips in a plea for silence she tried once more to make contact. 'Con, it's Grainne, honey. Try and make a sign of some sort if you can hear me. Try Con. Please try.'

Ellen Chester suddenly gasped and her body started in shock. She gazed at Grainne unbelievingly, uttering, 'It moved! I felt it. His arm moved!'

Grainne laughed with delight. 'There now, didn't I tell you it was my Con!' she exclaimed excitedly. 'Didn't I tell you that I'd got him back.' She leaned close to the bandaged head again.'Don't worry Con, I'm going to care for you. You're going to be moved to the North Dispensary either today or tomorrow, where I can look after you better, and help to make you well again.'

'Well now, you sound very happy this morning, Grainne.'

It was Malcom Galbraith, accompanied by two

porters, one carrying a wooden framed canvas stretcher.

'I've a cab waiting outside, Grainne. I'm going to transfer this poor fellow immediately.'

'Malcom, he knows me! It is my Con, without any doubt at all. It's my husband,' Grainne told the young man, and a faint frown creased his brows.

'How can you tell that he knows you?'

'Look, put your hand so.' Grainne took Galbraith's hand and placed it on the bandaged forearm. Once more she began asking the injured man if he knew her, begging him to move his arm if he did. After a few moments, Galbraith nodded.

'Yes, there was a definite movement of his arm then, Grainne.'

'I told you!' Her great green eyes shone with happiness. 'I knew he would come back to me. I knew he wasn't dead!'

She suddenly burst into tears and Ellen Chester quickly moved to her and held her tightly. 'That's it, *cariad*. Let it all come out. Hold nothing back. Let the tears flow,' she crooned comfortingly, but all the time her fine dark eyes were watching Malcom Galbraith's face.

In his turn he stole quick glances at the Welshwoman, and what he saw puzzled him. She was well dressed in costly-silken widow's weeds, with an expensive black bonnet trimmed with a black lace veil, now thrown back to show her pale handsome face.

'Now who might you be? You don't look like any slumrat, that's for sure,' he wondered, 'or like a tail. But if Grainne's staying with you, then you must be the one who she went to meet in Brunswick Street. And the only women who live there are the damned tails.'

When Grainne had composed herself once more, and had apologised for breaking down, she introduced Ellen Chester to the young doctor.

He bowed courteously. 'I'm honoured to make your acquaintance, ma'm.'

187

She inclined her head graciously. 'And I yours, sir.'

'Quite the lady, ain't you,' he thought admiringly, 'and considering that you're no longer a chicken, a damned good-looking woman. Once I've tired of Grainne Shonley, I might well give you a turn, Madam Chester, indeed I might.'

Then their eyes met, and he drew breath sharply as he saw the hostility in hers …

'Christ!' he wondered silently, 'can you read my mind, looking at me so?'

To cover his momentary discomfort he busied himself in giving instructions to the porters for the removal of the injured man to the cab waiting outside the Infirmary's main entrance. But before the porters actually lifted the man, Malcom Galbraith turned to the two women.

'Grainne, Mrs Chester, I think it best if you leave us now. Moving this poor fellow may well prove a very painful process for him, and witnessing that will only cause you undue distress. I also want to change his dressings when we arrive at the Dispensary. Therefore I consider that the best course for yourselves is to go now, and come to the Dispensary tomorrow. If you will arrive there at two o'clock in the afternoon I will meet you myself. I shall be able to advise you of his degree of healing after I have changed his dressings and examined him thoroughly.'

Grainne displayed some reluctance to leave, but Ellen Chester found herself agreeing with the doctor, and under her urging Grainne finally accepted Galbraith's suggestion.

As the two women were walking down Brownlow Hill the cab carrying Galbraith and his patient passed them, and Galbraith smiled and lifted his top hat in salute. Both women nodded in reply and Grainne asked her companion, 'Well, what do you think to Dr Galbraith now, Ellen? He's a real gentleman, isn't he?'

The Welshwoman's lips pursed. 'Grainne, I think you should be always on your guard with that *real gentleman*.'

188

'Why do you say that?' Grainne stared uncertainly at her friend.

Ellen Chester chuckled cynically. 'Because when he looks at women, his eyes are the eyes of a dog on heat!'

The casual brutality of this statement angered Grainne. 'I don't think you can have any justification for saying such a nasty thing about Dr Galbraith. He's been kindness itself to me, and has never in any way offered me insult.'

The dark eyes turned to her, and in their depths glimmered an utter certainty. 'He will, *cariad*. He will. So guard yourself. Believe me, I am speaking as a true friend, who only wishes you well.'

Grainne's anger rose, but not wishing to quarrel with this woman who had been so good to her, she bit back the sharp retort which sprang to her lips, and kept silent during the remainder of their descent of the hill.

It was Ellen Chester who broke the strained silence. 'I don't think it any use doing the rounds of the servants's registries, Grainne. Even if you found a place locally as a lady's maid, you wouldn't receive much above twenty pounds a year. And from that you would have to buy your uniforms to begin with.'

'But I must find work of some sort, Ellen.' Grainne's anxieties now crowded in on her. If she were alone, working as a servant would be a way out of her present predicament, but she was now forced to accept in the cold light of day that her idea of entering into service was an impossibility. Not only would she be unable even to visit Con with any regularity, but the money she would eventually receive would barely feed him, let alone provide him with decent shelter.

'How about your husband's family? Can they not help him?' Ellen Chester suggested.

'They would if they knew what had happened, I'm sure,' Grainne told her, 'but they've gone to India, and even if I knew how to contact them, by the time they could give me any help, it would be too late.'

During the walk back to Brunswick Street, Grainne

thought a great deal about what Ellen Chester had said concerning Malcom Galbraith. Reluctant though she was to accept the other woman's opinion concerning him, yet she found herself wondering afresh about his motives for helping her.

'Ellen,' she asked tentatively, 'do you really believe that Doctor Galbraith will offer me insult.'

'Perhaps insult was the wrong word to use, *cariad*.' The Welshwoman looked very serious, and she came to a standstill and took Grainne's arm to halt her also. 'Listen to me very carefully, *merch fach*, because what I am going to tell you is what I truly believe. You are convinced that the man we just saw is your husband, are you not?'

Grainne nodded emphatically.

'And you are determined that you will care for him for the rest of your days?'

'Yes, I am so,' Grainne declared positively.

'Then you will need money, and much more money than you will be able to earn no matter how hard you work, but you have many assets, *merch fach*: you have youth, intelligence and great beauty. Men desire you.'

Knowing what was to come, Grainne interrupted, 'You believe that I will have to become a prostitute, don't you, Ellen?'

The Welshwoman's pale face was very grave. 'Yes, child, I do believe that. Unless you give up this idea of caring for that man.' The breath hissed between Ellen Chester's teeth as she exclaimed, '*Iesu Mawr*, child, you don't even know for certain that he is your husband! How can you even think of caring for him? He could be a stranger. Supposing that you find out later that he isn't your man? What will you do then?

'He is Con,' Grainne said stubbornly. 'I know that he is Con.'

'How do you know?' The other woman repeated with mounting exasperation. 'How can you know?'

'He is Con,' Grainne reiterated doggedly. 'I know he is.'

190

'And are you really prepared to go with men in order to support him?' Ellen Chester demanded.

Grainne could make no quick reply. For the first time she really faced the possibility that she might have to do just that, in order to care for her husband. 'Could I?' She asked herself now. 'Could I give my body to strange men for money?'

She had come to her marriage a virgin, and had never known any other man's loving but Con's. She enjoyed sex, possessed a healthy sexual appetite, and was able to admit to herself that at times she had seen men who had stirred sexual desire in her. But she had always been physically faithful to her husband, and had always intended to remain so.

'Well?' Ellen Chester pressed for an answer, 'are you prepared to sell yourself.'

Grainne sighed deeply, and slowly shook her head. 'I just don't know,' she said slowly, 'I just don't know.'

'There is something else you must consider as well.' The older woman seemed determined to probe until she found a weak spot in Grainne's apparently steadfast resolve. 'Have you yet faced up to the fact that this man may well be blind for the rest of his life?'

'Dr Sinclair has already told me that he has lost his sight.'

'It doesn't seem to be grieving you overmuch,' the Welshwoman accused. 'Neither does the fact that your husband, if it is he, is going to be hideous to look at, and a virtual cripple.'

'I know he will be badly scarred,' Grainne muttered sullenly, and then lashed back, 'Why do you torment me in this way? What have I done that you should act so cruelly towards me?'

Angrily she began to stride away, then her steps slowed and she came to a standstill, and turned back. 'Why are you talking this way, Ellen?' Her green eyes were troubled. 'Haven't I got troubles enough, without you badgering me so?'

Ellen Chester's heart filled with pity, and she came

191

up to Grainne. 'I'm not acting towards you with any malice, *cariad*,' she said gently, 'I'm only trying to make you face reality.'

'I am facing it!' Grainne declared.

'Are you?' Ellen Chester challenged. 'Look into your heart, *merch fach* and face the truth of what you find there.' She took a long deep breath as she steeled herself to continue. 'You don't want to believe that when those bandages are taken off that man, then he will be monstrous to look upon, do you? You don't want to believe that his sight has really gone. You will not allow yourself to believe it. You are hoping that when those bandages come off, the husband you knew and loved will be there still ... Oh! You can accept that he'll be a little scarred perhaps, and will have some temporary difficulties in using his hands and arms, but you want to believe that he will still be the man you loved; that he will still be the man whose body you have enjoyed; still be the man that you hungered to fill your body in the darkness of night; still be the man whose good looks and pleasing personality caused you to be envied by other women because you possessed him.' She paused and grieved to see what effect her words were having. 'I have to do this *merch fach*,' she told Grainne sadly. 'I have to make you accept reality now. You must accept that the husband you knew and loved is dead, and that this man whom you wish to believe is your husband, is a stranger, even if his name is Con Shonley. He is no longer the man you knew. He is changed now; he is a stranger. Your husband is dead, Grainne. Con Shonley is dead!'

'Dead! Dead! Dead! Dead!'

The words ricochetted through Grainne's brain, and a darkness veiled her sight.

'Dead! Dead! Dead!'

She felt as if her head were a battleground and that the word had stormed through all her defences and was now rampaging through her being, mercilessly destroying all the hopes that had sustained her through the ordeal of the past weeks. Her body began to quiver erratically and her breathing became choking gasps.

'No!' She shook her head violently. 'No! No! No!'

Ellen Chester grabbed Grainne's arms and forced her back against the wall. 'Yes, girl, yes! Yes! Yes! Yes! He is dead! Dead!'

Grainne's face was a mask of torment, and from her lips came a howl of utter misery, then sobs tore from her throat, and her body sagged as if all strength had left her.

Ellen Chester's pale face was also twisted with pain, and she cradled the helpless sobbing girl in her arms.

'I'm sorry, *cariad*.' She was weeping now herself. 'I'm sorry. I'm sorry.'

Both women lost all track of time as they stood against the smoke-grimed, red-brick wall, clinging to each other, their tears smearing on each others cheeks.

It was Grainne who broke the embrace. Weak and spent though her grief had left her, yet she felt a new strength burgeoning as she moved her head back to look at the other woman, who was still weeping and muttering incoherent words.

'There now, it's all right. It's all right.' Grainne stroked Ellen Chester's wet cheeks with her fingers. 'It's all right, Ellen'

'I didn't mean to hurt you so, *cariad*,' The Welshwoman muttered brokenly, her breath catching in her throat. 'I only wanted you to realise what you're facing.'

Grainne remained silent for some time as she marshalled her thoughts. Then she said quite calmly, 'You were right, you know, Ellen. What you said was right. I was refusing to face reality. I was refusing to grieve for Con; to accept that the man I had married had gone for ever. I still believe that the man we have just seen is Con Shonley. I have to believe that, because I am just not strong enough to face losing him completely. But now at least, I think that I am strong enough to face what lies ahead for me; to face reality.'

The other woman's dark eyes shimmered with compassion. 'I'm glad, *cariad*. For I feared that you were on the road to madness. I feared the shock of actually seeing your man's injuries, seeing his flesh and not a swathe of bandages, would finally unhinge your mind.'

'I shall be all right now,' Grainne assured her, feeling confident that she would be so. The bitter outburst of grief had purged her of all false hopes, and where those hopes had been was now a rapidly burgeoning strength of purpose. She blamed herself for whatever had happened to Con, and she knew that she would never cease to feel guilt. But she was determined to make what amends she could, and while there existed any chance at all of the injured man being her husband, then she would do whatever she had to do to care for him. Whatever physical repulsion or moral scruples she might have against following the course that Ellen Chester prophesized, Grainne was now fully prepared to stifle, if she could find no other way of ensuring that the injured man was able to live his life in peace and comfort. And above all else she knew that to give way to her grief any more was a luxury she simply could not afford. Grief must now be buried deep within her, and only allowed to surface when she would be alone and unwatched. It must, for all their sakes, become a very private thing.

The Welshwoman studied Grainne's features, and she read in them the change that had come about in the girl's mind.

'Whatever you decide to do, then I'll help you all I can, *cariad*,' she promised, and Grainne hugged her gratefully.

'I don't know what I've done to deserve all your kindness, Ellen.'

The Welshwoman grimaced sadly. 'If I were really kind to you, Grainne, I would go right now and thrust a knife into that man's heart, to stop you doing what you intend doing for his sake.'

To her own amazement Grainne suddenly felt her heart lightening, and she was able to smile, and say jokingly, 'Don't do that, for God's sake. I couldn't bear to have you on my conscience, as well.' And, hugging the other woman fondly, she said, 'Come on now, let's go back to Brunswick Street. I want to see my new lodgings.'

Chapter Twenty-Five

The narrow court was enclosed on all sides by tall houses, their windows broken and stuffed with rags, some of the outer doors torn from their hinges. The cobbles underfoot were covered with a thick layer of stinking refuse and the ash-tip which dominated the court was an oozing mountain of filth.

Grainne's nose wrinkled at the vile stench and Ellen Chester told her, 'Your room is on the third floor, *cariad*, so you won't be able to smell this up there.'

'That's just as well!' Grainne smiled grimly. 'This would choke a pig.'

The two women entered one of the houses midway along the court and mounted the wooden stairs, which echoed hollowly under their boots. The walls were greased black by the countless bodies which had brushed against them in passing, and the plaster had fallen in great chunks to be trampled underfoot and create a rough uneven surface on each stair. The house itself reeked of damp and decay, and its dark narrow corridors and warped unpainted doors seemed to bear silent witness to the dreary hopelessness of the ruined lives that it sheltered within its rooms.

Grainne was pleasantly surprised by her own room when she unlocked and pushed open its cracked door. Its bare walls and floor looked to have been recently washed, and the sparse, shabby furnishings – large box-bed, a stuffed armchair, a battered chest of drawers, a small table and two stools – appeared reasonably clean. By the side of the rusty grate a big wooden box held coal, and a small pile of kindling lay on the hearth. A wrapped bundle of candles were on the mantelpiece next to a brass candlestick, and over the mantelpiece hung a cracked, fly-specked mirror in a very tarnished gilt frame.

'Was it you who had it cleaned up?' Grainne asked Ellen Chester, and the woman nodded.

'Mind you, the rooms in this house aren't normally too dirty. As I told you, all these rooms are rented by the judies, and most of the girls try to keep things as clean as they can.'

'It's very quiet, isn't it?' Grainne wondered, because above all else she had ever been aware of since she had landed in this city was its continual, unceasing clamour.

'They'll all be sleeping now, I should think. These girls here mostly work the dock area, and the sailors normally don't come ashore until evening time. There'll be noise and bustle enough then.' She smiled at Grainne apologetically. 'I'm sorry I couldn't find you a better place, *cariad*, but ...' She shrugged expressively. 'Anyway, when my man goes back to sea, you can always come and stay with me again.'

'Believe me, I'm grateful to you for this,' Grainne said warmly. 'Do I pay you the rent?'

'No, you pay Aggie Fields. She's the landlady, and she'll come calling on you quick enough, believe me. Anyway, the first week's rent is already paid, so you don't have to worry about that.'

'Oh but I do,' Grainne stated forcefully and insisted that the other woman take the money from her. Overriding her protests she declared, 'No Ellen, you have to take it. I can't let you do so much for me without return. I couldn't rest easy.'

Eventually Ellen Chester took the coins from Grainne. Then she smiled at the younger woman and told her, 'I don't think you'll ever know what your friendship means to me, *cariad*. You're like a breath of fresh air.'

Grainne laughed and briefly hugged the older

woman. 'Jesus, in this city a breath of fresh air is worth a king's ransom. I might do very well if I put myself on the market as fresh air.'

Ellen Chester's pale face became sombre. 'Listen, *merch fach*, I have to leave you now, because my man's ship has docked and he'll be coming to my room very soon. I shan't be able to come and see you for a few days. This one likes to keep me under his eye all the time he's on shore, and if I go anywhere without him he kicks up a terrible row, so I want you to promise me something.'

Grainne was happy to agree.

'I want you to promise me, *cariad*, that during the time we're apart, you'll think very, very carefully about what you intend doing. You might well hear and see things in this house which will fill you with disgust. You'll doubtless meet some of the girls who live here. Look well at them, *cariad*, and ask yourself if you could bear to be like them? Remember, that many of them were decent and God-fearing once, and many of them thought that they could deal with this sort of life and not take any lasting harm from it. Look at them well, *cariad*, and listen hard to what they say. Will you promise me that you'll do that?'

'I promise,' Grainne answered simply, and Ellen Chester leaned over and kissed her cheek, then left without another word.

Alone now, Grainne took her meagre belongings from her canvas bag and arranged them in the chest of drawers. She went to the bed, pulled back its coverings, and saw with relief that the sheets were clean and fresh. Unlike the corridors and stairs the room did not smell of damp and decay. Instead it held a faint scent of musk which was not unpleasant. Grainne went to the solitary sash-window pleased to find that all its unwashed panes were intact. From it she could see down into the court, and on impulse lifted the lower case, and almost instantly closed it again as the stench of the ash-tip rose in the warm, humid air.

She sat down in the armchair and, for a while, leaned back with her eyes closed and for the first time in many days allowed herself to relax completely. Her eyes closed and, listening to the buzzing of a large fly up and down the window glass, she drifted into a doze.

A brisk rapping on the door roused her, and stifling a yawn she went to open the door.

'Welcome to Africa Court, me duck. Just moved in, have you?'

The girl had a pert face and a great mass of frizzed, dyed ringlets which tumbled down her back. Her short, dumpy body was barely covered by a grubby, white night-shift, hanging so low from her shoulders that her large breasts were exposed to the nipples. 'You 'udden't ha' a drop o' the Oh be Joyful to spare, 'ud you, me duck? Me bleedin' froat's that dry I could spit fokkin' bricks.' Her accent was that of the city, and her artful blue eyes were too old for her years. 'I'm Binsy, I lives next door to you.'

Without waiting for an invitation she moved past Grainne and into the room, her eyes darting around her as if evaluating the contents. She perched on the edge of the bed, appearing very much at her ease. 'Mind you, I might not be living next door to you arter tonight, if fokkin' Aggie Fields comes looking for her rent afore I've done a bit o' business. How much is the old cow charging you?'

The young girl was so easily friendly that Grainne could not take offence at this invasion of her room.

'I'm paying four shillings.'

'What? Only four fokkin' deaners?' The girl exclaimed incredulously. 'Fokkin hell, you must have somtin' on the old bastard, mustn't you? I'm paying a deaner a night, and that's no gammon.' She grinned showing small, even, but badly discoloured teeth, and Grainne found herself thinking how pretty the girl would be if her hair were natural and her teeth clean. 'Still, good luck to you, me duck, that's what I says. I'll drink anybody's health what can do the old fokker down for a couple o' bob.' Again she grinned cheekily. 'And talking o' drinking your health, me duck, 'as you got a lush about the place? Me froat really is in desperate need.'

Grainne shook her head, and could not help but smile at the engaging girl. 'No, I'm sorry. I've no drink or anything else here at the moment.'

'Ah well, ne'er mind it, me duck. Arter all, you wasn't to know that you'd be having a lady visitor, was you?' Binsy grinned. 'What's your name, anyway?'

'It's Grainne; Grainne Shonley.'

'A Paddy arn't you? There's bleedin' fousands on 'um here. Allus has been. Fokk me, but youm pretty, arn't you though? Youm bleedin' daft to work the docks, me duck. Youse could be doing business wi' them rich fokkers up in the town.' She suddenly stopped speaking, and a broad knowing grin spread across her face. 'Hold on a minnit, me duck. That's where youse have been, arn't it? Up round the Theatre Royal and the Amphitheatre; that's where youse have been. That's why I'se never seen you afore down here. I bet you'se had a fella keeping you in a nice house, wi' your own carriage and all. That's it, arn't it?'

Grainne could not help experiencing resentment that she should be taken for a whore. But she accepted that to feel so was futile. Naturally this young girl would assume that any woman who moved into one of these rooms was a prostitute. A bitter pang cut through her as she realised that in the eyes of the world she would be regarded as a whore simply because she was living here. She pondered that point for some moments, and Binsy's blue eyes shrewdly studied the kaleidoscope of emotions fleeting across Grainne's face.

'Youse arn't a gay girl, are you?' Binsy suddenly said. 'Youse arn't on the game.'

Grainne slowly shook her head.

'What the fokkin' hell are youse doin' here in Africa Court then?' the girl demanded incredulously. 'Are youse running away from a husband or summat?'

'No, I'm not running away from anything,' Grainne told her.

'How did youse find this place?' The young girl seemed puzzled. 'Aggie Fields only rents to them she knows. How did you come to know Aggie?'

'I don't know her. It was a friend of mine who found this room for me.'

The girl winked salaciously. 'A gennulman friend?'

Grainne realised that she would get no respite from this constant questioning until the girl knew all the details. Although Grainne disliked having to tell strangers her own personal concerns, yet she also knew that while she lived here she would need to remain on good terms with the other inhabitants of the house. The world outside was hostile enough for her to contend with, it would be foolish to add the hostility of her immediate neighbours to that score.

'No, it wasn't a man. It was Ellen Chester. Do you know her?'

The pert features twisted in an effort to recollect, then grinned. 'Oh yes, Ellen Chester. That'll be Taffy Ellen. She's got a room just along Brunswick Street there, arn't she?'

Grainne nodded confirmation.

' She's a bit uppity, arn't she. Seems to reckon she's better than the rest o' the judies round here. She only goes with mates and captains, and you never sees her having the crack or taking a lush wi' the rest o' the girls. Mind you, she keeps herself to herself and don't interfere wi' anybody, and she'll allus drop you a deaner if youse are skint, so the other girls don't dislike her, for all her fokkin' snootiness.' The girl paused, then grinned cheekily. 'Could youse see your way to giving me the lend of a deaner, so I can wet me froat afore I goes trawling? I'll pay it back, cut me froat and swear to die, if I don't.'

Grainne gave her a shilling coin, which the girl bit down on with her teeth, then spun it up high in the air and caught it in her mouth. She spat it out into her hand, and grinned happily at Grainne, 'You'll do for me, me duck. See you later.'

Binsy went out whistling gaily, and Grainne smiled to herself, 'Well, at least I'll have lively company in this house, if nothing else.'

She decided to explore the premises to seek out the wash-house and whatever other conveniences it might possess. So after arranging her few belongings, she left the room and made her way down to the ground floor. A stone-flagged passage led to the rear of the house and Grainne heard voices and laughter, coming from the open doorway at the end of it. She went to the doorway and peeped through.

The room was the kitchen, with a big, rusty, iron stove which had a fire in its grate, and a table around which were lounging half a dozen girls and women, drinking and smoking cheroots and pipes. None of the women were dressed, they mostly wore only loose dressing gowns, and their hair hung shaggy and uncombed.

'Here's the new pal.'

It was Binsy who spoke, and she invited Grainne to enter with a beckoning hand. 'Come and join us, Paddy.'

Grainne accepted, and seated herself by Binsy's side.

'This is Doll, that's Fat Sal, Agnes, Charlie, Sophie, and this new pal's name is Grainne, girls.'

Binsy performed the introductions, and each woman named smiled at Grainne in a friendly way and offered her sips from their glasses or puffs from their pipes and cheroots. She didn't smoke herself, but to be sociable accepted a sip or two of gin.

'I'm looking to see where I can draw water, and where the privy is,' she told them.

'Old Molly 'ull get your water for ye, and ye'd be well advised not tae use the privy at all. Tell Old Molly tae bring ye a chamber-pot. She'll empty it for ye whenever ye need. We let her sleep here, and give her food and drink money, and she does the chores for us,'

Fat Sal, a freckled, sandy-haired Scotswoman informed her.

'Who is this Molly? Where can I find her?' Grainne questioned.

'That's her there,' Fat Sal pointed the stem of her short clay pipe towards the iron stove against the far wall.

The room was gloomy and at first Grainne took the huddled figure lying on the floor at the side of the stove to be a heap of old rags put there for burning. Then the heap moved and a resounding belch came from it, and Grainne was able to see that it was an ancient looking hag.

'She's fokkin' lushington at present, Grainne. But she'll stir herself by and by,' Binsy chortled. 'You'll know by the stink when she's moving. The poor old cow can't walk without farting. She reckons that when she was a gay girl some bugger shoved his walking cane up her arse one night and punctured it, so she can't keep any wind inside her now. It just blows out every time she walks.'

'Really Binsy, do you have to be so crude? Cannot you exercise some small degree of restraint when we have guests among us?'

It was the woman named Agnes who spoke, and Grainne looked at her with some surprise at hearing her well-bred voice. She was a thin-featured, emaciated looking woman of about thirty years, whose constant dry cough and unnaturally flushed cheeks bore witness to the consumption that was slowly killing her.

'Agnes is a lady,' Binsy informed sarcastically. 'She arn't a slumrat like me. Agnes was brung up proper, weren't you, Aggie, me duck?'

The woman stared down her long thin nose at Binsy and then told Grainne, 'My late lamented father was a clergyman, my dear and, had he lived, would now be a bishop.'

A gale of laughter greeted her words, and Fat Sal gibed, 'He was Old Moll's fancy man, that's what he was!'

'Only 'til the crushers locked him up for lifting little boys shirt-tails. Old Moll kicked the bleeder out then,' another woman joined in, and they all rocked with laughter.

Agnes regarded them with an expression of exaggerated pity, and smiled at Grainne, showing teeth that were sadly decayed. 'My father was buried in London in Saint Paul's Cathedral with all the pomp and ceremony that his exalted position deserved. Four Bishops followed his coffin to the grave.'

Binsy winked hugely at Grainne. 'That's right, that is me duck, and Old Molly was the chief mourner. She walked behind his fokkin' coffin roarin' her eyes out, and shouting, 'What the fokk shall I do now? He was me wairld! I loved his fokkin bones.''

Grainne was afflicted with a terrible urge to giggle, but tried to keep her face suitably solemn, as Agnes went on, 'I have it on the highest authority, that if my father had been of the Roman persuasion, then undoubtedly he would be a candidate for canonisation.'

Grainne could see the madness in Agnes' eyes, and felt pity for her, but that pity became tinged with alarm when the woman's clawlike hands suddenly reached across the table and grabbed her own hand in a tight grip, as she cried, 'I can save you, you know.' Agnes' voice throbbed with conviction. 'If you will but let me. We can pray together, and ask forgiveness for your sins. I shall call upon my dear father to intercede for you in Heaven. Would you like that?'

Binsy interrupted. 'Take care, Agnes, I think I hear Black Ezra coming.'

Immediately the thin woman wailed in fright, relinquished her grip and without another word scurried out of the kitchen, leaving Grainne staring after her in bewilderment.

'Black Ezra used to be her fancy man,' Binsy explained, 'and he served her fokkin' awful, so he did, the bastard. I reckon it was him a beating her so bad that sent her doo-lally-tap. All men are bastards, Grainne, but ponces are the worst bastards of all. You never wants to let any o' them get ahold of you.'

'This man, Black Ezra, does he still beat her?' Grainne asked with concern.

'He arn't able to beat anybody where he's gone, unless it's the fishes.' Binsy grinned. 'I was told that he picked on the wrong man one night, took a knife in his belly, and found a berth in the river. And a bloody good riddance too, because he drove more nor a few poor wenches to chuck themselves into the fokkin' river by his treatment of 'um. And that's no lie, is it, girls?'

The confirmation she sought came instantly.

'Are there many such men making the girls work for them?' Grainne wanted to know, fascinated by these aspects of a life she had never before heard about at first hand.

'Too many,' Fat Sal put in, 'but we won't have it in this house. There's no man comes through the door here unless he pays.'

'Apart from the fokkin' crushers,' Binsy contradicted.

'The police? Do they come here?'

Grainne's surprise caused the others to laugh, and it was the pretty mulatto girl, Sophie who answered with a flash of beautifully white teeth, 'O' course they does. They'm fokkin' men, aren't they. They gets tired o' fokkin' their wives, like all men does, and comes looking here for a bit o' fresh meat. We'em obliging to 'um, because then they leaves us alone, and if we has trouble from our customers, then they'll come and give the fokkers the heave-ho for us. And they'll have a word wi' any ponce who gets too pushy.'

'Do you get much trouble from the men who come here with you?' Grainne was enthralled.

'Not a lot really,' Fat Sal put in, 'and most times there's allus two or three of us about the house, so

205

when we hears any of the girls skriking, we all pitches in to help her. It 'ud take a champion pug to beat us lot, and he'd know he'd been in a fight, I'll tell you.'

'How many girls live here?' Grainne asked.

'Round about a dozen, usually,' Fat Sal said. 'They comes and goes, you know.'

Grainne lapsed into silence as she struggled to comprehend this strange world she had entered. She listened to the conversation between the women and girls and marvelled at how matter of factly they talked of what they did with men, and the types of men they encountered. Although she was a married woman, compared to this present company she was an innocent in sexual matters, and although she suffered the occasional twinge of disgust, she ruthlessly tried to suppress that emotion. Grainne was not a hypocrite, and refused to condemn these women for doing what they had to to survive. 'After all,' she reminded herself, 'aren't you contemplating joining their ranks yourself?'

'You arn't bin on the game afore?' It was Doll, aged twenty, with the sallow complexion and flat features of the slum child.

'Grainne shook her head. 'No, I haven't. Truth to tell, I don't really know if I'll be able to do it when the time comes.'

'You can come out wi' me, if you want. I'm going out shortly,' Doll offered. 'I'll show you the ropes.'

Grainne did not know what to say in reply. She found now that although she had become accustomed to the abstract idea of prostituting herself, the actuality of agreeing to accompany this girl this very evening appalled her.

Fat Sal's eyes, almost buried by her puffy cheeks and eyelids, regarded Grainne knowingly. 'You arn't ready for it yet, are you girl?'

Grainne sighed and bit her lips, then answered softly, 'No. I don't think I am.'

'But there's nothin' to it,' Binsy asserted cheerfully. 'Me and Doll and Sophie works the casinos and the singing rooms. We has some jinks I'll tell you! Dancing and enjoying ourselves.' She made a lewd gesture with her fingers. 'And if youm feeling randy, what's better than a good-looking sailor-boy to finish the night with? What's better than enjoying yourself, and getting fokkin' paid for it as well? It's money for jam, this work, I'll tell you no lie. Money for jam!'

All Grainne's hard-won determination was rapidly deserting her, fight though she did to retain it, her face mirrored that fact.

Fat Sal recognised what was happening to her, and scolded the two younger girls, 'Leave Grainne be! It's hard for a respectable woman to start on the game.'

'What's hard about lying on your back, and opening your legs to get fokked?' Binsy asked in genuine puzzlement.

Grainne suddenly realised the enormity of the crime that had been, and was being committed against the children of the slums every minute of every hour of every day. This girl before her was still only a child in years, but had never known a childhood. She had been born in filth and corruption, raised in filth and corruption and, unless some miracle occurred to save her, would spend all her living days, and finally die in the slums.

'And you? What about you?' a voice demanded in her mind, 'Are you now entering the same filth and corruption? Will you not be spending the rest of your days, and eventually die, in filth and corruption?'

'No!' She silently asserted. 'I'll enter that world, but I'll not let it destroy me.' A feeling of defiance flooded into her. 'If my fate is to become a whore, then I'll make being a whore pay me well. I'll not end my days like poor Old Molly by the stove there. If I'm to be forced into earning the wages of sin, then I'll make sure that those wages are good ones. I never asked to be put into this situation, and I don't think I deserved to be put into it either. If I had any other alternative, then I'd not do what I intend.' Her thoughts suddenly veered at a tangent, and she inwardly demanded of God, 'If you are watching over me, then you must know the situation I am in. If being a whore is such a terrible sin, then you show me some way I may avoid becoming a whore. Show me, I challenge you to show me!'

Fat Sal waited patiently until Grainne became aware once more of her surroundings, then told her, 'You listen tae me, hen, I know something of how you must be feeling right now. Ye must remember that for these girls and thousands o' wains like them, they've never known any other sort o' life at all. They've seen every sort o' wickedness that there is tae see, from the time they was birthed. They came to this trade like a bird comes tae flying. They've never had anything else that they could come tae. So in a way, I suppose it's easier for them, God ha' mercy on them.

But I was nae always a tail. I was reared by guid, God-fearing parents who loved me well. I married and had two bairns. My man was a sailor. He got drownded off the coast of Greenland. I worked at sewing, cleaning, anything I could to try and feed my bairns. But we all ended up in the bloody bastille, the bloody workhouse. Doing this is the only way I can get enough money to ha'e my bairns cared for. They're wi' my auntie back in Scotland, and I send money for them every fortnight.

The first time I went wi' a man for money, I felt so shamed I thought I'd die of it. But all the time I was laying under him I kept on telling myself that I was nae doing it for my pleasure. I was doing it for my bairns. It was all I could dae, and it was putting food in their belly, clothes on their backs, and keeping a warm roof over their heads. So it was nae wicked or evil what I was daeing, because I was daeing it for the right reason. Now, I can see that you're troubled by the thought of going on the game, but if you're daeing it for the right reason, then I canna see that there's anything wrong wi' daeing it.'

Grainne smiled wryly. 'The priests would give you an argu- ment about that, Sal.'

The other woman's face twisted scornfully, 'Oh aye! They bloody black crows point their bloody fingers at us, and call us scarlet women, and whores of Babylon, right enough. But where were all those bastards when my bairns were being torn away frae me in the bloody workhouse? Why didn't they gi' me some means o' fillin' my bairns wee bellies instead o' bloody stupid prayers and hymns? You can't eat prayers and hymns, hen. And ye canna use a sermon tae keep the wind and rain off ye in the night.' She paused, her lips still moving angrily as she relived old memories, then went on, 'Dae ye under- stand what I'm telling ye?'

Grainne nodded. 'I think so. What you're saying is that beggars haven't got the luxury of choice.'

For a moment the others around the table stared blankly at her, then Fat Sal thumped the table-top resoundingly and roared with laughter. 'That's it! That's just it! So you just dae whatever ye have to, hen, and tell them that don't like it, but that they can kiss your bloody arse!'

Grainne drew a deep breath suppressing any incip- ient self-pity she might feel at the cruel fortune which had brought her to this plight. During the famine back in Skibereen she had seen women prostituting them- selves for a piece of bread. Women who had always lived chaste lives. Grainne was tough-minded enough to accept that she would do whatever she had to in order to care for Con, and she would not waste strength in bewailing her lot, or in trying to find excuses for what she did, or, most important of all, allowing herself to indulge in self-condemnation.

She smiled to herself with a bitter irony. 'If I am to be a whore, then I shall be a proud whore, and hold my head high.'

Fat Sal stared long and hard at Grainne, then chuckled and held out her hand. 'Shake hands wi' one o' your new sisters, hen. We'll help ye all we can.'

Grainne took the proffered hand, and it seemed to her that she had crossed over a river, and left all her bridges burning behind her.

'So be it,' she accepted solemnly. 'So be it.'

'Whose got any push? Because I'm skint.' It was Charlie, who until now had been silently puffing on a long cheroot. She was another under-sized, sallow-faced Liverpudlian who looked about fourteen years old to Grainne's eyes.

'Fokk off, Charlie!' Sophie answered indignantly. 'You arn'r paid your wack for bleedin' days. You ought to be putting some money on the table.'

All the rest of the younger girls joined in, accusing Charlie, and she answered back with a spate of shrill denials.

Fat Sal winked at Grainne. 'Pay no heed to the silly besoms, Grainne. You come on up to my room and we'll have a little talk.'

On their way out Fat Sal stirred the motionless heap of rags that was Old Moll with her foot, and instructed her to look after Grainne as regards water and a chamber pot.

Fat Sal's room was very like Ellen Chester's, with a profusion of cheap crock ornaments, and a cluttering of furniture.

She produced a bottle of French brandy and two tumblers from a cupboard.

'We'll have a couple o' drams and a wee bit o' crack.' She smiled at Grainne.

When they were both settled in overstuffed arm-chairs with their glasses in their hands, Fat Sal asked Grainne, 'Where are ye thinking o' working?'

Grainne shrugged, and grimaced ruefully. 'I haven't thought of that really. I've been thinking more about if I can do it, rather than where!'

The fat woman nodded understandingly. 'I should-'nae worry overmuch about if ye can dae it, hen. When the time comes, make sure that ye're full o' drink. That way it 'ull be a sight easier to dae. Ye'll hardly feel it.

Now tell me all about yersel'.'

Although Grainne was normally a reticent person, she had noticed a change within herself since the wreck of the *Florida*. She had felt very lonely, and had welcomed company for its own sake. Before the wreck she had always enjoyed being alone. Now, she feared it. Before the wreck, although she had always been ready to be friendly to people she did not know, she had always been reluctant to tell them about her personal life. Now she found herself almost eager to tell even a comparative stranger such as this woman, all about herself and her life. She launched into her story, and Fat Sal listened with an avid interest. When Grainne had finished and lapsed into silence, the Scotswoman leaned forward and patted her hand.

'Ye've a tough old row to hoe, hen. But ye'll manage it, nae doubt o' that. If ye like, I'll come wi' ye the morrow tae the Dispensary. It might be as well for ye to hae some other body wi' ye when ye see your man being unwrapped.'

'Yes, I think you're right about that, Sal. I'd like you with me,' Grainne accepted.

'Right then, ye're on. And now I've got tae get dressed and do a wee bit o' trawling. Sitting here won't pay the rent. You take the bottle wi' you, hen, and take a few drams. It'll help ye tae sleep.'

Although Grainne had never been a heavy drinker, she welcomed the suggestion. 'But you must let me pay for the bottle,' she insisted, and despite Fat Sal's protests pressed the money on her.

Back in her own room she sat looking into the empty, rusty grate, sipping brandy and allowing her thoughts to drift where they would. She found herself remembering long-forgotten incidents and people of her childhood. Darkness fell and from within the house she heard doors slam at intervals, and voices, both male and female, raised in drunken singing. With a shock she suddenly realised that she had not thought of Con for several hours, and puzzled as to why that should have been. She felt curiously detached; her emotions numbed as she thought of what the next day might bring. And finally, she stretched out on her bed and fell asleep.

Chapter Twenty-Six

It was two o'clock in the afternoon and the weather was grey and dismal. The burly gate porter at the North Dispensary stared hard at Grainne for some seconds, then recognition came.

'Youse was here afore.'

'That's right. My friend died here.' Grainne could not shake the feeling of foreboding which had oppressed her senses since she had woken that morning.

'Hold on, Miss.'

The porter disappeared into his small lodge for a few seconds, then came out and told the two women, 'Dr Galbraith left a message consarning youse. It's Mrs Shonley, arn't it?'

'It is,' Grainne confirmed.

'Right, youse are to go round to the dead shed at the back o' the east wing there. The doctor will meet you there.'

'The dead shed?' Grainne queried, her heart thudding fearfully.

The man grinned reassuringly. 'Don't worry, missis, it's only a name. Youse had best get round their quick, because Dr Galbraith arn't a gennulman who likes to be kept waiting.'

Grainne and Fat Sal hurried through the gate and around the back of the building, where they saw a small tar-painted wooden lean-to.

'Dear God!' Dread struck through Grainne. 'Is that a mortuary?'

Even as she spoke the words her name was called, and a smiling Malcom Galbraith came walking to her with an outstretched hand.

'I've good news for you, Grainne.' His eyes swept over Fat Sal, and his well-shaped lips curled slightly. 'That's a tail alright!' he thought, as he evaluated the fat woman's tawdry, gaudy dress and shawl, her hair hanging down her back, contained in a long hair net festooned with bright ribbons.

'I've redressed your husband, and I'm happy to say that his injuries are not as bad as Dr Sinclair led me to believe.'

Simultaneous relief and delight caused Grainne to laugh aloud, and tears brimmed in her eyes.

Galbraith stared at her hungrily, his thoughts racing. 'You're consorting with tails now, aren't you, little Grainne? I don't think that you're quite the innocent you make yourself out to be, my girl! I don't think that I shall need to tread so carefully with you, as I thought I might.' But aloud, he invited, 'Please do step inside, ladies.' He bowed them through the door of the small shed, Fat Sal captivated by his good lucks and charming manners.

The white-washed interior contained only the box-bed of the patient and Grainne felt a pang of disappointment to see the bandaged man still lying motionless, looking the same as when she had last seen him.

'Is he all right, lying sae quiet?' Fat Sal asked in a whisper, and Malcom Galbraith chuckled genially.

'I keep the poor fellow opiated, ma'am. Burns are amongst the most agonising of injuries, and I have always considered that it is better to opiate, than to suffer.'

'Well you'd know the best thing tae dae, your Honour.' Fat Sal was rapidly becoming infatuated with this charming, handsome man.

Grainne stood gazing at the patient, and was again experiencing that curious sense of emotional detachment. When she spoke it was as if she were enquiring after a stranger.

'You said that the injuries were not as bad as you had feared, Malcom?'

He assumed an air of gravity. 'I must warn you to understand what I said was purely relative. When I said they were not as bad as I had feared, I meant only that. All being well, he will survive, and maybe even survive for the full span of his years. However ...'

He hesitated, reluctant to continue, and remained so until Grainne urged, 'Go on, I must know. Don't concern yourself about my feelings, I am strong enough to bear whatever you may tell me.'

Galbraith sighed heavily. 'Very well then, Grainne. If you so wish. He will live, but I fear that his sight is gone. His hands are so badly anchylosed that he will only be able to use them as hooks, and his head and face are badly damaged. He will not be pleasant to look upon.'

'Has his mind been damaged?' Grainne pressed.

The doctor shrugged. 'I cannot tell you that, Grainne. That will only become apparent as time passes. Hopefully, once the shock has worn off, he will be fully *compos mentis*, and, as we already know, his hearing appears unimpaired. As for his speech, I see no reason why he should not be able to formulate his words in some form or other. Perhaps he will be hard to understand at first, but you will accustom yourself to it as time passes.'

He pulled a gold hunter-watch from his waistcoat pocket and glanced at its ornate face. 'I'll have to leave you for a time. Please wait for me here.'

When the two women were alone, Fat Sal nudged Grainne suggestively. 'Ye never told me he was sae guid-looking, that doctor fella.'

Grainne shook her head absently. 'When I'm here I only really see my Con.'

'Aye, o' course ye would.' Fat Sal radiated sympathetic understanding. 'Jesus! The puir fella's in some bloody state, isn't he!'

She went to the side of the box-bed and lifted the

coverings so that she could see the patient's lower body. 'He looks tae be a well-made man, Grainne.' She swung her head to ask abruptly. 'Canna ye tell if it's your man or nae, by his legs and balls?'

Grainne grimaced wryly, and shook her head.

'Nae, perhaps ye canna,' Fat Sal said reflectively. 'Come tae think of it, all dicks look alike don't they, unless they're Jewish, or black.'

She dropped the coverings back and then looking searchingly at Grainne, asked, 'Would ye like me tae leave ye here by yerself wi' him, hen? It's nae bother tae me. I can take a walk through the wards and see if there's anybody I know here.'

'All right Sal, if you like.'

Grainne seemed almost indifferent, and Fat Sal looked at her closely. 'Are you all right, hen?'

'Yes, I'm fine.' Grainne tried to smile assurance.

'Aye, all right then. I'll come back in a wee while.' Still looking doubtfully at Grainne, Fat Sal went from the shed.

Grainne remained standing where she was, looking at the bandaged head and listening to the harsh stertorous breathing. The curious feeling of detachment persisted and strengthened, and she experienced no grief as she regarded the man who she believed to be her husband, only the sure knowledge that no matter how long he might live, she would do her utmost to care for him, and to ensure that his life would contain as much ease and comfort as she could procure for him.

She could not tell how long she had been alone, when Malcom Galbraith re-entered the shed.

'Has your friend gone?' he asked.

'She'll return shortly.' Grainne told him, and then added, 'I want to thank you for all your kindness to my husband and me, Malcom.'

He waved her thanks aside. 'It is my pleasure, Grainne. I have much to talk with you about.' He glanced around him deprecatingly. 'But this is not the place to suit. I want you to dine with me tonight.' He smiled warmly. 'Will you do so?'

When she made no reply, he frowned slightly. 'I am acting as your friend, Grainne. I have much to say to you concerning your future, and the future of your husband.'

'Can you not tell me here?' Grainne questioned, as she was very undecided about Galbraith's invitation.

The slight frown of annoyance creasing his broad, smooth brow momentarily deepened, then the lines smoothed as he smiled regretfully, and said, 'Alas, no, my dear girl. I am to perform an operation very shortly, so time is pressing, and what I have to say may take considerable time. That is why I ask you to meet me tonight. Besides, what is wrong about two friends sharing a meal? There is no impropriety in that, is there?'

Grainne smiled a trifle shamefacedly; inwardly angry with herself. 'Why must you be so suspicious of this man? Has he not always been kindness itself to you?' she thought and told him, 'Very well, I'll meet you.'

'Good.' He beamed happily. 'Do you know where the Lime Street railway station is?'

'Yes.' She nodded.

'We'll meet on the portico there at eight o'clock.'

Fat Sal came back into the room, and Galbraith made his goodbyes.

'Come, we'll go,' Grainne told her, and went over to the bed to whisper, 'Sleep well, Con darling. I'll come again tomorrow.'

On the way back to Africa Court Grainne was silent, immersed in her own thoughts, and Fat Sal respecting her feeling, stayed silent as well.

Chapter Twenty-Seven

When the two women reached Africa Court Grainne made the excuse of a bad headache and went to her room. She felt restless, her nerves jangled and she was tense. The bottle of brandy was still half-full, and filling a tumbler with the golden liquid she stood at her window sipping it, gazing at the seedy façades of the houses opposite.

Shouts attracted her attention and she looked down into the court itself. Two women were standing face to face, arms on their hips, shrieking insults at each other, and as Grainne watched frowsty heads appeared from windows, and a small knot of eager onlookers gathered in the court itself.

Suddenly the two women flew at each other and, biting, scratching, kicking, clawing at each others hair and faces, they went rolling over and over in the filth.

From one of the doorways a man came charging, dressed in shirtsleeves and trousers, a pair of heavy boots on his feet. He ran to where the women were fighting and began to kick them indiscriminately until, to escape him, they broke from their clinch and rolled away from each other. He grabbed one of the women by her long, streaming hair and dragged her across the cobbles, stopping only to kick her brutally when she screamed, until her face was a mass of blood and she fell limp and silent. Then he carried on dragging her across the broken doorstep and into the house.

The spectators excitedly discussed the event, laughing and joking, and then two of them lifted the other brawler onto her feet, and helped her to limp out of the court.

In Grainne's own house doors slammed, feet thumped on hollow boarding, and a shrill voice shrieked, 'Sophieeee? Sophieee? Sophieeeee? Sophieeeee?' over and over again until Grainne felt like screaming herself at every infuriating repetition.

'Could I keep Con here?' she asked herself. 'Could I expect him to be content to dwell here in Africa Court; to live amongst this savagery, and this noise, day after day, night after night?'

She lifted the bottle to refill her tumbler, and was surprised to see how much brandy she had drunk since returning from the Dispensary.

'Jesus Christ! I'm getting to be as big a drunkard as poor Denis.'

The thought of Denis Callaghan triggered a further chain of thought in Grainne's mind. 'Should I take Con back home? Back to Ireland?' But even as she thought of it, she dismissed it as an impossibility. People were fleeing that unhappy land in their millions to escape death from starvation and disease. 'And we've no one there who could aid us. God only knows what state Denis is in. He could be dead himself by now. And my Mammy, God help the poor soul! I could bring her nothing but more grief than she's got already. Could I somehow get word to Con's mother, and ask her to help?'

Dejectedly Grainne dismissed that possibility too. It would take months for any letter to reach the Mahoneys in India, and many more months before Grainne could receive any help from them. 'We would both be dead of starvation long before they could help us.'

She became aware of the uncomfortable emptiness of her stomach, and recollected that she had not eaten since breakfast, the previous day.

'Yes, I'll meet him,' she decided. 'I'll meet Malcom Galbraith and have a meal with him.'

She went downstairs to find Old Molly and have her

219

bring water to her room.

The drizzle of the afternoon had turned by the
evening into a hard rain, but Grainne was sheltered
under the huge Grecian canopy of Lime Street railway
station's entrance. She stood next to one of the massive
pillars, her shawl drawn over her head, and passed the
time by watching the many travellers enter and leave
the station.

A railway policeman, dressed in a dark-green
frockcoat, with a tall black tophat on his bullet head
came pacing ponderously past Grainne. His eyes
studied her suspiciously. She ignored him, and he
frowned and passed on. Then a short time later came
back, and this time stood next to her, rocking
backwards and forwards on his heels, humming
tunelessly to himself.

Grainne was uncomfortably aware of his constant
scrutiny, but at the same time pleased because his
presence kept at bay the persistent importuners who
infested the station.

At last the policeman spoke to her. 'Are youse
waiting for somebody?'

'I am,' she told him shortly.

'Who?' he wanted to know.

'For a friend.'

'What sort of friend?'

Grainne looked at him angrily. 'What concern is it of
yours?'

His heavy red face scowled. 'Don't gi' me any o' your
lip, Paddy. Or I'll be bloody well lifting yez.'

'For what?' Grainne demanded indignantly. 'I've
done nothing wrong. I'm only waiting here.'

'Is there anything the matter, Officer?'

The sound of Malcom Galbraith's voice made
Grainne to turn to see him standing behind her.

'This young woman, sir, she's loitering suspiciously.'
The constable saluted, when he saw Galbraith's fine
clothes, and heard his educated accents.

'This lady is waiting for me, Constable,' Galbraith informed the man, then ignoring him dismissively, he smiled at Grainne. 'My apologies, my dear. I was unexpectedly detained. Come, I've a cab waiting.'

He took her arm and led her across the wide street towards a hansom cab.

As the small vehicle rattled along Grainne sat stiffly in the corner of the leather seat, and gazed at the reflections of the gas lamps on the wet roadway and the diamond flashes of the rain caught in the light as they spattered into a myriad of tiny droplets. Deliberately she fought to control her thoughts, afraid that if she allowed her emotions to dominate, she would jump from the cab and run off into the darkness of the night. Sensing the turmoil that raged within her Malcom Galbraith made no attempt to talk.

The cab stopped in a quiet street lined with elegant houses, and Malcom Galbraith helped Grainne down from the vehicle, then paid the cabby.

'Where are we?' she asked.

He smiled at her, and she thought him very handsome in the gaslight.

'We are standing outside Number Fourteen, Rodney Street, my dear Grainne. My cook has prepared an excellent meal, and my man-servant is, I'm sure, waiting on tiptoe to lay it before us.'

Galbraith's rooms were on the second floor of the tall house, and were opulently furnished. The man-servant opened the door to Galbraith's knock, and registered no interest in Grainne's arrival.

The table was already laid, and Grainne was impressed by the fine plate and silver cutlery. Having been in titled service herself, she could recognise the quality of everything before her in the gas-lit dining room.

The impassive man-servant waited on them, and Malcom Galbraith proved to be a charming and attentive host. Grainne felt herself to be in some sort of limbo. It was as if she were outside of herself, watching a strange woman eat and drink, and talk with Malcom Galbraith.

When they had eaten Malcom Galbraith invited her into his drawing room and seated her on a lavishly brocaded armchair before the fire.

She took brandy and water, and they sat in silence for some considerable time. Then Galbraith asked her, 'What are your plans, Grainne? What do you intend doing now?'

Keeping her eyes on the flames darting and wavering, Grainne told him, 'I intend to care for my husband.'

'That does you much credit.'

Galbraith's handsome face was slightly flushed, and his eyes continually moved up and down Grainne's face and body. She wore only a plain, high-necked dark dress without any ornament or jewellery, and her dark hair was simply plaited and corded around her head; her face innocent of paint or powder. It was the natural beauty and quiet grace of her manner and appearance that attracted Galbraith above all else. Of course, he lusted for her firm high breasts jutting out against the thin fabric of her bodice, and the slender shapeliness of her body, but her beauty was of a type that also moved him romantically.

'Take care, Galbraith,' he reminded himself. 'Don't get smitten with this girl. She's only a slum-rat, after all.'

'I don't think caring for my husband can be called a credit to me,' she said quietly. 'I love him, and it is the duty of a wife to care for her husband in sickness and in health, is it not?'

The young man chuckled. 'I see a good many wives in my work, Grainne, and there's a high proportion of them who would not agree with you on that score.'

She merely smiled.

'I don't wish to talk about such painful matters now, Grainne, but it is very necessary that you make some arrangements to find shelter for your husband. He will not be able to remain in the Dispensary for very much longer, I'm afraid.'

The news shocked Grainne. 'I thought you wanted to study him?' she queried. 'And I assumed that it would be many weeks before he would be well enough to be discharged from the hospital.'

Galbraith's tone was regretful. 'You must understand, my dear, that there is a constant stream of applicants for entry to our wards, and that every day we are forced to turn cases away, who in all honesty well deserve admittance. Naturally, if it will help you, I will endeavour to keep your husband in the Dispensary as long as I possibly can. But I do not have the final decision on that length of stay, Grainne. The Head Surgeon decides in the end.'

'But if you knew that you would not be able to keep Con in your hospital, why then did you have him transferred there?' Grainne questioned.

'Because if I had not done so Dr Sinclair would have had your husband moved to the sick ward of the workhouse this very day. As it was I was forced to argue most heatedly with the fellow before he would allow me to take your husband as one of my patients.'

Grainne sat mulling over what he had told her. Then she asked, 'How long then, before Con is discharged?'

'A week perhaps, ten days at most.'

A thrill of real fear shuddered through Grainne. She now had only a few shillings left to her, and if Con was to be discharged within a week, she knew that she must somehow earn enough money in the next few days to prepare for him.

'Do you have any money, Grainne?' Galbraith asked her.

'I've some.' She dared not let herself compute how little.

'How much?'

'Some sixteen or seventeen shillings.

'That'll not last many days,' he told her.

Again they lapsed into silence, and the young man

223

became annoyed with himself for his own hesitance. 'Dear God, Galbraith, what a damn fool you are! Why are you acting as if you were some love-sick puppy, and she the highest born lady in the land? She's only a slum-rat! A damned slum-rat who lives with tails, and most likely is a bloody tail herself. And here's you, you damn fool, behaving as if she were some delicate flower.'

Grainne could sense the tensions in the young man, and mindful of what Ellen Chester had said to her, she thought she could guess something of what was causing his tension.

Nevertheless it still came as an unpleasant shock when he calmly proposed, 'Why not allow me to look after you, Grainne? Then I could ensure that you would be able to care for your husband. You'll find that I am a generous man.'

Despite all her rationalisations of the past days Grainne still couldn't prevent a sudden burgeoning anger and resentment. She stared at him levelly, and he seemed to become uneasy and have some difficulty in meeting her eyes.

'What do you mean when you say, *Look after me?*' she asked, determined to force him away from delicate allusions.

He flushed slightly, and his tone became edged with a blustering defensiveness. 'Exactly what I said, look after you.'

'But why should you do so much for me, Malcom, without any recompense?' She surprised herself with her own ability to act the shrew.

He scowled and, his blush deepening, he spoke angrily, 'Very well, you drive me to speak plainly. So be it. I'll speak plain. I want you to become my mistress. You would be well looked after, and you could afford to have your husband cared for.'

He rose to his feet and went to the sideboard to splash more brandy into his glass. Terrible humiliation burned through Grainne, and she wanted to cringe; to hunch her body as small as she could, and hide her face from the world. First her anger erupted and she wanted to shriek abuse at this man, and hurl the glass she held at his head. Then she had the desire to flee; to jump up and run and run and run until she reached an empty hidden place where she might escape from all trouble.

But she did none of these things. Instead she suppressed all her rampaging emotions, and forced herself to think.

Moodily Galbraith drained his glass and refilled it. He stared at the upright figure, head erect, silhouetted by the firelight, and gnawed his lower lip. His feelings were confused. He wanted this woman more than any other woman he had ever met. He was angry at his own inability to regard her as nothing more than just another affair. Yet he was forced to admit even at this moment there was that in her which stirred the poetry in his soul.

'Look, Grainne,' he gestured placatingly with his hand. 'I spoke too bluntly, and I'm sorry for it. My feeling for you overcame me. I ... that is ... I ... I want ...' He fumbled for words, but could find none, and faltered into silence.

Grainne did not turn her head to look at him, neither did she speak. She merely remained sitting, back straight, head held high, her eyes fixed on the flickering flames. A strange calm had come over her, bringing with it a curious sense of detachment and numbed emotions. She was able to think with a surprising clarity and precision, and consider her course of action.

She rose to her feet, and turned to face the man, saying, 'I should like to leave now, Malcom. Many thanks for the dinner,' she told him in a neutral tone.

He stared hard at her, wanting to detain her if he could, but instinctively his wide experience of women told him that at this moment he should not try and keep her there.

'Of course, my dear. I'll send my man to fetch a cab for you.' he said softly.

She shook her head. 'No, I'd sooner make my own way home, thank you.'

He spread his hands placatingly. 'Very well, my dear, whatever you prefer.'

He came to the fireplace and tugged on the silken bell-rope which hung at its side. When the man-servant came in answer to the summons, he told him, 'Mrs Shonley is leaving now. Show her to the door.'

Facing Grainne, he offered her his hand and not wanting to part enemies, Grainne took it briefly. He smiled then told her in a low voice, 'Remember, a message here will always find me,' and half-bowed in farewell.

The mood of detachment persisted in Grainne on her walk back to Africa Court, and she moved through the drunken, rowdy, crowds on the streets, hardly conscious of their presence. She thought dispassionately of what had occured that night.

'Despite what Ellen Chester told me, I still believed that Malcom Galbraith was only acting in friendship.' Her lips curved in a mirthless smile. 'A precious fool I was! But then, I keep on forgetting that where I live is a message to the world, Here is a whore!' A pang of bitterness pricked her. 'The only difference between me and the other girls in Africa Court, is that at least they've got the courage to be real whores and be paid for it. I only carry the name, and I haven't got the courage to take the benefits.'

A drunken man came from the doors of a garishly-lit gin palace, and tried to accost her.

'Hey girlie, d'you wanna drink? Come an 'ave a drink.'

Grainne side-stepped his clumsy lunge and ran on past him, quickly out-distancing his stumbling pursuit. She slowed to a walk, and found that she was actually considering the implications of Malcom Galbraith's offer.

'What did he mean, "well looked after"? What would that amount to, I wonder?' Again her lips curved in that mirthless smile. 'Well, he did say he was generous. I might make a fortune from him!'

She turned into Brunswick Street, and looked up at Ellen Chester's window, but all was darkness there. In the darker stretches of the road, huddled in entries and doorways, were the shadowy veiled figures of women. Grainne's lips twitched in mingled pity and disgust. These were the casualties of the game. Those who were too disfigured by age or disease or both to be able to attract men in the light, so they lurked here in the darkness, ready to perform any perversion for mere pennies; ready to risk their hopeless lives with any degraded, bestial man who would buy their wares. Grainne shuddered as the thought struck her that there but for the Grace of God, she could end her own days.

She reached Africa Court and turned into the dark covered entry. As she did, she collided with a human body and shrieking, jumped back into the roadway. Then peering back into the gloom, she saw that she had bumped into a man with his trousers around his ankles, his hips driving into the woman he had got crushed against the greasy, damp wall, her skirts bunched up to her waist. Grainne retreated across the road, and waited until the couple had finished and left. Then she hurried through the entry-way and up the stairs to her room.

She lit no candle, but fumbled in the darkness until she had found the bottle containing the last of the brandy. She drank from the bottle itself, and the fiery liquid caused her to splutter and cough. She sat on the armchair with the bottle clutched to her breasts.

From Binsy's room next door to her own she could hear through the thin walls the rhythmic creaking of a bed, and the mingled grunts and gasps of Binsy and the man she was with.

Once again Grainne was racked by indecision and

doubt. 'Can I really do what Binsy is doing even now? When it comes to the actual moment, will I be able to lie down with a man and let him do whatever he wants to me?'

She drained the last drops from the bottle and dropped it beside her on the floor. 'If I accepted Malcolm Galbraith's offer, then in a way I would be like his wife. He would expect me to sleep only with him.' Ruthlessly she forced herself to be honest. 'He's very handsome, and if I were not already married, and he came courting me, then no doubt I'd enjoy making love with him. But that's the problem. If I agreed now to become his mistress, and then found that I enjoyed sleeping with him, I'd be a whore in the real sense. I would be unfaithful to Con in my heart, as well as with my body.'

She stood up and began to pace restlessly up and down the room. From next door the creaking of the bed increased in tempo, and the loud grunting erupted into a drawn-out wailing moan, then all was abruptly silence. The silence was finally broken by Binsy's shrill voice, 'Hey, jack, don't you fokkin' fall asleep on me. Get up, willya!'

Grainne came to a sudden decision. 'That's the only way it can be done; to go only with faceless strangers who can make no demands on me other than the few minutes they have paid for the use of me. That way, in my heart, I shall always be faithful to Con, because there will be no danger of any emotional attachment. It will, purely and simply a business transaction.'

Her foot caught the empty bottle and sent it spinning across the floor. 'That shall be my tool,' she told herself. 'I'll drink before I go with anyone, and then I'll be better able to bear what I'm doing.'

She moved to the window and stared through the cracked panes at the lights glimmering through the windows of the houses opposite, and was still standing in that same position when the dawn finally paled over the roofs of Liverpool.

Chapter Twenty-Eight

Four days had passed since Grainne had dined with Malcom Galbraith, and every afternoon she had visited Con in the Dispensary, but had seen nothing of the young doctor himself. She had made contact again with Liza Davis, the fat nurse, and had given her half a sovereign so that she would keep watch on Con, and do whatever she could for him.

Now it was Thursday afternoon, and Grainne was sitting on a stool by the side of Con's box-bed in the small shed. She had a single shilling left to her, and knew that this coming night she would have to finally face what she dreaded. It was for this reason that she had eaten nothing that day, but had kept her last shilling intact. She intended to deaden her feelings with drink, before she went in search of a customer.

During the hours that Grainne spent by Con's bedside she had talked to him almost continuously, but had received no response of any kind. Liza Davis told her that Dr Galbraith had insisted on keeping the patient deeply sedated with frequent administrations of the tincture of opium, and gave it as her personal opinion that this was the best thing for the injured man.

'He arn't feeling no pain, is he. You should be grateful that Dr Galbraith is a kind-hearted chap. If he weren't, then this poor bowsy 'ud be hollerin' day and night, I'll tell youse. Burns and scalds is the most trying of all injuries. Some I'se seen has screamed themselves to death wi' the agony of it,' she had said.

Liza Davis came bustling into the shed now, and greeted Grainne cheerily, 'How bist, Mrs Shonley?'

Grainne tried to smile, but her spirits were sadly depressed and the smile was more of a grimace. 'I'm well, Mrs Davis.'

The woman had brought with her a small bladder, a tube and a pannikin containing a mixture of milk, brandy and the opium tincture.

'I'm going to gi' my lord here, his rations,' Liza Davis informed Grainne.

'Has Dr Galbraith mentioned anything more about my husband being discharged?' Grainne asked.

"The House Surgeon 'ull be making his rounds tomorrow, Mrs Shonley. He'll decide then who'se to go and who'se to stay,' the nurse told her.

'And if he decides Con is to go, when will I have to move him?'

'On the day after. That 'ull be Saturday won't it? We usually gets 'um up and ready to leave by midday. I should think youse'll be looking forrards to that, having your man back home wi' youse.' Grainne nodded, but inwardly her heart quailed at the prospect.

'I've still got nowhere to take him, except Africa Court,' she voiced her thoughts, and Liza smiled bluffly.

'You hark to me, my love, he won't be knowing where he is iffen you keeps on dosing him with the opium. Anyways, what's wrong wi' Africa Court? Where is it exactly?'

'It's off Brunswick Street,' Grainne told her.

The fat face mirrored surprise, and the half-buried eyes peered questioningly at Grainne. 'You lives down Tiger Bay?'

'Yes, I do. You seem surprised by that?' Grainne was instantly defensive.

'Oh nooo,' the fat woman appeared slightly flustered, 'it's just that you don't look the type o' young woman to be living there. You looks too respectable for that area.'

Grainne could think of no reply to make, and instead pointedly changed the subject.

'Do you notice a different sort of smell coming from my husband's bandaging, Mrs Davis? From there,' she indicated a large damp, foul-smelling area covering his right shoulder and upper arm.

The fat woman put her nose close to the discoloured stain and sniffed, and her face registered a doubtful frown. 'It smells almost like rotting meat, Mrs Davis.'

Grainne's own vague anxiety concerning the freshly appearing stain and smell crystalised into alarm as she saw the other woman's reaction. 'Could it be gangrene?'

'Nooo o' course not,' the fat woman assured bluffly. 'Nooo, it's just the natural discharges, that is. It's just the badness a-coming out of him. It's a good sign, Mrs Shonley. It shows that his body is throwing out all the pus and such like.'

'Are you changing his dressings as I asked you to?' Grainne wanted to know.

'O' course I am!' the fat woman seemed ready to take offence at this aspersion on her professional integrity. 'I promised youse that I'd look arter him, and that's exactly what I'se done. I been nussing here for more years than I cares to remember, Mrs Shonley, and I'm known as a good nuss, and a woman of her word. You can ask anybody about that.'

Grainne did not wish to quarrel with the woman, so she tried to mollify her. 'I don't doubt you, Mrs Davis. It's just that I'm worried about him. Did you see anything wrong with his shoulder and arm when you changed his dressing last?'

'No I never!' the fat woman snapped. 'If I had, then I'd ha' bring it to the Doctor's notice, 'udden't I?'

Suddenly Grainne felt that she could not bear to remain in this cramped, foul-smelling space for a moment longer. She had to get out into the air and be by herself. With a mumbled farewell she hurried from the shed and headed around the building towards the gate lodge.

In the main entrance of the Dispensary Malcom

231

Galbraith was standing in conversation with one of his colleagues. He saw the dark-gowned woman with the shawl drawn close about her face hurrying throught the gates, and knew it was Grainne Shonley. Quickly he excused himself and went after her.

'Grainne? Grainne?'

The sound of her name being shouted brought Grainne to a halt and she stopped and turned around. When Galbraith reached her, she asked immediately, 'When is Con being discharged?'

His handsome features were uneasy, as he told her, 'I think that the House Surgeon will want him gone by Saturday, Grainne. There is nothing more that can be done for your husband here. It is now only a question of waiting for him to heal. I cannot truthfully justify to my superior any necessity to retain your husband here any longer.'

'Very well, I shall come for him on Saturday,' Grainne said quietly.

'Have you now found somewhere to take him?' Galbraith asked.

'He'll have to share my room at Africa Court. I'm sure we'll manage very well.' Grainne smiled ruefully. 'After all, in this city there's precious few who have the luxury of only two to a room.' She did not say that in any sarcastic sense but only as a simple statement of fact.

'Goodbye, Dr Galbraith. I shall always be grateful for your kindness to Con.'

She turned on her heel and hurried away, leaving Malcom Galbraith staring after her with very mixed feelings.

Chapter Twenty-Nine

It was early evening and only Fat Sal and Grainne were in the kitchen of Number Three, Africa Court. A candle was smoking on the table next to the bottle of gin that Grainne had purchased earlier. Fat Sal had tried to persuade Grainne to paint her lips and rouge and powder her face, but Grainne would not.

'It's bad enough, what I shall be doing tonight,' she thought, 'without me advertising shamelessly to all the world what I have become.'

The raw spirits she had been tossing down her throat on an empty stomach made her feel tipsily light-headed, but did nothing to dull her sense of shame.

'Now, you've got your sponge-box tucked safe away, have ye, hen?' Fat Sal sought confirmation. 'Whatever ye dae, don't forget to use them.'

Grainne nodded wearily, and her fingers felt the hard outlines of the small box in the pocket of her gown. It contained small sponges soaked in vinegar which she would insert into her vagina before intercourse as a preventative against impregnation.

'I always use a bladder and flood meself straight after doing it, as well,' Fat Sal went on. 'That way ye can be double sure that ye have nae copped for a bloody sprog. Have ye put the water and things in your room, like I told ye to?'

Again Grainne nodded, and her eyes brimmed with tears.

'Hey now! Come on, lassie! No skriking now. Ye'll

not earn any pennies if ye're going to be roaring your bloody eyes out. The customers are looking for a good time, not a bloody funeral.'

Fat Sal was not being unkind. She remember her own first time out on the streets, and she knew well how this young girl was feeling at this moment. She patted the limp hand lying on the table before her.

'Now you listen, hen. Once ye get the first one over and done wi', then it'll get easier with each one that ye dae. It's only the first one that's hard, after that it's naething! All ye dae is lay back, open your legs, and shut your mind to what's happening. Honest, it's naething like sae bad as youse are fearing it'll be. I swear on my bairns lives, it is'nae.'

She poured more gin into Grainne's glass. 'Drink up, hen. Things look better through the bottom o' a glass.' She took a swallow herself, smacking her lips with relish. 'It's nae bad this. I've drunk worse.' She leaned across the table confidentially, the candlelight casting strange shadows among the fat folds of her face. 'Now tonight I'll stay wi' ye, hen. We'll work together. There's a lot ye have tae watch for, in this game. Some o' the bowsies ye'll be meeting have crawled out of the fokkin' middens, so they have, and there's some that are purely evil. But most of them are just out tae have a guid time, and there's nae harm in them. When Jack's ashore he just wants tae dance and drink and sing, and have a woman in his bed when he's done wi' carousing for the night. So don't ye go worrying your head, hen. I'll find ye a nice sailor-man for your first time.'

Grainne tried to shake off her depression, and to be business-like. 'What should I ask? I mean, how much?'

Fat Sal's yellowed teeth gleamed as she laughed uproariously. 'You ask for as much as ye can get, hen, and get anything else from them that ye can do, as well. We're not daeing this for friendship, hen. We're daeing it for money. Keep that in the front of your mind all the time, and never forget it. You and me, we're not like a lot o' these girls. We've got people

234

depending on us for their roof and bread. You and me can't afford not to be greedy.'

Grainne blinked owlishly, and her head was spinning dizzily. 'But how do you ask them for the money, Sal? I mean, do you ask before you do it, or afterwards, or what?'

The other woman smiled sadly. 'Jesus, ye're unco' innocent, for all that ye're a married woman, arn't you, Hen? There's an awful lot about this game that ye'll only learn with experience. But don't worry, ye'll learn all there is to know gey quick. Just remember one thing only, and that's never tae be backward in coming forward for your money. Have ye ever met a bloody shopkeeper who is slow to ask ye for the cash? Well that's what we're daeing in a sense. We're shopkeepers selling something. So always get the money first, if ye possibly can.' She laughed raucously. 'And never, ever gi' the bastards tick.' She swallowed the last of the gin in her glass, and told Grainne, 'It's time we went, hen, and did a bit o' trawling.'

She made Grainne drink another glass full of gin, then took her by the arm and led her out into the night.

The wooden floor shook and the very walls themselves seemed to quiver as the horde of dancers stamped round and round and round to the music of a gay Polka, dispensed by a German band. Flaxen-haired, fresh-faced men, their complexions bright scarlet, played their sax-horns, clarinets, trombones, cornet-a-pistons, and French horns in the over-heated room, thick with tobacco smoke and gin fumes, the smells of sweating bodies and sulphurous gas-lights.

'What d'ye think of Tibbet's Dancing Casino then?' Fat Sal asked, the sweat already trickling down her face to smudge its thick layered powder and rouge.

Grainne felt dazed by the tumult surrounding her, and her body was already damp with sweat beneath her dark gown. She shrugged her slender shoulders, and tried to smile.

'It's all right.'

The other woman stared keenly at her, and then from inside her bodice produced a flat silver spirit-flask and unscrewed its cap before handing it to Grainne. 'Here. Take a dram. It'll cheer ye up.'

Grainne swigged the tepid brandy without enjoyment, knowing that she needed the alcohol to enable her to get through this night.

'Come on, pretty.'

A tall, sun-bronzed young sailor beckoned her onto the floor, and Grainne stared at him in amazement, marvelling at his physical likeness to Con, with his oiled black curls, dark eyes, and lean muscular build. Half-dazedly she felt Fat Sal give her a push, and allowed herself to be propelled forwards into the welcoming arms of the man. He smelled of sweat and tar and sea, and the ale and spirits he had drunk reeked from his mouth.

'*Boom ta Booom. Ta boom boom boom. Boom ta Boom ta Boom!*'

Another lively Polka tune came from the band and Grainne was swept away into the midst of the dancers. She possessed a natural talent for dancing and even half-drunk as she was, was able to match the steps and rhythm of her partner.

The young sailor grinned down at her with tobacco-stained teeth, and sang out the words of the tune,

> *For I love you well,*
> *My own sweet girl.*
> *And no matter how I seem,*
> *When I come home from sea again,*
> *It's then you'll be my queen …*

Boom ta Boom. Ta boom ta booom. Boom ta boom ta boom.

The band tootled and blew and the crowd danced and sang, and the hours passed, and Grainne was lost in a world of glaring lights, pulsating music, stamping feet and her own reeling senses. Then she felt the cool night air on her face and felt the sailor's strong arm supporting her as she stumbled back to Africa Court.

In her room she offered no resistance as his fingers fumbled to undress her, and then his hard lithe body was crushing against her own nakedness, and his hands were cupping, kneading, stroking, his lips smothered her mouth. Through her drunken confusion a single thought suddenly penetrated, and she fought him off until she could find and insert the vinegar-soaked sponge. Then she was lying beneath him, and she felt his knees bludgeoning her thighs apart, and she moaned in shame and misery as he entered her body.

When he had done, and was lying on his back beside her, mouth open, snoring loudly, Grainne rolled on her side and drew herself up into a foetal position. Then she wept and wept and wept as if her heart was breaking.

She awoke long after dawn, her head throbbing, her stomach heaving with nausea. The space beside her was empty. Only the indentation in the pillow was left as silent witness to her companion of the night. That, and a single gold sovereign lying in the indentation. Grainne sat up in bed and took the gold coin between her fingers, then held it up before her eyes and examined it curiously, fancying that money earned as she had earned this, must in some way show its tainted origins, but it showed nothing except the head of the monarch, regal and proud.

'It's just another coin,' Grainne told herself with a curious sense of relief. 'It's just a coin. No different from any other coin. Except that it belongs to me!'

She rose and washed her body using a flannel and the bucket of cold water. As she sponged her smooth white skin Grainne examined herself, seeking signs of the lovemaking of the night. Superstitiously she believed that her wickedness must have left its mark on her body, but apart from a barely discernible reddening where his fingers had dug into her flesh in the moment of his climax, there was nothing else to be found.

She brushed her teeth, and brushed and combed her hair before plaiting it once more and coiling it around her head. Then she dressed and sat down in her armchair, trying to evaluate her feelings concerning what she had done. To her own mystification, she found that the overriding emotion, was that of numbed indifference. The woman of the night was like a stranger to her. It was as if she were two distinct personalities, and the Grainne Shonley of the morning had nothing to do with the Grainne Shonley who was a whore.

'That's what I am now ... a whore ... a real whore,' she told herself, but with only a pang of sadness and regret. 'I've no choice in the matter, have I?' She found that she was able to accept that fact with dispassion. Again she held up the gold sovereign and stared at it long and hard. 'Five weeks rent,' she marvelled. 'Last night, with just one man, I earned five weeks rent. I could work one night only, and earn enough to keep me and Con in ease and comfort for a week.'

She made her way down to the kitchen, and was greeted with a chorus of mocking applause from the girls already gathered there. She blushed furiously, and for a few moments her mood of indifference threatened to desert her, and the shame of what she had done burnt deep, but she defiantly forced that shame away.

'I had no choice,' she reiterated constantly to herself. 'I had no choice.'

'Well, how much did ye get from the goodlooking jack?' Fat Sal wanted to know.

'He left a sovereign on the pillow,' Grainne told her.

'Is he meeting you agen?' Sophie enquired.

Grainne shook her head. 'I don't know what he's doing. I was asleep when he left.'

'Asleep?' Fat Sal frowned, 'And you still found a bloody couter on the pillow? Fokk me, but ye were lucky, hen. Most o' the bloody jacks 'ull gi' leg bail if ye're sleeping. How much did ye ask him for anyways?'

Again Grainne was forced to shake her head. 'I can't remember if I did ask him for anything, for truth to tell, I was drunk.'

'Now what was the last thing I telled ye, hen?' Fat Sal scolded. 'Didn't I tell ye to make sure o' your money, first, last and always? Didn't I tell ye that?'

'Yes, you did,' Grainne admitted, and felt suitably chastened at her own professional shortcomings.

'Aye, I did so,' Fat Sal spluttered angrily, as though she regarded Grainne's failing as a personal insult to herself. 'Ye're no' a bloody dollymop, hen, giving it away for a supper and a few gins. Ye're a tail, a judy, it's your living we're talking about here. Ye cannae afford to gi' nothin' away in this game. Because what ye have to sell does nae last over long. It's only fresh goods that fetch the high prices in this trade, hen, and they goods does nae stay fresh for very long.'

'I wished I looked like you, Grainne,' the sallow, flat-faced Doll said wistfully. 'I'd be working the toffs places then, I 'ud.'

'Yes, that's where you ought to be, Grainne,' Binsy said excitedly. 'Youse are a lady. Iffen youse wore nice gowns and jewelry you could be sitting in your own box at the Amphitheatre or the Theatre Royal. You could be drinking wine and scoffing nice scran at the Adelphi, wi' your looks, couldn't she girls?' she appealed to the rest of the bleary-eyed, slip-shod gathering around the table.

'O' course she could!' Sophie's teeth flashed white in her dark, pretty face. 'That's what you ought to do, Grainne. Buy yourself some really nice clothes, and then try up town and see what you can trawl there.'

Mad Agnes came falteringly into the kitchen, still clad in her tawdry finery of the night, her feathered bonnet crazily askew on her lank greasy hair ... A chorus of exclamations and eager questions greeted the sight of her blood-caked swollen face.

'What the fokkin' hell happened to you, Aggie?'

'Where did you cop that lot from?'

'Who did it, Aggie? Who did it?'

The woman slumped down on the bench and leaned forwards with her elbows on the table top.

'Have you got a lush?' she begged.

Fat Sal pushed a bottle of gin towards her. 'Here, take a dram, and then tell us what's happened tae ye.'

Wincing as the raw spirit stung her swollen lacerated lips, Agnes' gullet bobbed up and down as she greedily sucked from the bottle. Then she begged for a cheroot, and Binsy passed over the one, half-smoked, she had between her lips.

Mad Agnes inhaled feverishly, coughing even as she did so. Then she told them, 'I went aboard a ship with my gentleman friend, and his shipmates did not use me with any good manners.'

Grainne could hardly believe that this well modulated, cultured voice was issuing from the human wreckage across the table from her.

'Were they lascars?' Fat Sal wanted to know.

Mad Agnes shook her head. 'I believe them to be Greek.'

'Fokk me, Aggie!' Binsy snarled in disgust. 'Arn't you learned any fokkin' thing since you bin on the bleedin' game? Don't youse know no better than to get on board? You deserves all youse got for being so bleedin' stupid!'

Grainne stared questioningly at Fat Sal, and the Scotswoman explained.

'You never goes on board wi' the jacks, hen, unless it's your real sweetheart. And even when ye know the jack well, we're still risking a gey lot. The crew all uses you, and then chucks you off wi'out a penny piece. Sometimes the bastards even robs whatever you might have on you yourself. It's only the green young girls who gets caught like that. Or the bleedin' night owls who daren't show their faces by daylight. But them poor buggers has got nothing else left that they can

240

lose, have they, 'cepting their lives.' She turned to Mad Agnes. 'How many had ye, and how much did ye earn?'

The mad woman visibly shuddered, but answered evenly enough, 'God knows how many, Sal. They took turns all night long. Then they bundled me into a row boat this morning, and dumped me on the quay. One man felt sorry for me and gave me a sixpence.' She rolled her eyes heavenwards and said with a woe-begone expression, 'The policeman was going to lock me in the Bridewell for loitering. He accused me of trying to rob the warehouses.'

Roars of laughter erupted from the other women, and Grainne could not stop herself from giggling.

'Who gi' you the walloping!?' Binsy wanted to know.

'It was my gentleman friend, when I asked who was to pay?' Tears suddenly trickled down the worn cheeks, and the mad woman sobbed out, 'And I thought he loved me. He told me he did.'

Pity welled up in Grainne's heart for this pathetic creature, but before she could utter any words of comfort, Fat Sal had gone to the other woman, and was cradling the bonneted head against her huge stomach.

'Now no greetin', hen. Ye know that all men are bastards. So dinna waste your strength by greetin' over them. Here now, you take a wee dram o' this.' She held the gin bottle to the lacerated lips. 'And then I'll take ye up tae your room, and see you settled in your bed. Come the night, ye'll be feeling as chipper as a bloody squirrel agen. Ye know ye will.'

She asked Grainne to help her, and between them they half-carried the unsteady Agnes up to her room, undressed the emaciated body and put her into bed.

The stayed watching her until she fell asleep, and Fat Sal said quietly, 'This is the other side o' the coin, hen. This is what can happen to a tail iffen she's not gey careful. There's an awful lot o' puir girls found in the river, or lying in some midden. There's evil out in those streets, hen, and it finds all too many of our sort, and leaves us dead, or even worse.' She paused, her normally jovial features troubled. 'And there's sight worse things can happen tae ye than death, Grainne. I know, because I've seen some o' them. Agnes was lucky to come off as light as she has.'

Grainne's own fears were rousing. She had not bargained for the awful dangers that now rose up to present themselves to her imagination.

As if she could read the girl's mind, Fat Sal told her, 'Now ye dinna' hae to walk terrified, hen, but what ye must always dae, is tae walk wi' great care. It's always a guid idea to hae a knife wi' you, and be ready tae use it if needs be. Like I told ye, most men just want a fuck. But there's some who want other things, and it's them ye must learn to recognise, and tae keep well away from.'

Grainne nodded thoughtfully.

Fat Sal regarded her in silence for some moments, then told her, 'The girls are right, Grainne. You should nae be working the docks. Wi' your looks and the way ye conduct yersel', you should be looking for toffs, not jacks ashore. Ye could trawl them easy, hen. I seen the way that yon doctor at the hospital was looking at ye. He'd gi' anything to have ye, I'm gey sure o' that. It's fellas like him ye should be going wi'.'

Grainned smiled mirthlessly. 'As a matter of fact, Sal, he's already offered to make me his mistress.'

'And what did ye tell him?' Fat Sal pressed.

Grainne's mind went back to that memorable occasion, and she could only shrug, and smile ironically. 'I acted like a virtuous wife should act ...' But she abruptly broke off as she realized that she had not given a single thought to Con since the night before. In her mind she was aghast. 'What is happening to me? What am I becoming?' she wondered. Badly shaken, she could only tell Fat Sal, 'I have to go.'

She ran from the room and from the house, and went out into the bustle of the crowded noisy streets, and with her mind in a confusion of conflicting emotions she walked on and on in what seemed endless, aimless circles.

Chapter Thirty

Grainne felt that she could not face seeing Con that day even though the injured man could have no notion of what she had done. Instead she paid Doll two shillings to go to the Dispensary and see Liza Davis on her behalf. The girl came back with news that was both a relief and a worry at the same time.

The House Surgeon had decided that Con should remain in the hospital for another week, but Liza Davis had not given a reason. She had only sent a jumbled message of reassurance that Con was going to be all right, and that it was merely a minor complication which necessitated his staying.

Although Grainne was greatly concerned about that complication, still she was forced to admit that Con's prolonged stay at the hospital was something of a relief. It would give her that much more time to find a suitable place to bring him to. She knew that she could never bring men back to Africa Court if Con was there. The thought of having sex with a man with her husband close-by filled her with horror.

By early evening Grainne was already tipsy, having spent most of the afternoon drinking in the kitchen with the other women. She went up to her own room to prepare for going out, and after she had washed, she lit a candle and by its light examined her face closely, seeking for visible changes to complement the moral changes that she feared were taking place within her. She could find none, but imagined that her eyes were somewhat harder, and more wan.

She, Binsy and Fat Sal went out together, and although Grainne's heart was heavy, she tried to put a bold face on it, joining in with her friends crude humour and raucous laughter.

They called in at several ale houses and gin palaces, where Grainne was introduced to other prostitutes, and some of the men who lived off and preyed upon them. Three times during the course of the night Grainne took men back to Africa Court. After the third man had left she again washed herself with a flannel and cold water, and once again saturated the sponges with fresh vinegar. Then, she slumped down in the armchair and buried her face in her hands, sobbing with self-loathing. When all her tears were spent, she remained sitting in the armchair, staring blankly before her at the spluttering candle flame. Then a sharp knocking at her door broke into her reveries, and she called out to know who was there. A man answered, and Grainne was startled to hear Malcom Galbraith's voice.

Opening the door she asked him, 'What are you doing here?'

He smiled uncertainly, and removed his tall top hat. 'Aren't you going to invite me in, Grainne?'

She moved back and he followed, his eyes flickering around the mean room. Grainne was sure that the smell of men and sex hung heavy in the air, and she could not help flushing with embarrassment and shame.

The young man's manner was diffident, and twice he seemed about to speak, but although his lips opened briefly, no words came. Then his eyes fell upon the small open box containing the sponges, and he frowned.

Grainne's shame prodded her into a defiant challenge. 'Why do you look so disgusted? How else am I to live?' she cried.

His own manner hardened. 'I offered to look after you, Grainne.'

'You offered me this!' she stated flatly.

He shook his well-groomed head. 'I did nothing of the sort. I offered you my protection.'

245

Grainne suddenly realised the unfairness of blaming him for what was happening to her, and her tone softened a little, as she said wearily, 'No matter. What's done is done, and there's nothing to be gained in arguing about it. What did you want of me, coming here like this? How did you find me?'

He spread his hands in the gesture she was coming to know well. 'It wasn't difficult to find you, Grainne. Liza Davis told me that you were living in Africa Court.'

A cruel urge swept over Grainne; one which she could not control. 'So, you have found me! And you know now that I am become a whore. So what is it you wish to say to me?'

His own quick temper rose. 'Only that you are behaving like a damn fool,' he snapped heatedly. 'You are prostituting yourself with the very dregs of society. I'll give you three months at most before you find yourself in the lock ward.'

Grainne knew what the lock ward was. It was the ward set aside for the treatment of venereal diseases. An angry retort rose to her lips but she did not utter it. She knew that he was speaking the truth, and one of the major reasons for her present self-loathing was that she risked becoming infected every time she went with a strange man.

'Listen to me, Grainne,' he appealed. 'When I offered you my protection, I spoke very clumsily, and failed to express my real feelings towards you. I am not going to shower you with protestations of love and life-long devotion, because I truly do not know if I love you. What I do know is that you are constantly in my thoughts, and I care very deeply about what happens to you.

'Yes, I do want you for my mistress, that I freely admit to. But you would not be simply a sexual plaything for me, Grainne. I would offer you kindness, friendship and respect.' He smiled and added ironically, 'That in itself is a deal more than many men offer their lawfully wedded wives!' He paused as if considering his next words, then said slowly, 'Financially, I would make you a generous allowance, sufficient for you to live well and have your husband cared for properly. I would take a small house for you, if you so wished, and if in the course of time I found that I was no longer able to continue with our relationship, then I promise that I would not leave you destitute.' He stopped speaking and regarded her keenly. 'Surely Grainne, you would be better off with me, than in continuing this present course?'

Grainne's thoughts were a hopeless confusion. Naturally in many ways his offer was tempting. She was already beginning to doubt her own capacity to continue in this present life-style. She already knew that the only way she could face selling her body was to be half-drunk when she did so. And she also realised that her drinking would inevitably and quickly bring her down into the gutters. She experienced a sudden impulse to accept Galbraith's offer, but could not bring herself to speak the words of acceptance. 'Perhaps I fear that I might become too attached to him,' she thought. 'Because he is handsome and charming enough to win most women's hearts. I know that it is hard to understand, but I really do think that I am not being unfaithful to Con in my heart, when I go with strangers. Because I only go with them in order to earn money to look after Con with. But if I were to accept this man's offer, I fear that I might well become overly fond of him, and if that happened, then I would be truly unfaithful to my Con.'

'Well, Grainne,' Malcolm Galbraith asked gently, 'what do you say?'

She shook her head helplessly. 'I don't know … I just don't know.'

He smiled to mask his disappointment, and told her, 'Listen, my dear, think about it for a few days.'

'Tell me, why is Con being kept in the Dispensary for another week?' she questioned, feeling an acute sense of guilt because she had not asked immediately on seeing Galbraith.

'I prevailed on the Head Surgeon to leave him be,' the young man answered casually enough. 'He appears to have developed an infection.'

'On his right shoulder and arm?' Fear lanced through Grainne as she sought this confirmation.

Galbraith looked surprised. 'Yes, that is so. How did you know this, since you haven't been to the Dispensary today, have you?'

'Mrs Davis sent word to me,' Grainne explained, 'that Con was to stay, and yesterday I noticed the bad smell myself coming from his bandages.'

'It's nothing to be concerned about.' The young man reassured her. 'It's merely a localised infection, and I've left instructions with the fellow who is walking the wards this weekend to keep an eye on it for me.'

'You're very kind,' she whispered. She felt near to tears yet again, and was angry with herself for what she regarded as her own weakness, castigating herself, 'Will you stop crying like a baby! All the weeping and wailing in the world is not going to alter anything, or make it better.'

'I must go,' Galbraith told her. 'Will you think about what I've said, Grainne?'

She nodded. 'I will.'

Abruptly he reached into his pocket and pulled out a handful of coins, which he laid on the chest of drawers.

'Take this, so that you'll not need to go out in search of a man again tonight.'

Before she could even reply he was clattering down the stairs, and by the time she reached the landing, he had gone from the house.

Grainne stood for a long time gazing down at the small heap of coins.

'If I touch them, if I use them, then I will have committed myself,' she thought. 'I shall have committed myself to becoming his mistress ... And why shouldn't I become that? At least I would be living in some sort of decency.'

Her mind seemed to become a dichotomy of two distinct and opposing entities, disputing for and against acceptance of Malcom Galbraith's offer; and that dispute raged within her all through the remainder of the night and, even when sheer fatigue overcame her and she slept, her dreams were troubled with it.

She awoke shortly after dawn, and lay staring up at the cracked, stained plaster of the ceiling, and found that she had reached her decision.

'I cannot become Malcom Galbraith's or any other man's mistress while Con lives. He must remain first and foremost in my heart.' She accepted without bitterness the prospect of perhaps a lifetime of degradation stretching before her. 'What's to be, will be and I shall bear it with as much courage as I can muster. I can do no more than that.'

Chapter Thirty-One

The rancid smell in the small shed was thick in the air, and Grainne knew that this was not a localised infection.

She went to the side of the box-bed and looked down at the motionless, bandaged figure, whose only sign of life was the stertorous, ragged breath rasping in and out of the black holes of the mouth and nostrils, and with a sinking heart saw the wide spreading stains of body fluids covering the right arm and shoulder.

She laid her hand on the man's left arm, and spoke softly, 'Con, it's me, Grainne. Can you hear what I'm saying to you? Can you understand me?'

There was no answering movement from the arm, and Grainne suddenly experienced the deep rooted certainty that there would never again be any answer from this man.

Nevertheless she still spoke to him.

'I'll not be long away, Con.'

She went in search of Liza Davis, and found the fat woman in the ward where Maggie Nolan had died.

'Well now, and how are you, Mrs Shonley? Come to see your man, have you?'

Grainne nodded, then drew the woman to one side. 'Listen, Mrs Davis, I need to know the truth. So for the love of God, please give it to me. Has my husband got gangrene?'

At first the woman made no answer and Grainne gripped the fat arm fiercely and urged, 'Tell me Mrs Davis. Tell me the truth, for pity's sake!'

Reluctantly the fat woman nodded. 'I fear so, Mrs Shonley. I didn't want to tell you afore, because I know how hard youse have been having it. I just didn't want to add to your troubles.'

'Did Dr Galbraith know?' Grainne demanded, and again in answer there came the reluctant nod of the fat woman's head.

'Will he die?'

In her mind Grainne already knew the answer to that question, but still a shock of pain hit her when the woman confirmed her thoughts.

'He'll not last long, Mrs Shonley. But perhaps that's a blessed relief for the poor soul, because if he was to live, then his life could only ever be a burden to him.'

'How long will it be before it's over?' Grainne asked softly.

The other woman shrugged doubtfully. 'That's hard to say, dearie. Mayhap a week, mayhap a day. There's no way o' telling for sure.'

'I want to stay with him.' Grainne said firmly. 'Am I allowed to?'

A mirthless grin twitched the other woman's lips. 'If you've money to gi' the porters, then they'll not throw you out from the shed, dearie. But I'm sure if you was to ask Dr Galbraith, he'd arrange for you to stay with your husband, and then you'd not need to gi' the porters anything.'

Grainne shook her head emphatically. 'No, I don't want to involve Dr Galbraith. I've money I can give the porters.'

Liza Davis examined the young woman closely. She saw the pale, drawn face, the shadowed eyes, the nervous twining of her fingers, and sensed the suffering that could not be seen because it was hidden deep in the young woman's heart.

'You go on back to your man, dearie. I'll be coming in presently to gi' him his medicine.'

When Grainne had hurried back to the shed, Liza Davis went down into the cellars, and there unlocked a small wooden chest that she kept hidden there. From it she took a small glass phial which contained a dark, pungent-smelling liquid. She visualised Grainne's face, and her own face was pitying.

'Well,' she decided, 'at least I can do this much for you, girl. I think youse have gone through enough already. I'll be doing you and him both a mercy.'

Later that morning Malcom Galbraith came to the shed, and Grainne asked him as he entered, 'Why did you lie to me about my husband's condition?'

The young man's handsome face was troubled, then he sighed heavily. 'I lied for two reasons. The first was because I did not wish to add to the burdens of your suffering.' He hesitated, and she pressed him.

'Go on, finish it.'

He spread his hands. 'Very well, I'll speak plain. I wanted you to come to me. I thought that if you knew that your husband had such a short time to live, then you would spurn my help.' Again he paused, his eyes studying her features, his expression still showing a troubled sense of guilt. 'I meant it only for the best of motives, Grainne. I only wanted to be of service to you, and to help you in any way that I could.'

Grainne accepted what he said as the truth. 'Very well, Malcom. Let's leave it at that, shall we?'

'What will you do now?' he wanted to know.

'I shall take Con back home, and bury him with his father. That is where he belongs, lying in his native soil by the side of the man he loved above all other men.'

Abruptly she took some coins from the pocket of her dress and handed them towards Galbraith. 'I can't accept the money you left with me, Malcom.'

He lifted his hand in rejection. 'No. You must keep it, Grainne. If you intend to return to Ireland with your husband's body, then you'll need it. Look, if it makes you feel better, then regard it as a loan, and pay me back when you can. Please, Grainne, allow me to at least do this much for you.'

The note of appeal in his voice was genuine, and not

wishing to gratuitously wound his feelings, Grainne accepted.

'Many thanks, Malcom. I shall pay it back to you as soon as I'm able.'

'I must go now, Grainne, I am called to Edinburgh on urgent family matters. Will you write to me at my address in Rodney Street if ... if ...,' he tried to express himself with the utmost delicacy, 'if you should have gone to Ireland before my return here. Please, Grainne, write to me as a friend.'

She nodded gravely. 'I will.'

His smile lit up his features. 'Do you promise?'

'I promise.'

'We shall meet again, Grainne, in happier circumstances,' he stated positively. Leaning forward he touched his lips gently to her cheek, and left without another word.

All through that day Grainne sat by the side of the motionless man. Only Liza Davis came into the shed, and deftly used the bladder and tube to administer the mixture of milk and opium. Then she smiled kindly at Grainne, and gently squeezed the girl's slender shoulder.

'I'll be here 'til late iffen you needs me for anything, dearie.'

Grainne smiled wanly, and thanked her.

The injured man died just as dusk deepened into darkness, and Grainne bowed her head and breathed a prayer for the salvation of the released soul. She felt no acute grief. Instead she experienced an increasing sense of relief that he had been set free, and that nothing could hurt or harm him now.

The thought struck her that perhaps this man had not been Con after all. There was no proof that he had been, and only her instinct, or desperate need to believe that he was, had made her think that this man was her husband.

'If that should be the case, then I prostituted myself

for nothing,' she thought sadly. 'And now he's dead, then it was all for nothing anyway, wasn't it? I degraded myself for nothing.'

And then it seemed that a voice spoke to her, and that voice was Con's.

'You didn't degrade yourself, honey. You acted out of love for me. Nothing that you did for love, could ever degrade you. I love you, Grainne. I'll always love you ...'

'And I'll always love you, Con. Always.' Grainne whispered, and the tears that fell from her eyes were tears of healing for her broken heart.

Chapter Thirty-Two

A fresh wind was blowing up the Mersey Estuary bringing with it the clean freshness of the open sea.

The paddle steamer, *Athlone* was preparing to leave the dock and sail for Cork, and the usual swarms of porters and dockers and passengers crowded the quayside.

Grainne Shonley stood with Ellen Chester on the dockside watching the porters carry Con Shonley's coffin up the gangplank.

'What will you do after you've laid him to rest, *merch fach*?' Ellen Chester asked. 'Surely you'll not stay in Ireland.'

Grainne's face was very pale and thin, but her eyes were calm and although shadowed by sadness, they radiated a hard won strength and confidence.

'Do you know, Ellen, I honestly haven't given thought yet to the future. There'll be time enough for that after I've laid Con by the side of his father.' She smiled wryly. 'After these past weeks, the future can hold no terrors for me.'

'Will you write to me, *cariad*? I'd like to know how you are, and what's happening with you.'

'But of course I will, and maybe I'll visit you someday,' Grainne promised, and Ellen Chester took her hand warmly.

'Yes, do that, *cariad*.' Her fine, dark eyes shimmered with tears, and quickly she kissed Grainne's cheek.

'Goodbye, *merch fach*.'

Grainne watched the dark figure until she had gone

In 1848 – the most ruinous year of the potato famine – Grainne Shonley and her husband, Con, leave their native Ireland for the promise of the New World. Arriving in Liverpool, gateway to America, they encounter the squalor of Paradise Alley, the most treacherous part of the docklands. In this corrupt world no one can be trusted – especially their sinister landlord Tom Tracey and his henchmen. But their passage overseas is soon confirmed and the Shonleys leave with relief.

As *The Florida* sets sail Grainne feels sure that their luck has changed. But she hasn't bargained for the vile conditions below deck, the tyrannical Captain Lockyer, or for the fearful night when disaster strikes the ship . . .

Also by Sara Fraser in Futura:
TILDY
TILDY: POORHOUSE WOMAN
TILDY: NURSING WOMAN
TILDY: POINTING WOMAN
TILDY: RADICAL WOMAN
TILDY: GANG WOMAN
THE BITTER DAWNING
YOUNG JETHRO
THE KING'S BOUNTY

FICTION

UK £3.50

ISBN 0-7088-4766-8

00350

Australia $10.95*
New Zealand $13.95* (incl. GST)
* recommended price only.

9 780708 847664

SARA FRASER

From the
bestselling
author of the
Tidy series

The Harsh & Noontide